MYS
THURLO

Thurlo, Aimee.

Bad samaritan.

WITHDRAWN

DATE			

7-10

BAKER & TAYLOR

Bad Samaritan

Bad
Samaritan

AIMÉE AND DAVID THURLO

Minotaur Books ✠ New York

This is a work of fiction. All of the characters, organizations, and events portrayed in this novel are either products of the authors' imaginations or are used fictitiously.

www.minotaurbooks.com

ISBN 978-0-312-36732-9

First Edition: July 2010

10 9 8 7 6 5 4 3 2 1

To our friends at the Archdiocese of Santa Fe—
Rita Lucero, Rosalie Romero, Sandra Kay Rael,
and Fran Andersen; you guys are terrific.

ACKNOWLEDGMENTS

With special thanks to Di and Phillip Uzdawinis
for always taking time to answer our questions.

Bad
Samaritan

I

FAITH COULD MOVE MOUNTAINS AND CAST THEM INTO THE
sea, but although Sister Agatha's faith was strong, it was far
from impregnable. There were too many chinks in her armor,
and lately it seemed as if God had decided to test each and
every one.

At the moment, it was one thirty in the morning and she
was barely awake. Yawning and shaking the cobwebs out of her
head to stay alert, she drove toward the small town of Bernalillo,
creeping down the narrow blacktop at forty-five miles per hour.
The anemic headlights of the Antichrysler—the monastery's
rickety old station wagon—barely parted the black curtain trying to envelop them.

Pax was sitting up straight on the passenger's side. A former
police dog, he was now the monastery's pet and companion to
the externs—nuns who didn't take a vow of enclosure. Sister
Agatha wondered if the old boy had somehow managed to

understand the seriousness of their current situation, and his personal connection to it.

Until tonight, she hadn't really believed that things at Our Lady of Hope could get any worse. For the past few months their monastery had been bravely fighting against a death sentence. Though the final curtain hadn't yet fallen, barring a miracle, the end was now near.

One slim hope still remained, but the threads that bound it were so fragile it didn't seem wise to cling to them. That was why Sister Agatha had chosen to protect herself by preparing for the worst. *Piensa mal y acertarás.* It was a local Spanish saying that meant "Think the worst and you'll be right." Yet her attempt to remain realistic just left her feeling even more empty inside.

With effort, Sister Agatha pushed aside those concerns for now and focused on the matter at hand. Late phone calls to the monastery—like the one less than thirty minutes ago—ran the risk of not being heard and answered, since their only phones were inside Reverend Mother's office and the parlor. However, tonight's caller had been insistent and the ringing had eventually awakened Sister Bernarda.

That frantic call for help had come on behalf of one of the monastery's most loyal friends, and Reverend Mother had dispatched Sister Agatha immediately. As Mother had explained, Sister Agatha was the extern most used to handling "difficult" situations—and that description certainly fit the situation at hand.

Forcing herself to focus exclusively on what she had to do next, Sister Agatha drove directly to the sheriff's station. The nearly full parking lot attested to the importance of what was taking place.

After finding a parking space at the end of the row, she put the big white German shepherd on his leash, then hurried down the sidewalk to the front entrance. The foyer led to an equally small lobby, where a young male deputy was attempting to calm a shirtless and extremely irate older man in plaid shorts and flip-flops. He'd obviously had too much to drink. Drunks of all ages, sizes, and shapes abounded on the Fourth of July holiday, when celebrations usually went well into the wee morning hours of the fifth.

Ignoring the ruckus, she led her curious dog around the duo and stepped up to the front desk. Sergeant Millie Romero rose from her chair and nodded to her.

"I'm glad you're here, Sister Agatha," she said loudly, trying to be heard over the noise the drunk was making. "Sorry for the circumstances. I imagine you want to see him now?"

"Yes, I do. While we're walking there, could you tell me what the department plans to do with him? A high-profile officer like he is will need extra care. The second they put him in with other prisoners he'll be in mortal danger."

"That's why he's not in a cell. For now at least, he's being held in one of the interrogation rooms," Millie said, coming out from behind the counter. Holding open the half-door that led into the bullpen, she added, "Do you want to leave Pax here while I take you to see him?"

"That's a good idea. This *is* his second home." Sister Agatha unfastened the leash and saw Pax go beg a cracker from one of the sergeants at a cubicle.

As Millie walked down the hall with her, Sister Agatha could feel the woman's tension.

"He could sure use your help," Millie said in a quiet voice. "Officially, there's not much we can do right now. Captain Chavez will keep an open mind, but things don't look good."

"Where's Captain Chavez now?" Sister Agatha asked, looking around.

"He's still at the crime scene."

Sister Agatha slowed her steps. "Before we go in, can you tell me how he's dealing with this?"

"Not well at all," Millie said, nodding to another officer in the long passageway.

Sister Agatha swallowed back the sense of outrage that filled her. This man, of all men, deserved better. Nothing about the incident made sense to her.

A second later they stopped in front of a door that read INTERVIEW ROOM A. A thick window revealed the prisoner sitting in a wooden chair in front of a small table. His chin was resting on the table, and he looked half asleep.

Hearing the lock being worked, her old friend looked up, and Sister Agatha saw his face clearly for the first time.

Sheriff Tom Green looked exhausted. Bleary eyed and disheveled, he barely resembled the spit-and-polish professional his officers were used to confronting.

She and Tom went way back, and at rare times, Sister Agatha could still catch fleeting glimpses of a Tom Green the others couldn't even imagine. Tonight, for one of those brief moments, she actually saw the reflection of her old college boyfriend. He had been a vulnerable, sensitive young man who'd claimed her heart before she'd been compelled to follow a higher calling.

He stood, squared his shoulders, and nodded to Millie. "How did you hear?" he asked Sister Agatha.

"One of your people called the monastery," she said. "We were told you'd been detained."

"Arrested," he corrected. "My opponent in the sheriff's race, Robert Garcia, has been murdered. The evidence at the scene and the facts I know to be true don't match, but I didn't kill Robert."

"I believe you, Tom," she said. "Your people know that's true, too. So let's see what we can do to straighten this mess out."

"I'll be down the hall if you need me," Millie said.

Once the door shut, Sister Agatha focused on Tom. "I come into town often enough to know all about the campaign—the name-calling and the rest of it. But how—"

"Did I end up in this mess?" he interrupted, finishing her thought. "I wish I could tell you exactly what happened, but the details are all jumbled up in my mind. Worst of all, they don't match the physical evidence—at least the bits I've been told about."

"Tell me what you remember," Sister Agatha said, taking a seat across the table from him.

He nodded. "I was in the park celebrating the Fourth, shaking hands, and basically meeting the public. Out of the blue Robert Garcia came up to me, carrying two hot dogs. He handed me one and asked if we could talk privately. He suggested that we go to the southwest corner of the park past the swings once the fireworks started. Nobody was likely to disturb us there at that time. I agreed. He then stepped away to speak to some of his people, and I continued talking to my constituents. After that, I picked up a glass of lemonade and kept campaigning. I'd started feeling really drowsy by the time I was supposed to go meet with Robert."

"Your symptoms . . . were they like food poisoning?"

"No, not really. There was no nausea or stomach problems."

"So what did you do about it?"

"Nothing. I sucked it up and went to meet Robert. When I reached him, everything was spinning, and I knew I was going to pass out. I wanted to tell him to get help, but I was having trouble putting words together. He said something just as my knees gave way. The last thing I remember was the startled look on Robert's face."

"How are you feeling now?" Sister Agatha asked, leaning forward and looking more closely at her old friend.

"I'm okay, and before you ask, I had a physical a few months back. No blood pressure issues. I'm in perfect health, so I'm guessing I was drugged. It was either in the hot dog or the lemonade. That's all I had."

"Didn't you say that Robert had a hot dog, too?" Sister Agatha asked, clarifying.

"Yes, they looked like ones from the city's kiosk. They were wrapped in those red, white, and blue napkins."

"Okay," she said. "Now tell me what happened after you regained consciousness."

"I was flat on my back, and Millie Romero was crouched beside me. Millie said that Al Russo, Robert's campaign manager, had called 911. According to her, Russo lost track of Robert, so he went looking for him. What he found was Robert's dead body—killed by a gunshot—with a blood-smeared club in his hand. Since I have a bloody bruise on my head, the blood's probably mine."

"So basically, they'll say you shot him before you went down," she said, deep in thought.

"It's as if someone framed me but gave me an out. I could plead self-defense, but since a club's no match for a pistol, I'm vulnerable to charges of excessive force."

"Which you would still beat. A police officer is authorized to use deadly force when he's attacked."

"Yes and no. I'd have a legal battle on my hands."

"I wish I could visit the crime scene now while everything's fresh," she said.

Tom shook his head. "A crime scene needs to be worked by specially trained officers. You'd be in the way and might even unknowingly compromise evidence."

"Even now you're sticking to the rules?"

"Those rules were made and put in place for a reason."

She sighed. *That* was the Tom she knew. "Anything else you can tell me?"

"I was told that they'd found a single footprint—a size ten and a half—that had been left in a muddy patch near the body. It doesn't match my shoe size or pattern, or the victim's. The thing is, it could have been left there anytime after the sprinklers got things wet. They go on every morning at seven."

"The presence of a third person at the crime scene could help clear up some of the apparent inconsistencies," Sister Agatha said.

"Maybe, or maybe not," he muttered sourly. "All I know is that I have this bruise on my head, but I can't remember getting it," he went on, gingerly feeling the lump by his left temple. "Had I been conscious, I would have remembered a blow like this, and it wasn't caused by the fall when I passed out. There was nothing in the grass that I could have hit my head on. I looked."

"Verifying that you were drugged is crucial now. Have they given you a blood test?"

He shook his head and winced. "I've been asking for one ever since I was brought in. To me, it's obvious. That's the only way I can explain my inability to remember things more clearly. I'm being framed, but I'll need a tox screen to back up my story."

"So what's the holdup?" Sister Agatha asked.

"Budget constraints. Our department has a policy that doesn't allow for extra tests when the evidence appears so straightforward. In this case, it indicates that I shot Garcia about the same time he clubbed me," he said. "My people will help me push for one, but what worries me is that by the time they get a tech here, it'll be too late."

"How can I speed things up? Is there someone I can speak to on your behalf?"

"I don't think so. Gloria and my lawyer, Doug Sanchez, are working hard to get things rolling. They spoke to Captain Chavez, who's acting sheriff right now, and he's for it, but DA Springer is apparently throwing a million legalities in their way." He rubbed the stubble that now covered his chin. "Springer owes his job to the Garcias."

"No one who knows you will believe you're guilty of murder," Sister Agatha said firmly.

"That's what I'd like to think, too. Problem is, with this run for office against the Garcia machine, I've now got as many enemies as I do friends."

"I'm your friend, Tom, and trust me—I'll find out what happened."

"I know you will. Thanks," he said with quiet gratitude.

"This is a very complicated frame-up, Tom. We need to find out why anyone would go to all the trouble, and exactly what's behind this."

"I wish I could tell you."

"The evidence indicates that you were a bonus—but not the target. You were even struck on the head to give the impression that you'd acted in self-defense—a way out for you. Robert had to have been the real target, so I'm going to concentrate on him. As far as I'm concerned, the puzzle starts there."

"Robert had a lot of enemies."

"I imagine so, but nothing about this case—not even the logistics—makes sense. Why would Robert invite you to a secluded corner of the park, then attack you—an armed officer—with a big stick?"

"Exactly. Also keep in mind that if I'd wanted to take that branch away from him, I wouldn't have needed a gun. I'm at least a foot taller than he was, and well trained in self-defense. But the bruise on my head and the fact that the branch in his hand had blood on it back up the wrong version of what went down." He paused, then in a slow, deliberate voice added, "If Robert hadn't been the victim, I would have sworn that *he* was behind the setup. He liked playing people."

"You and he had differences even before the campaign, didn't you?" she noted, accurately reading his tone.

"Robert used to be a deputy. He and I have a history that dates back to his years in the department." He lapsed into what became a long silence.

"I'll need to know more," she prodded.

"I wish I could help, but those details are sealed. I'd just make my position worse if I told you. As it is, I've probably said too much already."

"I'll keep whatever you tell me confidential," she assured him.

He considered it for several moments, then answered. "Here's what I can tell you. Robert and I went head-to-head on just about everything. He quit about a year after I was elected sheriff and set up his own security firm. I figured he was out of law enforcement for good. Then came the primaries, and suddenly he was the other party's candidate and in my face again."

Sister Agatha felt a sinking sensation as she listened to Tom. Things *were* looking bad. Their current mayor, JD Garcia, was Robert Garcia's brother, and no friend of Tom's. Tom's refusal to play small-town politics had made him an outsider—one certain people would be happy to see go down.

"The only thing that makes sense to me is that a third person was there—the killer," Sister Agatha said. "We need to act fast and find out who that was. The longer the truth stays hidden, the worse it's going to get for you."

"I didn't fire my weapon unassisted. I know that, but I have to prove it. Somehow, I've got to find a way to remember everything that led up to the moment I passed out." He took a slow, deep breath and added, "Can you get me a list of everything that was found at the crime scene? It might help me."

"Millie was there, so I'll ask her. If she has orders to withhold that information from you, maybe Doug Sanchez can request it. They're supposed to give the defense access to that information, aren't they?"

"With Tivo Chavez on the case, Doug'll probably be given a copy of whatever the deputies gathered up. I never thought much of defense attorneys—until now," he added in a taut voice.

"You've got a lot of people that'll be working hard to establish the truth, Tom. Hold on to that."

"I've also got enemies who are ready to do whatever it takes to get a piece of me," he countered quietly.

"Maybe so, but working from the standpoint that you're innocent, I'll be able to see things that others may miss." She pointed to his hand. "Like that injury. Why is your hand bruised? The web between your thumb and forefinger is down to raw skin."

Tom flexed his hand, making a fist, then opening it again. "Even after hours of practice at the range, I never bruised my hand firing my own weapon. This is evidence that supports my claim. The killer wrapped my hand around my pistol, then squeezed my finger against the trigger. That's how he shot Robert. What he forgot to take into account was the recoil. That, coupled with an unconscious man's sloppy grip, completely explains this type of bruising."

"Did you point that out to the deputies at the scene?"

He nodded. "I had them take photos, too."

"Good. Firing the weapon while it was in your hand tells us that the killer is savvy enough to know about gunpowder residue," Sister Agatha said.

"Yeah, and the blow to my head offers an easy explanation for me being unconscious."

They heard footsteps coming down the hallway, and a second later Millie Romero unlocked the door for John Ramirez. Sister Agatha recognized him as one of the department's senior crime scene investigators.

"I'm here to draw blood, Sheriff," he said with a grin. "We need to get that done now to increase our chances of finding detectable traces of whatever drug they used on you. Then, by the time the bureaucrats get around to authorizing the tests, we'll already be a step ahead on the results. Hopefully, we're not too late already."

Tom already had his sleeve rolled up. He looked at his watch. "It's been at least six hours since I ate. How late is too late?"

Ramirez looked up and shrugged. "Lots of variables, Sheriff. Wish I knew."

"Let's hope my time hasn't run out," Tom said.

"You'll be fine, Tom," Sister Agatha said, although she wasn't feeling particularly hopeful. Even if the tests proved what they all believed, they would still have a long way to go.

"Look for a type of knockout drug that can result in partial amnesia. My memory of the events is too jumbled to be explained otherwise."

Sister Agatha watched silently. It was said that after the first twenty-four hours, the chances of solving a crime dropped precipitously. Yet never in her investigative experience had time been such a critical factor on every front. She couldn't even guarantee how long she'd be able to investigate before the monastery was closed and her order left New Mexico.

It was absolutely imperative that she find answers quickly. Praying she wouldn't fail her friend, a man who was now counting on her help, she left the tech to his work and slipped out of the room.

2

SISTER AGATHA WALKED DOWN THE HALL DEEP IN THOUGHT. First she checked on Pax, who was now asleep on the floor beside one of the desks. Then she went to the break room and poured herself some coffee. She wasn't used to being up at this hour and didn't trust herself to remain alert enough not to miss something important.

Millie Romero joined her about five minutes later. "We're done, Sister. Would you like to go back?"

"First I need to talk to you, if you have a minute," Sister Agatha said.

Millie nodded wearily. "Even if I didn't, I'd make time," she said quietly.

"We need to find out who else was in that area of the park when Sheriff Green met with Robert Garcia," Sister Agatha said. "Someone must have seen them leave the crowd—then followed."

"Like the killer, you mean," Millie observed. "Captain Chavez is working the case and will make a list of people to interview. Since there were so many people at the event last night, it's going to take a while."

"It might go faster if I get some names from the sheriff and start checking on my own. Also, Tom and I will need a list of everything that was found at the crime scene. Can you get a copy of that for us?"

"I don't know what the procedure is in a case like this, but once the reports come in, I'll make sure the details go to the sheriff, or to his attorney," Millie replied. "Worst-case scenario, I'll get somebody ticked off. Of course, if charges end up being filed, he will be entitled to the information. If not, then he's the sheriff. It shouldn't matter in the long run, and the sooner this matter is resolved, the better."

"Don't worry, Millie. I'll make sure it all stays confidential."

"Thanks," she said quietly. "The sheriff's run this department as a team. We're like family—at least most of us—and I, for one, am totally convinced he's being framed."

Sister Agatha glanced down the hall. "Take me back to Tom for a few more minutes. Then I'll pick up Pax and be out of your hair for a while."

A few minutes later, Sister Agatha sat across from Tom in the interview room. "You've already mentioned some of the people you remembered dealing with at the festivities. Now think back carefully, Tom. Who saw you walk away with Robert?"

He paused, a faraway look on his face. "I'm not sure," he said at last. "I spoke to some of my constituents, had a lemonade, then went to meet Robert. By then, the fireworks were starting, and people weren't moving much, just looking up."

"Okay. Who gave you the lemonade?"

"I don't know the guy's name, but he was one of the city employees working the food stands," Tom said. His forehead furrowed and his eyebrows knit together as he struggled to recall more details. "He was Hispanic looking, with short, curly black hair and a mustache. He had a rough complexion, too, like someone who had had severe acne as a teen."

"There'll be a list of the workers somewhere, so I'll find him," Sister Agatha said firmly. "One more question. How well do you know Al Russo?"

"He was Robert's campaign manager. I've met him a few times at local events and around the town hall, but I don't know him personally. All I can tell you is that he's effective at his job and reputed to be honest—unlike his boss."

"Thanks. I'll be speaking with him soon," she said. "Before I go, Tom, is there anything you need right now?"

He started to speak, then glanced away from her and looked down at his hands, which rested on the table.

"What's on your mind, Tom?" she asked gently. "You can ask me anything."

He met her gaze with a steady one of his own. "Gloria . . . She's high-strung, and right now she's probably terrified," he said.

"I'll go talk to her. Is there anything else?"

"Just find out what really happened. If anyone can do that, you can."

Sister Agatha saw the shadow of fear that crossed his eyes, but in a heartbeat he forced himself to relax slightly and gained control again. "Lies never stand up to close inspection," she told him. "I'll find the truth."

"I believe you. God's always on a nun's side," he said with a hint of a smile.

"It sure seemed that way back in high school when Sister Assumpta would catch us passing notes."

He laughed.

"Don't worry," she said growing serious again. "God *will* help us."

After giving him a reassuring smile, Sister Agatha followed Millie down the hall, stopped by the bullpen, and picked up Pax, who was awake again. As they stepped outside together she took a deep breath.

Beyond the glare of the station lights, the night sky was clear, and a full canopy of stars twinkled overhead. Yet despite the beauty and order she saw above her, fear nipped at the edges of her mind. Her calm, orderly world was coming apart at the seams, and as it unraveled, so did everything else she'd taken for granted. Her friend and her beloved monastery were fighting for their very existence, and both could lose the battle.

Feeling small and helpless in the face of what lay ahead, she began to tremble. Her sudden prayer was simplicity itself and came straight from her heart. "Oh, dear God, help!"

The Maria bell rang at 4:30 A.M., gently waking the sisters from their rest. Matins, a prayer that would counter the evils that roamed the night, was said before daybreak. It was also symbolic of brides who'd remained alert waiting for their bridegroom.

"Now is the time to rise from sleep. Let us open our eyes to the Light that comes from God," Sister Agatha recited in silence.

Struggling to become fully awake, she went to the washbasin and rinsed her face. After leaving the station last night, she'd visited Gloria Green, Tom's wife. She'd been unable to do much more than calm the woman down, but by the time Sister Agatha had returned to the monastery, she'd been wide-awake. All in all, she hadn't had more than three hours of sleep.

She soon joined the sisters in chapel, ready to take part in their communal prayer. After Matins came Lauds. Those prayers were said at dawn and gave praise to God. It was all followed by Mass. These daily affirmations helped her restore order to her thinking. As long as she placed God before everything else in her life, she'd have the strength to face whatever lay ahead.

At seven thirty, when they adjourned for breakfast, Sister Agatha looked around the refectory and saw the same concerns that plagued her mirrored on the faces of the other sisters. Change was never easy. Sister Clothilde, who'd faithfully fixed their meals and had been their laundress for as far back as anyone remembered, was already living at Agnus Dei, the monastery outside Denver that was their almost certain future destination. Sister Gertrude had gone up at the same time, both driven there by Sister de Lourdes. It was hoped that the elderly sisters would find the warm welcome at Agnus Dei Monastery easier to bear than packing up the remains of their lives here at Our Lady of Hope.

Unless an all-out miracle happened, their beautiful monastery would be closing its doors for good in another few weeks, and those who were still here at that time would move north as well. As the Bishop had pointed out in his last paternal visit, there weren't enough nuns at Our Lady to justify the expensive renovation their old building would require to remain habitable.

Had they been able to afford it, Sister Agatha was certain, Mother would have allocated the funds to save their home. Unfortunately, they were close to broke. With the foreign outsourcing of the NexCen mail order business—filling orders for electronic components produced at the local factory—they'd lost a major source of income. Their scriptorium operation, where they'd worked converting text and images to digital format, had also suffered from outsourcing, stretching their current budget to the limit.

"According to the bean counters, we're not cost-effective," Sister Bernarda had grumbled privately.

Sister Agatha's heart twisted as she thought of having to leave the home she'd so loved. Most of the sisters had lived here for the past twenty years or more. Sister Agatha herself had been born and raised in this community and had never lived more than a half hour's distance from the monastery.

Yet the facts against them were seemingly indisputable. The invitation from Agnus Dei had come at just the right time, too, a sure sign that it was God's work. The Colorado monastery was doing well—thanks to several endowments.

Yet, deep in her heart, it felt as if God had played favorites. Agnus Dei had great abundance, while they struggled. Though she knew she was looking at things from the wrong perspective, she could see the same feeling in the eyes of the sisters that remained.

Once they'd finished breakfast, Sister Agatha hurried to the parlor, where she knew Sister Bernarda would already be. When she arrived, the former marine was seated behind the desk, her battle face in place. It was her lack of expression that told Sister Agatha just how difficult her fellow extern was finding the reality of their circumstances.

"Has Reverend Mother heard anything new from the archdiocese?" Sister Agatha asked.

"They're considering our final appeal, but Luz del Cielo Winery next door has made an offer. They want to expand the vineyard and turn the monastery into a bed-and-breakfast. They've even offered to respect our cemetery if we sell. The Archbishop is in favor of us accepting the offer. He believes we'll all be better off at Agnus Dei, so I doubt he'll change his mind. Money's too tight in this ailing economy. As much as we love it here at Our Lady of Hope, I'm sure we'll be serving elsewhere soon," Sister Bernarda said in a heavy voice.

Sister Agatha sighed softly. "That's all the more reason for me to get busy," she said, trying to bolster her own spirits. "There's a lot to do between now and then." She quickly reported the events of last night.

"Reverend Mother's in the infirmary this morning," Sister Bernarda said. "The burden she carries is twice as heavy as ours, and it has taken a toll on her health. Sister Eugenia has insisted on keeping her under observation for a few hours this morning."

Sister Agatha smiled. Their infirmarian, Sister Eugenia, didn't take no for an answer, but Reverend Mother was a formidable opponent.

Just as the thought formed, they heard the grille slide open. The wooden, windowlike opening allowed the cloistered sisters to remain inside the enclosure while visiting with family and friends who entered the parlor.

"Child, what's the news from town?" Reverend Mother asked Sister Agatha. To Reverend Mother, the sisters were all her spiritual children, and she called each of them "child."

The weariness in Mother's voice tugged at Sister Agatha. The move to Agnus Dei would be hardest on her. Though it wasn't her fault, Reverend Mother still felt responsible for Our Lady of Hope's current economic quagmire.

Sister Agatha briefly explained the situation, then said, "Sheriff Green's in real trouble, Mother. Although the evidence against him is mostly circumstantial, it's still impressive. Unless the person who really killed Robert Garcia is caught, Tom Green could end up being charged with murder."

"You firmly believe he's innocent?"

"I have no doubt of that, Mother. After talking to him, I'm convinced he's being framed for the crime. What's worse, even if he isn't charged and convicted of murder, the real killer could go free."

"Sheriff Green has served our community with honor and has stood by Our Lady of Hope Monastery through some very dark moments. Do whatever's necessary to restore his good name. Our prayers will support you every step of the way."

"Thank you, Mother," Sister Agatha answered.

Reverend Mother stood, wavered slightly, then, grabbing the back of her chair, eased herself back down again.

In an instant, Sister Agatha went through the enclosure door and was at her elbow. "Mother, let me walk you back to the infirmary."

She shook her head. "No time for rest. There's too much work to be done."

"But Mother—" Sister Agatha started. The ringing phone interrupted her.

Sister Bernarda, closest to it, answered. "Mrs. Green, I'm so sorry to hear the news about your husband," she said, then, after a beat, added, "Yes, she's here."

Sister Bernarda gestured to Sister Agatha, then hurried out the enclosure door to Mother's side. "I'll help Mother," she said. "Gloria Green would like to speak to you."

Leaving Reverend Mother in her care, Sister Agatha hurried into the parlor to answer the phone. "Hello, Gloria. I've been praying for both you and Tom. What's the situation this morning?"

"They're still holding him. According to his attorney, Tom'll be arraigned within seventy-two hours. By then they'll have decided what the charges will be—either manslaughter or murder. Doug says they're within their rights to keep him for more questioning, but it's driving me crazy. Most of the department's on Tom's side, but there are others . . ."

"I was planning on coming over this morning to talk to you again. Is that all right?"

"I'll be here."

"Good. I'll see you soon," she said, then hung up. As she turned, Sister Agatha realized that Reverend Mother was still at the grille.

"Go with my blessing, child," Reverend Mother said. Then, refusing Sister Bernarda's help, she went down the hall as silently as she'd arrived.

"The trip to Denver will be very hard on her," Sister Bernarda said softly.

"Once we're there, Pax will help. He'll be a great therapy dog for her and a touch of home, all in one package." Seeing Sister Bernarda's surprised look, she added, "Did I mention that Agnus Dei has welcomed Pax? I can't tell you how relieved I was when I heard that."

Pax had washed out of the police department because he'd lost his aggressive edge. Yet he'd earned his keep at the monastery by protecting them.

As she stood at the window, Sister Agatha could see Pax playing outside, nosing something on the ground. When it hopped, she realized he was teasing a toad.

"Gloria sounded so defeated on the phone. Please assure her that we're all here for her," Sister Bernarda said as Sister Agatha opened the door leading out into the front grounds.

Sister Agatha walked across the enclosed grounds to where the motorcycle and sidecar were parked and whistled for Pax. The dog came running, jumped into the sidecar, then waited as she fastened her helmet.

"We'll be riding up to Agnus Dei in this motorcycle, Pax.

That should be fun—better than nudging toads. Something to look forward to, don't you think?"

Maybe it was something in her tone of voice that tipped him off, but the dog looked at her, his ears pricked forward—almost as if waiting.

"Can't fool you for a minute, can I?" she muttered. "Maybe we better just take things one day at a time."

It was just after the morning rush hour, and the air was cool and dry. By this afternoon, however, temperatures would soar and hit the high nineties. When the thermometer climbed like that, even their summer habits felt hot and heavy. Summers in New Mexico—that was one thing she wouldn't miss in Denver.

Glad to have found at least one positive thing about their move, she continued the drive south toward Bernalillo in better spirits. The sheriff's home was on the northern outskirts, less than fifteen minutes from the monastery. Gloria, Tom, and their children lived in a modest home with a silver corrugated-metal pitched roof. Just east of the main irrigation canal, it was at the end of a shady graveled lane lined with enormous cottonwoods that must have dated back fifty years.

She arrived in short order and pulled into the driveway behind a blue SUV. The Harley had a distinctive putt-putt, and by the time she'd turned off the ignition, Gloria was already at the courtyard gate. Her hair color had changed many times over the years, most of them variations of blond, but right now it was a truly unattractive auburn that startled rather than flattered. Her eyes were puffy, an indication that she'd been crying.

"Come in," she invited Sister Agatha as the nun removed her helmet. "I brewed fresh coffee, and I've even got some leftover meat loaf Pax might like."

Hearing the words "Pax" and "meat loaf" immediately got

the dog's attention. He barked twice and jumped out of the sidecar.

"Now you're stuck. He'll hound you until he gets what you promised, no pun intended," Sister Agatha said, laughing as she placed the helmet on the saddle.

As they stepped onto the brick floor of the Territorial-style home, Sister Agatha glanced around. The living room was impeccable, a rare sight. With two boys—one a teenager and the other in middle school—she'd expected to find the usual clutter of sports equipment and shoes lying around, but today everything looked in perfect order. From what she could see and smell, Gloria had been cleaning the leather sofa and chairs with a spray dressing. The surfaces gleamed, even in the subdued light.

"The boys took a flight out last night to my mother's in Phoenix. They protested like crazy, but I didn't give them a choice. There's no way I wanted my boys in the middle of all that's happening." She looked around the room and shook her head. "When I got up this morning I found that I couldn't stand the silence, so I started looking for something to clean." She met Sister Agatha's gaze. "The quiet at the monastery—does it ever get to you?"

"It's a different type of quiet," Sister Agatha answered after a moment. "It doesn't mark the absence of something. To us, it's a reminder that He is ever present, and we commune with God in that peace. If anything, I'd call it . . . soothing."

Gloria sighed softly, walking toward the marble-topped island on the kitchen side of the room. "This kind of quiet—the absence of my children—is driving me nuts. The really frustrating part is knowing that with the Internet, my guys can contact their friends and find out what's going on instantly. There's no way I can stop that. Even if I said no, they'd find a way. Well, at least the distance will give them some protection from the constant back-and-forth of allegations and the overall nastiness that's bound to surface."

She waited for her hand to steady, then picked up a carafe from the counter and poured Sister Agatha a mug of coffee.

Pax, who'd been very patient up to now, sat right in front of Gloria.

"Oh, sorry, boy, I nearly forgot." Gloria opened the refrigerator, brought out a chunk of meat loaf wrapped in clingy plastic, then opened the cupboard. A few seconds later, Pax was busy gobbling up cold meat loaf from an aluminum pie pan while the women were seated at the breakfast bar.

"I know you're scared and worried, Gloria, but you've already come a long way from last night. Keep your spirits up. Tom needs you to believe in him."

"He didn't tell you about us, did he?" Seeing Sister Agatha's puzzled look, she continued. "Tom and I are having major problems, and I was getting ready to move out. The only reason I'm still here is because of Tom's attorney. Doug said that it would make things even worse for Tom if I left now. People would think I moved out because I thought he was guilty."

"You were going to leave Tom?" Sister Agatha repeated, stunned. "Gloria, why? He loves you, and you have such a lovely family."

"Tom loves his *job*, Sister. The boys and I finish a distant second."

For a moment, words wouldn't come. Sister Agatha understood better than most what drove Tom, but she wasn't sure there was a way to explain it. "He *does* love you and the boys, Gloria," she answered at last. "You're at the very center of his soul. It's true that his job takes much of his time, but he sees his work as his mission in life. It's what he was put here to do."

"Is that the way you feel about being a nun?"

She nodded. "It gives me purpose. Tom's work is very different from mine, though. It's not all-encompassing. Tom needs you—as much as you do him. The job keeps his blood pumping, but you and the boys *are* his heart."

"Tom and I will have to settle a lot of things after this is over," Gloria said, wiping a tear from the corner of her eye. She drank her coffee in silence for several long moments, then, in a stronger voice, continued. "In the meantime, we're both counting on you to help him prove his innocence."

Realizing that Gloria didn't want to discuss her marital problems any longer, Sister Agatha didn't press. "The first thing I want to do is find out more about Robert's campaign manager, Al Russo. He's the one who found Tom and Robert."

"His ex-wife, Jayne, and I were friends for a while before she left town. Jayne told me once that Al and she divorced because they didn't have enough in common to stay together. They never really talked. They also never went anywhere together except to dinner, and then it was always to a sports bar. All he ever wanted to do was watch games on TV, play golf, or work. She wanted . . . well, a husband and a friend she could do things with. He was neither."

"Who's Al dating these days?"

"Nobody, according to the gossip. He hits the sports bars, but mostly for the guy talk and the big-screen TV. From what I hear, Al likes keeping his life simple. I assume he still dates occasionally, but it hasn't been often enough to catch anyone's attention."

"Thanks for the information, and the coffee," Sister Agatha said, standing up. "Come on, Pax, we've got a long day ahead of us."

"You sounded like Tom just then." Gloria walked with Sister Agatha and Pax across the room. "If you hadn't become a nun, Tom would have married you in a heartbeat."

The statement, under the circumstances, surprised Sister Agatha, and she stopped to meet Gloria's gaze directly. "Tom and I were together a lifetime ago, Gloria—our last year in high school and for a few semesters in college. Since that time neither one of us has ever looked back."

"You sure?" Gloria asked, an edge to her voice now as she reached for the door handle.

"Completely. My heart belongs to my Lord, and Tom's love is yours and the boys. It's the way things were meant to be."

Gloria nodded, opening the door.

"I have one last question for you before I go," Sister Agatha said, turning in the entrance to face her. She repeated the description of the man who'd handed Tom the drink. "Does that remind you of anyone in particular?"

Gloria thought about it for a moment. "Yes, as a matter of fact, it does—Mayor Garcia's new son-in-law. His name's Matt, Mike, or something like that.

"The guy's trouble, Sister Agatha. I've heard that JD nearly had a coronary when Cindy married him. According to Tom, the kid's been arrested for possession of dangerous drugs—I think he was dealing—about a year or two back," she said, her eyebrows knitting together, "but I'm not one hundred percent sure about that timing. Tom will know more."

"I'll check on that. Thanks." Sister Agatha stepped out onto the porch, Pax at her side.

"Just so you know, nobody in the Garcia clan is a fan of Tom's. It wasn't simply a personal thing between him and Robert. Every single one of them would be happy to see Tom go down. He's been a thorn in the side of their political-crony network for years now."

"Tom has enemies—it goes with his job, Gloria. But he's also got some very good friends," she added with a confident smile. "I'll tell you another thing I've learned over the years. The truth *always* comes out if you're willing to keep digging, and that's exactly what I intend to do."

Her confident words had their intended effect. Sister Agatha could see Gloria's spirits lift. Yet experience assured her that things would get a lot worse before they got better.

3

BEFORE SHE PUT HER HELMET ON AGAIN, SISTER AGATHA called the station and asked to speak to Millie. After her late night, Millie would probably have the day off, but she wanted to make sure.

Having verified that Millie was at home, Sister Agatha turned to Pax, and smiled. "We're on our way to make pests of ourselves. We'll probably wake Millie up, but under the circumstances, I don't think she'll mind."

They were soon driving down a badly maintained graveled road. Sister Agatha went slowly, not only because of the rocks that covered the roadway but in an effort not to spook the horses and llamas in an adjacent pasture. Pax barked happily at them, but then, seeing Sister Agatha signal him, quieted down almost instantly.

A minute later, they pulled up at the end of a dead-end street and turned right. The small, unpaved driveway was covered with adobe-colored rocks and lined by big chucks of black volcanic lava—a popular landscaping material found locally in abundance.

As Sister Agatha climbed off the motorcycle, she saw Millie coming though a gate that adjoined a horse stall at the rear of the property. In her hand was a green plastic feed bucket.

After closing the gate behind her, Millie looked up and, seeing them, waved. "I thought I heard a motorcycle. What are you two doing here this early?" she asked pleasantly, joining them. "I guess you don't sleep late much either, huh?"

"The Maria bell at the monastery is always on time," Sister Agatha answered. "But what are *you* doing dressed and working already? You were at the station until well after midnight."

"I can't sleep in, ever. No matter how late I go to bed, I always wake up at six thirty in the morning," she said, wiping the sweat off her brow with a tissue. "It's starting to warm up already, so we'll probably reach close to three digits today. Let's go inside. We can relax and have something to drink." She added, "You're welcome, too, Pax. I've got some leftover chicken you might like."

Pax whined in eagerness, and Sister Agatha laughed. "Pax, you're really a pig." Glancing back at Millie, she added, "I want you to know that he eats a whole huge bowl of kibble every night on top of all the treats he gets in town. He's a bottomless pit."

Several moments later, they sat in Millie's homey kitchen. A collection of decorative ceramic cows lined the countertops, and collectible kitchen gadgets from bygone eras covered the walls. As Millie poured the coffee, Sister Agatha waited, looking at a shelf containing sets of salt and pepper shakers all in the form of pigs and hogs.

"Crime scene work has been completed. I got the list of all

the evidence they found and gave the sheriff a copy before I left last night—well, earlier this morning," she said at last.

"After looking at the list, did he remember anything new?" Sister Agatha asked.

"Not to my knowledge, but I didn't stick around long after that. You might want to go back and talk to him again. No telling how things look to him this morning now that he's had a chance to recover from what happened and been given time to think."

Sister Agatha sipped Millie's blend of coffee. It was smooth and better than any she'd ever tasted. "This tastes wonderful."

"Thanks," she answered. "It's one of my favorites." She took a sip, then met Sister Agatha's gaze. "The sheriff asked me—off the record—about the crew who worked the refreshment stands yesterday. In particular, he wanted to know about the mayor's son-in-law, Mike Herrera."

"Is it true that Herrera was arrested for possession and for dealing drugs?"

"Yeah, but except for that one offense, his record's clear. From what I've seen and heard, the guy's really cleaned up his act since that bust," Millie said. "Supposedly, Robert went to bat for him with JD before the wedding as a favor to his niece, who needed someone in her corner. JD didn't want Cindy to marry him, for obvious reasons, but they sorted it all out."

"You know, it's funny. Mayor John David Garcia goes by JD, and his daughter goes by Cindy, not Cynthia. Yet Robert's never been called Bob."

"You never met him, did you?" Millie observed. "If you'd known him, you wouldn't have asked me that question. Nobody took shortcuts around Robert. He was particularly that way around the station. Once he made lieutenant, Robert began demanding accountability to an impossible degree. He wanted to control everyone and everything around him. That attitude extended to his personal life, too. I've heard that he had his wife completely cowed. All throughout his campaign she stood in the background, smiling but never saying a word. I have a feeling that nothing she ever said was quite good enough for Robert, so she figured it was easier to stay out of the way."

"Robert sounds like a tyrant, but he obviously had people who were loyal to him. From what I've already heard, Al Russo was working quite hard to get him elected."

"That's true enough," Millie conceded. "Then again, that was Al's job."

"Has Robert's body been released to the family yet?" Sister Agatha asked.

"No. Maybe in another two days or so, depending on how long OMI—the Office of the Medical Investigator—takes with the autopsy," Millie said. "That's my guess, anyway."

Sister Agatha finished her coffee, then stood. "I'm going to go over to the park and take a look around. It'll help me put things into perspective. Thanks for your help, Millie."

"The area around the crime scene's still taped off," Millie warned.

"I figured that, but maybe just being in the vicinity will spark an idea or two for me. I'm hoping to spot something the others have overlooked."

"With your journalist background, you don't look at the scene with the same eyes as a police officer, so I guess that's possible."

Millie's tone said far more than her words did. The sergeant doubted that Sister Agatha's efforts would be fruitful.

After saying good-bye, Sister Agatha drove to downtown Bernalillo, stopping in one of the parking spaces beside the multiacre park and community center. There was plenty of shade, with all the old trees and shrubbery, and the lawn was lush and green despite the previous day's heavy foot traffic.

City employees were taking down some of the tents that had sheltered vendors. Volunteers in red safety vests were scouring the grounds, picking up discarded food containers and napkins. As she strode across the grass with Pax in the direction of the swings, she saw a mobile camera unit from an Albuquerque TV station driving up the road leading to the southwest corner of the park. The vehicle parked at the curb, and two people got out. By the time she was halfway there, they'd disappeared behind a hedge of reddish orange trumpet vines.

Soon, she came around the end of the vines to a large area cordoned off with yellow crime scene tape tied and wrapped around several trees. Keeping Pax at heel and leashed, she stood and watched a TV camerawoman and well-dressed male reporter film a segment just outside the tape. Two other individuals with still cameras stalked the permimeter, angling for the best shots and taking several each. Curious townspeople who'd walked up the road or hiked across the park, as she had done, stared at the area with morbid fascination.

"Hey, Sister Agatha, Pax!" Chuck Moody called out, then came jogging up to them from behind.

Chuck, one of the two employees at the Bernalillo newspaper, the *Chronicle*, had more energy and bounce than anyone else she'd ever met. Chuck stood five foot four and had recently adopted a new haircut that made him look a bit like a Chia Pet. His head was completely shaved except for a thin line of reddish hair that grew out of the very center of his skull.

"I had a feeling I'd be catching up with you here today," he said, then continued with barely a pause to catch his breath. "The Garcia political machine is putting serious pressure on local law enforcement to close this case. They're after Sheriff Green's blood."

"Tom didn't murder anyone," she said calmly.

"Yeah, that's what most people I've talked to believe, too. The fact that Robert was holding a bloody club in his hand when he died makes no sense. Robert wouldn't have taken on an armed man with a club. Too great a chance of failure, if nothing else. Robert Garcia *always* had a plan. If he'd really wanted Tom dead, he would have contracted it out, being careful not to set up a trail that could lead back to him and making sure he had a perfect alibi. The sheriff would have been taken out of the picture for good, and Robert would have been in the clear. But grabbing a piece of broken branch off the ground and duking it out with a pistol-packing officer? No way. Garcia was a planner and manipulator, not some hothead."

"Yeah, the entire scenario has a definite smell to it," she said. Her eyes narrowed as she noticed the absence of his equipment bag. "What, no camera? So what really brought you here today?"

"You know me too well," he said with a quick little smile. Glancing around to make sure no one could overhear, he continued. "I have an idea. It's possible that there might have been a witness to the murder, someone the deputies wouldn't know about. I bet you anything that Scout was here yesterday."

"Who?"

"Scout's a homeless guy who has been hanging around town for months. He apparently avoids the shelters, but he's getting by, stealing food and raiding garbage cans."

Sister Agatha nodded, remembering the stories she'd heard. "They call him Scout because he wears a Boy Scout neckerchief beneath his gray cap. He protects his neck from the sun that way, like some French Foreign Legion soldier." Smitty, the town's grocer, often left day-old sandwiches on a window ledge at the back of his store for Scout. They'd always be gone by morning. Others in the community also left out food for him.

"That's the guy. With all the chow at hand yesterday, he'd have been here," Chuck said. "No way he'd pass up the chance to scrounge for food. Mike Herrera, who was working at one of the refreshment stands, told me that he saw him filling a grocery bag with hot dogs and buns snagged from paper plates."

"People tend to ignore the homeless, or just look away, not wanting to make eye contact. There's no telling what Scout might have seen," Sister Agatha said.

"Exactly. Like maybe the killer?"

"Would Scout return here so soon, though? Particularly with the police and media so interested in the place?" she asked as an afterthought.

"The police *were* here, but they've been gone for hours now. I was hoping he'd come back to look around some more."

"Let's take a walk, look around, and see what we can find," Sister Agatha said.

Chuck fell into step beside her. "The sheriff and you have been good friends for years. This has got to be hard on you—particularly in view of the recent bad news at the monastery," he added, deliberately not looking at her.

His words and the implication took her by surprise. The townspeople hadn't yet been told that Our Lady of Hope Monastery would probably be shut down.

"What are you referring to?" she asked, careful not to give anything away.

"I've heard that your cook, one of the really old nuns, passed on."

She stared at him and blinked. "Huh?"

"Sister Bernarda told Smitty that your meals were a lot

more basic now because the nun that used to cook is no longer with you."

"She's not at the monastery, but she's not dead," Sister Agatha said, laughing, then realized that her statement would require more of an explanation than she'd been prepared to give. Well, it was too late now. She had to say something. "Sister Clothilde is very elderly. She needed to go to another monastery that has more resources and is better able to cater to her special needs. She moved away, that's all."

"You have retirement homes for nuns?" Chuck asked, his gaze continuing to take in the area around them as he searched for Scout.

"We have retirement homes, yes," she answered, grateful that he hadn't specifically asked if Sister Clothilde was now living in one of them. She wouldn't have wanted to lie.

They'd been circling around the perimeter of the park and were getting close to the community center, a large one-story block structure, when Chuck stopped and turned to face her.

"What's up?" Sister Agatha asked him quickly.

"Somebody's standing behind that cottonwood tree next to the community center's trash bins. I think it's Scout, but don't look over there now," he warned. "If we spook him, he'll just disappear."

Sister Agatha leaned down to pet Pax, then glanced sideways. There was a flicker of movement as a shape backed farther into the shadows.

"Scout's jumpy and usually won't let anyone get close. I think we need to box him in real subtle-like. If we try to approach him directly, he'll bolt and we'll never catch him. He knows the ditch banks and the bosque like the back of his hand."

"What's your plan?" she asked.

"Stay here for a minute or two, Sister, then walk off. Pretend you're training Pax. I'll head for the community center, but instead of going inside, I'll circle around and wait at the corner. Give me a few minutes to get in place, then stroll toward the back of the building. Work with Pax and keep your attention on him, and don't even glance in Scout's direction. Once you're within five or ten yards of the trash bins, I'll come out of hiding, and he'll be between us."

"Okay. We're ready anytime you are," she said, her hand on Pax's head.

"Well, good-bye, Sister Agatha. You, too, Pax," Chuck said loudly, waving his hand, then walking away.

Sister Agatha pretended to examine Pax's paw for stickers, then stood. Walking at a leisurely pace with Pax at heel, she made her way slowly to the rear of the building, near the area where two staff cars were parked. Beyond, Scout stood near the cottonwoods, searching the trash.

She'd come within twenty feet of the trash when Chuck stepped around the corner. He was actually looking the other way, pretending to be talking to someone else, but Scout, seeing him, suddenly panicked. Realizing that she and Chuck were approaching him from separate directions, he yelped and, breaking from his hiding place, took off, racing past Sister Agatha.

Pax lunged at the running man, yanking hard at his leash. Sister Agatha could have stopped Pax from chasing Scout, but that would have defeated any chance she might have had of catching up to him. Allowing Pax to tug her along, she hiked up her skirt and ran across the grass.

"Wait!" she called out to Scout.

The frightened man jumped a hedge and raced down the wide ditch bank, which also served as a flood levee for the river, a quarter of a mile away.

Chuck hadn't exaggerated. Scout could sprint faster than

anyone else she'd ever seen on two legs. Despite Pax's enthusiasm, she could barely keep up. Scout was already fifty yards down the bank. He never looked back, intent on his escape. Then he swerved and headed straight toward the ditch.

At the opposite bank of the five-foot-deep muddy stream was a dirt road that gave access to the conservancy district vehicles. The gap was at least ten feet wide.

"Don't! You won't make it!" she yelled. Wearing a dusty backpack bulging with perhaps all his worldly possessions, he had no chance.

Scout jumped. His arms and legs flailing wildly, he landed on the steep opposite bank about a yard above water level. He then flopped forward up onto the road, landing on his belly and the palms of his hands. Completing a comical-looking somersault, he rolled up onto his feet, crossed the road in two bounds, then crashed through the stand of willows along the edge of the woods. Within seconds he'd disappeared into the bosque.

Sister Agatha caught a glimpse of something on the opposite bank where the man had landed and walked toward it for a closer look. Seeing it made her chest tighten.

"What did you find?" Chuck asked, panting as he jogged up and looked over Sister Agatha's shoulder.

She pointed. "Two hot dogs in a plastic bag. Probably his lunch, and maybe dinner. That poor man!"

Chuck stood at the edge of the ditch bank, appraising Scout's amazing leap. "He's in pretty good shape. I'll say that much for him."

"The man has the wings of an angel," Sister Agatha agreed. "Even as a kid I couldn't have made a jump like that."

"The nearest bridge across must be half a mile from here," Chuck said, turning to look both ways down the ditch. "We've lost him."

"I've got to figure out a way to get Scout to talk to me," Sister Agatha said, fingering her rosary thoughtfully.

"That's a tall order, Sister, especially after today. From what I've heard, he rarely allows anyone to get too close, even those who offer him a meal. That's probably why he never shows up at any of our homeless shelters, even during the winter." He paused, then continued. "We may have a lead on a crime that no one, short of an Olympic sprinter, can pursue."

"I'll ask Our Lord to help me, and He'll find a way," Sister Agatha said.

"I sure wish I had that kind of faith, Sister," Chuck said.

"So do I," she said without thinking. Seeing the confusion on his face, she managed a wry smile. "I'm far from perfect, Chuck."

4

ALTHOUGH THE ODDS OF FINDING SCOUT WERE SLIM TO none, they decided to walk to the bridge anyway and cross over. Together, they searched for footprints or anything else that might give them an indication of which direction Scout had gone.

After a half hour, they were forced to give up the search. The ground was too dry and hard to track man or animal here at the edge of the bosque. Hoping that Scout would come back later and retrieve it, they left the bag with the hot dogs resting in the crook of a tree branch.

"Do you happen to know Scout's real name?" Sister Agatha asked Chuck as they headed back into the park.

"Sister, I don't think that the guy himself remembers anymore. A lot of our homeless people have some serious psychological problems. Whenever I see Scout, he's usually searching garbage cans. The closest I've ever gotten to him is maybe fifty feet."

As they walked back across the grass, not much was said between them. Finally, as they reached the parking lot and the monastery's motorcycle, Chuck broke the silence.

"What's next on your agenda?" he asked.

"Funny you should ask," she said with an impish smile. "I'm still not getting a clear enough picture of what happened here yesterday. I haven't been to an Independence Day celebration outside the monastery in over twenty years. If you covered the event, I'd sure like to see the photos you took."

"I was here most of the day and night. My boss even paid for my three hot dogs and two cans of soda. How American is that? Follow me back to the office," he said, walking off to where his beat-up old sedan was parked.

As Sister Agatha headed back into town, Pax in the sidecar, she tried to come up with a strategy for finding Scout. He probably hadn't gone far—the bosque was undoubtedly his home— yet locating him was going to be anything but easy. He now knew they wanted to speak to him, and that would make it even harder. He'd make it a point to avoid them. Yet in her gut she knew that finding him and getting him to talk would be well worth the trouble.

Sadness crept over her. She'd met many of God's wounded children over the years, and although the world had broken them into pieces, they remained surprisingly resilient. Scout, for example, had shown remarkable resourcefulness surviving by his own rules.

Sister Agatha felt a twinge of guilt for having worried so much about the future of her own home. At least she knew she was going to be welcomed with open arms when the move took place, as, barring a true miracle, it most certainly would.

Sister Agatha parked in front of the small newspaper's office as Chuck got out of his car, attached Pax's leash, then walked inside. The adobe building had been completely rewired and modernized. It felt good to walk into a place cooled by refrigerated air instead of swamp coolers. Those all too often barely made a dent in the heat, and everything felt muggy from the moisture in the air.

"I've decided that I'm a winter person," Sister Agatha said, leaning back and making the most of that heavenly cold blast of air. Pax sat beside her, panting.

"Considering that habit you wear, I don't blame you," Chuck said, "but I like summer. Clothes don't have to be as heavy or bulky. My clothes, that is," he added with a grin as he reached for a small laptop computer. "All the photos I took that day have been uploaded into this laptop. I can preview and edit the shots at home, then send the results back here electronically."

As he retrieved the image file, Sister Agatha sat on the chair beside him and began to study the thumbnails of more than two hundred photos. Whenever she saw one she wanted to examine more closely, she'd give him a nod and he'd enlarge the image.

"This is my initial file, so you're looking at everything, including the rejects. I thought you'd want to see the entire day's shoot."

"I do, thanks," she said. "I can see many people I recognize, like Smitty, and of course almost every member of the Garcia family. There's Millie in the background of that shot. Her husband, too. Who's this gentleman by the podium?"

"That's Monty Allen, Robert's business partner. I've heard that he was the one who finally convinced Robert to run for sheriff. I don't think it was a tough sell, though. Whenever I've been around Robert, he's always come across as an arrogant know-it-all who insists on being in charge."

"What else do you know about Robert?"

"He and Sheriff Green had a truckload of problems back in the days when they were both in the department. My sources are pretty good, so you can trust that."

Sister Agatha knew that Chuck took pride in the accuracy of his information. He was an excellent reporter with a good handle on the facts. She couldn't help but wonder how long it would be before he found out that their monastery might soon be shutting its doors for good.

"Who's this woman standing behind Robert?" Sister Agatha asked him, focusing. "The one with the pasted-on smile."

"His wife, Victoria. She comes to all the community functions. The boy pulling on her hand is their son, R.J. He's obviously hard to control."

"Probably one of the reasons she doesn't look like she's having any fun," Sister Agatha muttered under her breath. "I guess it's just something that the spouse of a candidate has to do. . . ."

"Or else? From your tone, I guess you've heard the gossip," Chuck said. "Whether she enjoys it or not, Victoria always accompanies her husband when he's campaigning—but only she knows how bossy he really is at home."

Sister Agatha looked at a second photo, obviously taken before Victoria knew someone was taking snapshots. In that unguarded moment, the way Victoria was looking at Robert revealed much about their relationship.

Love and hate . . . opposite sides of the same coin. Maybe that explained Victoria's feelings for her husband. Love for what was right—a son, a fine home, social status and prestige. Hate, too—for broken dreams and a loveless marriage? Like everything else in life, emotions were seldom clear-cut.

Studying Victoria's crisp pantsuit and her expensive gold

necklace, Sister Agatha wondered just how much worldly goods and financial security mattered to the woman.

She took a deep breath and let it out slowly. Money seemed at the center of everyone's troubles these days—whether from too much or too little, though she imagined that too much would make the troubles easier to face. Her thoughts drifted to the situation facing Our Lady of Hope. Although she was deeply ashamed of herself, the truth was she was angry with God for abandoning them. Suddenly realizing the turn her thoughts had taken, Sister Agatha brought them to a screeching halt. They were His servants and would go wherever He asked.

"You're a million miles away," Chuck observed.

"Just trying to put things into perspective." At that moment Chuck's cell phone rang, sparing her any further explanation.

Chuck answered the call, then listened to the caller for fifteen seconds. "Who else is there now?" he snapped, his tone all business. "What about Victoria? Have you seen her?" There was another pause before he said, "I'm on my way."

"What's happening?" Sister Agatha asked. "Anything I'd be interested in?"

"Half the town's shown up at Mayor Garcia's home. Victoria's apparently staying there with him and his wife, Alyssa, and word got around. Neighbors, relatives, and friends of the family are paying their respects—bringing food, flowers, and condolences—the *pésame*, as they say around here."

"Those things go on for hours. I should drop by, too," Sister Agatha said, then, after a beat, added, "But not without Sister Bernarda."

Chuck smiled. "Makes sense. Mayor Garcia is a marine, and so's Sister B."

"There's that, and also the fact that the mayor is going to know soon enough that I'm looking into this case on the sheriff's behalf," she answered and stood. "Let's go, boy." Sister Agatha attached Pax's leash, then walked out with the dog just ahead of Chuck.

"JD *wants* the sheriff to be guilty. That's going to make things real interesting for both you and Sheriff Green."

Chuck had spoken softly, almost under his breath, but the warning was clear. Worst of all, she knew it was the truth. Tom and she were both in for a major battle.

Once Sister Agatha arrived at the monastery, she joined the sisters at the refectory for their main meal of the day, served promptly at 1:00 P.M. Sister Maria Victoria was reading from the Martyrology that detailed the ultimate sacrifices made by the saints for the love of God. Hearing about their travails could curtail even a healthy person's appetite, but that wasn't a problem for Sister Agatha today. She was famished.

As she ate the broccoli and corn casserole that Sister Clothilde had lovingly prepared and left frozen, ready to reheat, she remembered the older nun with fondness. Until her departure, Sister Clothilde had been an integral part of daily life at Our Lady of Hope Monastery.

Now, the monastery was in a state of suspension. Their peace was an uneasy one—the quiet before the storm of upheaval struck.

As Sister Agatha glanced around the room, she saw that Sister Eugenia's worried gaze was focused exclusively on Reverend Mother. Their prioress looked worn-out and frail, a result of the constant pressure she'd battled this past year. Too many bills, not enough donations. Although their lifestyle was simple, costs had soared, and their funds were barely sufficient to cover basic needs.

As Sister Agatha tried to push back the darkness that burdened her soul, her gaze fastened on Sister Ignatius, whose face mirrored only peace. Even now her faith hadn't wavered. In trying times, she was a lesson to all of them. Though her prayers never went unanswered, she hadn't asked the Lord to keep their monastery open. She'd only prayed that they'd be given the strength to accept His holy will, and asked that His angels camp around them and keep them safe.

After their meal, Sister Bernarda met Sister Agatha in the corridor. "I spoke to Reverend Mother, and she has given me permission to go with you to pay our condolences to Mrs. Garcia."

"Good," Sister Agatha said. "I doubt that the mayor will be pleased to see me, but if both of us are there, it'll defuse the situation and give me a chance to talk to a few people."

They were on their way in the Antichrysler moments later, Sister Bernarda at the wheel. This time Pax had to remain behind. Unhappy about that decision, he raced after the car. True to his training, however, he came to a sudden stop at the gate and stared mournfully at them as they continued down the dusty road.

"Sister Gertrude e-mailed us this morning. She can't wait to see Pax again," Sister Bernarda said.

Sister Agatha shifted the box of cookies she held on her lap as she turned toward her companion. "How are our other sisters doing up at Agnus Dei? Have you heard?"

"They're settling in. Agnus Dei's horarium is identical to ours, so not having to adjust to a new daily schedule is helping them feel more at home. Everything's working out." Sister Bernarda paused, then added, "I think we've been worrying over nothing. It's not as if we're losing our home."

"Aren't we?" Sister Agatha asked her, surprised.

"No, our *real* home is in God, and He can't be taken from us. The monastery's just a building," she answered, turning onto the highway.

"Is it really so easy for you to start anew someplace else?" Sister Agatha whispered.

Sister Bernarda hesitated, then, in a slow voice, answered, "No, but it's a matter of duty. Honoring that requires us to follow where He leads." Sister Bernarda pulled to the right to allow a faster-moving vehicle to pass.

Sister Agatha stared out the window, lost in thought. Although she knew that Sister Bernarda was right, the prospect of leaving Our Lady of Hope was still heartbreaking to her.

Twenty minutes later, they entered a long asphalt driveway that led to Mayor Garcia's home. Vehicles were parked almost everywhere. People in their Sunday best could be seen walking toward the house with flowers or food containers, and others were returning to their cars, having ended their courtesy calls.

The sprawling ranch-style home was surrounded by an enormous lawn, and the circular drive had a large fountain in its center. Though vehicles lined both the inside and outside curbs, Sister Bernarda saw a driver pulling out and was able to slip into the vacated place.

Once they'd stepped out of the car, Sister Agatha glanced across the hood at Sister Bernarda. "After I present the Cloister Cluster Cookies to whomever is accepting the food, I'm going to stay in the background as much as I can. I'll track you down when it's time for us to go."

"Roger that," she said, in her best Marine Corps bark.

Sister Bernarda's stride was purposeful and steady as she made her way through the foyer into the spacious kitchen/family room. Flowers of every variety and color rested atop nearly all the flat surfaces. There must have been a hundred people at the house, most of them gathered in small groups and speaking in hushed tones. The majority of them had either a cup or a plate of food in their hands. Three women in white coats stood behind the black marble breakfast counter, helping serve food to the guests.

True to her word, Sister Agatha took an offered cup of tea, then hung back, getting close enough to each group to get the gist of their conversation before moving on to the next. There was one overriding theme—Robert's sudden and unexpected death—and nearly unanimous agreement that the sheriff was guilty of his murder.

One woman, whom Sister Agatha recognized as a florist, briefly floated the theory that Robert had struck the sheriff, then committed suicide. Her companions quickly squashed that by calling for a motive the florist couldn't produce.

Moving on, Sister Agatha heard the name Mike being called by a young man standing next to the open French doors. In response, a twenty-something man next to the mayor moved across the room. Sister Agatha made her way toward him and soon was standing beside a floor lamp near the corner of a seating area, close enough to eavesdrop.

"There's no way Green is going to get away with this, bro," Mike said. "My father-in-law's out for blood."

Sister Agatha smiled. Her guess had been right. This was Mike Herrera.

"From what I've heard, it was self-defense," the other one said. "If someone came up and clubbed you across the skull, you'd fight back, wouldn't ya? I can understand that Robert was a relative, and you have to look after family and all, but Green was just protecting himself. The mayor needs to face facts and move on."

"Green and my father-in-law have a history. JD doesn't like anyone who disrespects the Garcias, and Robert and the sheriff have been in each other's faces for years now. I've got a feeling that there's a lot more to it than I've been told. I'm not very tight with JD, in case you haven't noticed. There's no way I'll ever be considered part of the Garcia family. Hell, if I hadn't married Cindy, he wouldn't hire me to mow the grass."

"Hey, *she* chose you. JD'll just have to live with it," the taller one said.

A moment later, a young brunette came into the room from the patio. "There you are, Mike. Hi, guys." She nodded to Mike's friends. "We need your help outside, Mike. No one can find RJ," she said, taking his hand in hers.

"Victoria needs to give that kid some space, Cindy. Your aunt's smothering him," Mike said.

"That's not our problem. *Our* problem is that Dad's having a fit because RJ's not here with his mom greeting people, and when Dad's unhappy, he takes it out on everyone."

"That's for sure. Okay, Cindy, I'll go help you look," he said, rolling his eyes. Mike nodded to his friends, then left with his wife.

"His ol' lady leads him by the nose," one of the men muttered.

"Hey, you gotta pay your dues. Mike'll never worry about money again, but he can kiss his cojones good-bye."

As they moved off across the room toward the food, Sister Agatha saw Mike and Cindy come back inside from the patio. The two stopped to talk to Al Russo, whom Sister Agatha had noticed earlier seated in an armchair. When Mike and Cindy continued upstairs, presumably looking for the boy, Russo stood, glanced around the room, then proceeded outside. Sister Agatha followed him and, standing by a red plum tree, saw him leave the brick patio and make his way across the spacious grounds.

Russo seemed to know precisely where he was going. Sister

Agatha followed him across the lawn, keeping her pace slow as if she were simply going for a stroll. Soon she saw Russo enter a fenced-off area containing a riding arena and horse stalls.

Taking a seat on a cedar garden bench, she turned to one side, her right ear in the direction of the stables, watching out of the corner of her eye.

Russo stopped by a hitching rail and called out to the boy. A moment later, a small, dark-haired seven-year-old boy with glasses peered out over the solid wooden gate of one of the stalls.

"I don't want to go inside," he yelled.

Al nodded calmly. "Me neither, RJ. Just a lot of strangers in suits and Sunday dresses hanging around, eating and looking bored. It's pretty awful right now."

The boy, looking relieved, nodded. "Yeah."

"What did you do with your ball, slugger? We can play catch."

RJ shook his head. "Dad took it at the picnic and gave it to Mom to put away. He said I'd have to crush a bunch of cans for the charity drive to get it back. It was signed, too."

"You get in trouble again?"

"Nah. Just the same old thing," he said with a shrug. "He takes my stuff, then I have to earn it back by learning some kind of lesson. He says I'm 'building character.'"

"Yeah," Al said. Sister Agatha watched the man's face harden.

"Mitch the Missile signed it himself," RJ said indignantly. "Plus he signed a 'Topes roster for me, with my name on it and everything, and Dad took that away, too."

Al smiled at the boy. "You mean this one?" Russo produced a pamphlet with the distinctive Albuquerque Isotopes logo from his inside pocket. The kid's face lit up instantly. "Just remember to put it in your special place when you get home. If you ask your Mom, she'll give you back the ball."

"Thanks, Al!" He looked at the roster, then back up at Russo. "Do I still have to go back inside?"

"Whatever for? I never saw you. A word of advice, though. Stay out of sight for a while. Mike and Cindy are on your trail."

As Al Russo headed back inside, Sister Agatha avoided eye contact with him, looking down as if praying. The little boy had a good friend in Russo. Yet what she'd just heard from RJ had raised even more discouraging questions about Robert Garcia's character.

Sister Agatha walked back across the lawn and entered the main room off the patio. Spotting Sister Bernarda, and not seeing the mayor anywhere, she went to join her fellow extern. Sister Bernarda was standing near Victoria Garcia, who was seated at the end of one of the big leather sofas, a plate heaped with food on her lap.

As Sister Agatha drew near, Victoria turned, and their eyes met for a moment. Although a trail of tears marked the makeup on her cheeks, Victoria's eyes were dry and clear, not red.

Victoria then turned to accept condolences from an elderly woman. She dabbed her eyes, and Sister Agatha heard Victoria's voice break as she spoke to the woman.

"There's something not quite right there," Sister Agatha whispered, coming up beside Sister Bernarda.

"I know what you mean," Sister Bernarda said in a barely audible voice. "Maybe the enormity of what's happened hasn't hit Victoria yet, so she's just doing her best to act the part."

Sister Agatha looked down at Victoria's plate. On it were lettuce, cherry tomatoes, cucumbers, and spinach leaves, topped by two big fresh, pungent onion rings. The serving looked untouched, and the woman had no eating utensils, at least none visible.

"Looks like she's getting help producing those tears on command," Sister Agatha replied, nodding toward the plate.

A murmur went around the gathering as JD Garcia and Al Russo stepped into the living room from an adjoining hall.

"You still want to stick around?" Sister Bernarda whispered.

Before she could answer, Sister Agatha saw Al Russo's gaze fix on Victoria Garcia. Their eyes met for an instant, and Victoria gave him a gentle, knowing smile. For those very brief seconds, Sister Agatha saw awareness shimmering there, and something more . . . perhaps intimacy.

"Now *that* was real—and very interesting," Sister Agatha said.

5

I'D SURE LIKE A CHANCE TO SPEAK TO VICTORIA BEFORE WE go," Sister Agatha said.

"Don't look now, but Al Russo's coming over," Sister Bernarda warned, looking over Sister Agatha's shoulder, then back at her.

A heartbeat later, Sister Agatha felt a hand on her shoulder. "Sister Agatha, under the circumstances, I'm surprised to see you here. JD's been told that you're working to clear the sheriff," Al Russo said quietly.

"Though he may not realize it, Mayor Garcia and I are on the same side. We all want justice, and that's going to require looking well beyond the surface of things," Sister Agatha said, walking out to the patio.

Al followed as she stepped outside. "If you're here to question people, you couldn't have picked a worse time," he added pointedly. "It's in very bad taste."

"Murder is never in good taste, is it, Mr. Russo? But please don't be concerned. I'll be leaving shortly." Before he could comment, she added, "Do you mind if I ask you something before I go? You were the first to arrive on the scene, and you called the authorities, right?"

"Yes. It was a big campaign day for Robert, and I noticed his absence almost right away."

"Think back. Do you remember seeing any transients wandering around the park?"

Al considered it for several long moments, then shook his head. "I didn't notice anyone, but that's not to say they weren't there. I had my attention focused on other things."

"How did you happen to arrive on the crime scene when you did?" Sister Agatha asked.

"One of our biggest campaign contributors showed up late, just in time for the fireworks. I wanted him and Robert to meet face-to-face, but by then Robert had slipped away. I searched around the park looking for him, but . . . I was too late," he added, shaking his head.

She was about to press him for more details when she saw Mayor Garcia working his way toward them from across the room. His look made it clear that she was as welcome as bubonic plague.

"If the sheriff's claiming it was self-defense, Sister, he's got a big credibility gap to cover," Russo continued. "Even with the stick Robert was holding, the sheriff could have easily overpowered him. He could have just sprayed him in the face, for one. I saw the can of Mace, or whatever, on the sheriff's gun belt." He paused. "If I were you, I'd concentrate on saving souls and let law enforcement officers solve the crimes. Your interference will only complicate matters in this community. Why don't you go home, Sister Agatha?"

"We came to let the family know we'll be praying for them and everyone who's involved in this tragedy, Mr. Russo."

"That's not the only reason you're here. You came hoping to learn something that might help you get the sheriff off the hook. I'm used to putting spin on just about everything, Sister, so don't try to kid a kidder."

Glancing past Russo, Sister Agatha saw the mayor pointing her out to another man, probably one of his security staff.

"I don't want to be responsible for unsettling the family, so I'll leave now," Sister Agatha said.

"Excellent decision," Russo answered.

Signaling Sister Bernarda, who'd been watching them, she hurried to the door. Less than five minutes later, they were in the Antichrysler heading down the highway.

"I think the mayor would have had you escorted off the property if we'd stayed even two more minutes," Sister Bernarda said.

"Yeah, I saw what was going on. That's why I figured it was time for us to go."

"I'm going to stop by Smitty's on our way back," Sister Bernarda said. "I promised to pick up a few things for Maria Victoria."

"Please tell me it's not more salsa," Sister Agatha said with a groan.

Sister Bernarda smiled. "No, we lucked out on that. Maria Victoria wanted us to see if Smitty could be persuaded to donate some fresh green chiles. One of our neighbors brought us a huge roasting chicken, and Sister is making chicken enchiladas tomorrow."

"Make real sure that they're *mild* chiles, will you?" Sister Agatha asked. "Those last burritos of hers nearly burned through the roof of my mouth."

"That's because Maria Victoria used green chiles from Mrs. Serna's garden. To the Sernas, that *is* mild."

"I grew up eating green chiles in this part of the country," Sister Agatha said, "but if that wasn't hot, I'd sure hate to taste what is. I was sweating, and my eyes were tearing. And did you see poor Reverend Mother's reaction? She took a bite, gasped, and reached for her water—which, of course, is the worst thing she could have done. Crackers or bread puts out the fire; water just spreads it around."

Sister Bernarda's lips twitched; then she burst out laughing. "The only one who came out okay that day was Sister Ignatius, who'd been feeling under the weather and decided to have Sister Clothilde's chicken soup instead."

"I really miss Sister Clothilde," Sister Agatha said quietly. "Despite her vow of silence she was always there for us whenever it mattered most. She has such a loving nature."

"I miss her, too," Sister Bernarda admitted. "We're a family, and being separated from any of the other sisters makes everything twice as hard. I think once we're all in the same place things will settle down, and we'll adapt. Agnus Dei will be a good place to live, too. Their monastery is involved in a mail order crafts business called Heavenly Goods. It sound like fun work. They have everything from woodworking to quilting."

"When it becomes 'our' monastery instead of 'their' monastery, that's when we'll know we're really home," Sister Agatha said gently, wondering if it would ever feel that way to her.

"I need a favor," Sister Agatha added, as they pulled into the parking lot beside Smitty's Grocery Emporium. "Can you help me get Smitty to myself for a few minutes? He's always busy, but I need to speak to him privately."

"I'll do my best. What kind of information are you looking for?"

"Smitty knows a transient they call Scout who lives in the bosque," Sister Agatha explained. "I'm hoping Smitty can suggest a few places where I might find Scout and, more importantly, give me an idea of how to approach without scaring him off. When Chuck and I tried to talk to Scout before, he took off like a jackrabbit."

"The homeless are often . . . damaged people. If he doesn't want to talk to you, you can't really force it," Sister Bernarda said.

"Still, I have to find a way. There's no telling what he saw the day of the murder. Finding a witness may be the only way we have of clearing the sheriff."

"Even if Scout told you precisely what you wanted to hear, you'd still have to find someone who could corroborate his story," Sister Bernarda said. "A person like that is rarely a credible witness. If you can't even get him to talk to you, imagine how he'd be with the police or on a witness stand."

"You're right," Sister Agatha admitted grudgingly. "Still, even if no one else believes him, it's possible he'll be able to give me a lead I can follow. At the moment, he's the only shot I've got. The Garcias certainly don't want to cooperate. In fact, they've made it clear they'll do all they can to get in my way."

As Sister Bernarda turned off the engine, the Antichrysler backfired loudly. An elderly man carrying groceries to his car nearly dropped his bag. Apologizing as they climbed out of the car, Sister Agatha and Sister Bernarda made sure he was all right, then entered the large grocery store.

Smitty's office was in the back, and, walking down the first aisle, they headed directly there. Sister Agatha knocked on Smitty's open door.

Smitty, a tall, slender, bald-headed man in his early sixties, looked up from his computer and smiled broadly. "I've never been so happy to get an interruption!" he said. "My bookkeeper's on vacation, and I'm trying to keep our accounts updated. Unfortunately, I can't understand her instructions." He gestured toward a spiral notebook with a long list of commands and keystrokes. "Bring back the adding machines, please!"

"I wish I could help," Sister Agatha said.

Smitty regarded her for several seconds, his kind blue eyes narrowing. "Ah, but you're the one who needs help. I recognize that look on your face. What's up?"

"While you two are busy talking, do you mind if I pick up a few things, Smitty?" Sister Bernarda asked him. "Like some green chiles?"

"Go ahead, Sister Bernarda," he answered. "Just give me a list so I can enter it in the books."

"Thanks," she said and left, closing the door behind her to give them the privacy Sister Agatha had asked for.

"Okay, 'fess up, Sister. What's on your mind? Something to do with Sheriff Green's situation, right?" Smitty asked, scooting his chair closer.

Sister Agatha laughed. "I didn't think I was that easy to read, but you nailed it." As she told him about Scout and the possibility that he'd witnessed something, she saw Smitty's expression change.

"I know who you're talking about, Sister, but I have no idea how you're going to track him down. He's a very troubled man—and with reason."

"What can you tell me about him?"

"His name's Daniel Perea, and he used to live a normal life in this community. The family owned a video rental store and seemed to make a decent living. That was about ten years ago, if my memory's correct."

"What could happen to a man to turn his life so upside down?"

"You mean how did he become Scout?" Seeing her nod, he continued. "Daniel always had a problem with alcohol. One evening he was behind the wheel and got into an accident. His wife and two kids were in the car with him, and they were all killed. Daniel was drunk at the time and somehow managed to survive it all without a scratch," Smitty added.

He shook his head slowly. "After that, Daniel fell apart. He drowned himself in a bottle, lost his business, then his home. Eventually, he ended up on the street and disappeared for a few years. He came back last March, still a transient. He lives in the bosque and roams the backstreets, mostly in the early mornings and evenings. He survives thanks to some of us who make sure he gets something to eat." After a long pause, he added, "Daniel—the man he used to be—is long gone. I don't think he even recognizes his name anymore. I've never seen him with a bottle, so I think his demons have conspired to take away his memories. Scout's all that remains."

"Have you ever tried talking to him one-on-one? If he knew you once . . ."

"I know what you're thinking, that maybe I could reach him. Unfortunately, I've already tried—and failed. I know he usually comes around late to pick up sandwiches and whatever else I leave out on the windowsill for him," Smitty said. "That's why I decided to hang around one night. I figured he and I would talk, but the second he saw me, he bolted. Then I tried leaving him a note and a pencil and pad, asking him to write me back. I got nowhere with that either."

"I'm really sorry to hear it," Sister Agatha said, wishing for everyone's sake that things could have been different.

"One morning I came around the corner and saw him up close," Smitty said in a hushed tone. "His gaze was completely blank, Sister Agatha. Daniel's not home anymore. All that's left is madness, coupled with the survival instincts of a wild animal."

"Would you mind if I hung around here some night and waited for him to show up?" she asked him.

He considered it, then answered her. "I'd rather you didn't. Once he spots you, he may be too afraid to stop by and get his food. Then he'll go hungry, and I'd hate to see that happen."

"Maybe I can back him into a corner—"

"*Bad* idea," Smitty said resolutely. "Like a wild animal, he might panic and strike out. Is talking to him really that important to you?"

"Yes," she answered simply.

"Then give me a chance to think about this some more. I'd hate to scare him off for good. He needs to eat, Sister, and I'm in a position to help him with that." He paused for a long moment, a faraway look on his face. "When I was growing up in the south valley, we were dirt poor. Six of us lived in a rented two-bedroom mobile home. If it wasn't for food stamps, we would have starved. When I see someone like Scout, I can't turn away. I still remember what it was like to try to sleep when your stomach's so empty it hurts."

"You have a good heart, Smitty, and God has blessed you in so many ways because of that. As soon as you come up with a plan, let me know," Sister Agatha said, going to the door.

Smitty followed her into the store. "For now, you might find it helpful to talk to the man who just came in."

"Who are you talking about?" Sister Agatha asked, looking around at the customers and past the full shopping carts near two busy cashiers.

"See the tall guy in the tan sports coat browsing in the deli sandwich cooler? That's Frank Marquez, a detective for the state police. He was just put in charge of the Robert Garcia case. The

62

mayor insisted that someone outside the sheriff's department handle the investigation."

"I know Frank, but I had no idea he was running the investigation," Sister Agatha said. Interestingly enough, chances were good that Al Russo had known about this when they'd spoken earlier but had chosen to keep her in the dark. "Thanks for the tip. I'll go talk to him."

As she walked over, Marquez turned and gave her a taut smile. "Mary—uh, sorry, Sister Agatha. I was wondering how soon it would be before you and I ran into each other," he said.

"And here we are!" Sister Agatha said pleasantly. "You're looking well, Frank." He'd never looked anything but fit. A former all-star jock, he'd been a man's man from day one.

He laughed. "I'm looking old—but you know, despite the habit, you haven't changed that much since the days when your brother and I hung around together."

The memories made her eyes grow misty with tears, and she had to look away and compose herself before finding her voice again. "You and Kevin spent hours working on your motorcycles in the driveway or in the shade of that cottonwood."

"You were always there, too. You liked working on bikes as much as we did. You didn't mind getting oil on your sleeves or dirt under your fingernails."

Memories crowded her mind. She'd adored her big brother and would have cheerfully gone with him to the ends of the earth—but ultimately he'd gone to a place where she couldn't follow. His death had come after a long, hard illness, and the ravages of grief had eventually led her into the arms of God. Only by drawing closer to Him had she been able to rise above her sorrow and find purpose in her life again.

"Now here we are," she said softly.

He nodded. "You and Tom are good friends, so I know that

telling you to leave this case alone is a waste of time—but here's a word of warning. This is *my* investigation, and I won't tolerate anyone undermining or interfering with my job. If you find out anything relevant, I want you to tell me immediately. If I find out you've withheld evidence, I'll throw the book at you— my friendship with you and your brother notwithstanding."

The words didn't surprise her. They were typical of Frank, who'd practically raised his three brothers alone. After the death of their father, his mother had sunk into an alcoholic's version of hell. Frank had then stepped up to do what had to be done. If Frank could be said to have a trademark, it was that he never let a challenge go unanswered. Frank, simply put, was a man to whom strength meant survival. He'd chosen the right job.

"I would never keep evidence from the police, Frank. You don't have to worry about that. I just want to help you uncover the truth," she said, then added in a gentle voice, "We all went to high school together, and you're Tom Green's friend, too. How can you possibly believe Tom's guilty of murder?"

"I have information you don't, and unfortunately it doesn't look so good for Tom, Sister," he said in a voice so quiet it was almost a whisper. "I know you want to poke around, but by doing that you're making some serious enemies."

"It won't be the first time," she answered. "Good thing I have a powerful ally." She pointed upward to heaven.

6

MARQUEZ PAID FOR THE SANDWICH HE'D SELECTED, then left in the black-and-white state police unit. A second later, Smitty joined her at the door.

"You don't look happy," he commented.

"I'm afraid for Tom," she admitted. "The Garcia family wants someone to hang for this, and Tom's the obvious target."

"You didn't tell Marquez about Scout, did you?"

Sister Agatha looked at him and blinked. "No, we never got around to that. At this point, I'm not even sure Scout saw anything. If I find out differently, of course I'll pass it on."

Smitty nodded, but before he could answer, a tall, stylishly dressed brunette wearing an overload of fine Zuni-style turquoise and silver jewelry approached them.

"You're Sister Agatha, right?" she asked, glaring though yellow-tinted designer glasses.

Sister Agatha nodded. "Yes, can I help you?"

"I'm Elena Mora, a friend of Victoria Garcia's, and I just wanted to say shame on you, Sister! People trust you because of the habit you wear and what you represent. By helping the guilty, you're not only undermining law enforcement in our community, you're siding with the devil."

"You're badly misinformed, ma'am. I'm searching for the truth and taking care not to condemn anyone on circumstantial evidence alone. *Nobody* but Our Lord knows what really happened last night—not me, and certainly not you."

"Putting a different spin on the facts isn't going to excuse the sheriff for what he did, Sister."

"Are you really so sure that he's guilty? Unless you were an eyewitness, you should wait for the facts before you judge—and condemn."

"You're the one who refuses to see what's right there in front of your face," she said. "Also, Sister, there's something you might want to keep in mind before you muddy the waters. Your monastery depends on donations to get by, and the people in this town want to see justice—not watch a killer set free."

"Then we're in agreement. I want to find a killer, too, and that can't be done with a closed mind."

"Sheriff Green *is* the killer. Wake up, Sister."

As the woman walked away, Smitty gave Sister Agatha a worried frown. "You're going to have to be careful, Sister. A lot of people are indebted to the Garcias in one way or another. That includes me, too, by the way."

"*You?*"

"Yeah, I got into a financial bind a few years ago, and thanks to JD's character reference I was able to get a loan."

"I'm glad he helped you—but the mayor's not my enemy, Smitty. If anyone deserves to learn the truth about how Robert died, it's his family." She paused and took a breath. "Believe me,

I'm going to find the answers even if I have to pursue this case twenty-four hours a day."

Smitty's eyes narrowed. "That hurry you're in . . . it's not just the murder, is it? I've had the feeling that there's something you're not telling me. You and Sister Bernarda haven't been your usual cheerful selves lately, and your shopping habits have changed, too. What's going on? If I can help, all you have to do is ask."

"We're trying to work out some problems at home, that's all," she said vaguely. "As soon as I can, I'll tell you all about it."

Eager to avoid more questions, Sister Agatha went to meet Sister Bernarda, who'd already gone outside and was standing on the sidewalk.

"Come on. Let's go," Sister Agatha said, walking quickly back to the car.

"What's your hurry?" Sister Bernarda asked.

Sister Agatha filled her in as soon as they got under way.

Sister Bernarda exhaled loudly. "It's hard to hide what's never far from our minds."

Sister Agatha nodded. "Speaking of our move, why don't we stop at the Ship and Mail Store on the way home? The manager offered us some sturdy boxes when I mentioned that we were in the middle of packing away some office supplies."

"We can use whatever she has to spare," Sister Bernarda said with a nod.

"Our computers will need to be double boxed in order to make the move to Agnus Dei safely," Sister Agatha said. "That statue of the Blessed Mother in Reverend Mother's office, too, will need special handling."

"I think most of our statues will probably end up in St. Augustine's chapel here in town. It looks like Father Mahoney is going to get the funds for the renovation he wanted."

"Where did you hear that?" Sister Agatha said.

"At the mayor's house. His wife said that the Garcias intend to make a big donation so the chapel can become a permanent memorial to Robert—bronze plaque and everything."

"That family's reach extends far and wide, doesn't it?" Sister Agatha asked, not expecting an answer.

Bernalillo was a small town, so it took less than five minutes for them to reach the Ship and Mail right across from city hall. The second they walked inside, Sister Agatha felt the change in the air. Conversations stopped abruptly, people stared for a moment, then voices began again, hushed, like people talking in the back row of church.

Sister Agatha spotted Kris Anderson, the owner, behind the register. The redhead's usual friendly smile was missing today.

"Good afternoon, Kris!" Sister Agatha said brightly. "We came to pick up those boxes you set aside for us."

"Sister Agatha, I'm sorry, but we had to recycle every last one of them. We can't help you," she said in a monotone.

Kris glanced quickly at a man standing at the counter several feet away. Sister Agatha followed her gaze and saw Monty Allen, Robert Garcia's business partner, attaching a label to a carton.

A moment later, Allen brought the box over and set it in front of Kris. "It's ready to go," he said. Giving Sisters Agatha and Bernarda an excessively polite nod, he headed out the door.

The second Allen left, the atmosphere in the room changed. Almost as if a collective sigh of relief had gone around, voices suddenly rose, and Kris flashed Sister Agatha a smile.

"I'm really sorry about being so abrupt, Sister. With Monty here, I couldn't afford to look *too* friendly."

"It's okay," Sister Agatha assured her. "I understand. Any friend of Sheriff Green's is the enemy right now."

"Unfortunately, yes—and the last person I want to cross right now is the man the Garcias are thinking of supporting in the race for sheriff. He'll be a write-in candidate, of course."

"When was all that decided?" Sister Agatha asked, surprised.

"My sister works at the mayor's office. She overheard Al Russo reminding JD that if Sheriff Green managed to avoid being charged with a crime, he was now unopposed and guaranteed four more years in office. JD went ballistic and called Monty Allen. The man has the qualifications, apparently. He served with the Albuquerque Police Department for twenty years, the last ten as a detective."

"Do you think there are many people out there who still believe Sheriff Green is innocent?"

"Yeah, I do, but the Garcias make a lot more noise."

"Now that the coast is clear, do you think you can find any of those boxes for us?" Sister Bernarda asked.

Kris smiled and nodded. "Sure. Just go out back to the loading dock. They're there against the wall, folded, stacked, and tied together with twine."

Sister Bernarda and Sister Agatha drove the Antichrysler to the back loading dock and saw Kris's teenaged daughter, Jaime, waiting at the door.

While they worked getting the boxes into the back of the large station wagon, Jaime didn't say a word. Sister Agatha wondered about it, but trying to load all the boxes became quite a chore. It wasn't until Sister Agatha went up the steps one last time to ask Jaime to thank her mother that the girl finally spoke.

"We depend on this city's business to stay open, Sister Agatha. Please don't put my mom on the spot again by asking for help. Okay?" Without waiting for an answer, Jaime closed the door behind her.

"Sister Agatha, you need to see this," Sister Bernarda said. "Can you come over?"

Sister Agatha joined her by the driver's side door. "What's wrong?"

"This was on the seat," she said, handing Sister Agatha a scribbled note that read, *Answers come at a price.*

"Exactly what do you think that means?" Sister Bernarda asked. "Are they telling us to stop asking questions, or offering to sell answers to us?"

"I'm not sure," Sister Agatha answered.

"Should we stop by the sheriff's department and turn it in?"

Sister Agatha considered it, then shook her head. "No, there's no direct threat involved, and right now they've got their hands full. Let's hang on to it, though."

"All right, then. Let's go home."

"Excellent idea," Sister Agatha answered.

Long after the Great Silence had begun, Sister Agatha sat alone at one of the few computers that hadn't been packed away. With so much going on, she hadn't even bothered to check e-mail. Despite the long list of ads that still managed to slip past their antispam software, one e-mail caught her immediate attention. It was from State Police Detective Frank Marquez.

As she opened it, Sister Bernarda came into the scriptorium wordlessly. Sister Agatha nodded to her, turned her attention to the letter, and gasped. Instantly, Sister Bernarda came over and began reading over her shoulder.

Frank's letter—what he was calling a "courtesy" to Kevin's sister—let her know that news that Tom's hand had tested positive for gunpowder residue had been leaked to the press.

Sister Agatha considered it in silence. Either someone at the sheriff's department couldn't be trusted, or the information had come from the killer himself.

She sat back. The person who'd framed Tom knew about forensics, so it was likely that he also knew the damage that leaking incriminating information could do. The frame was on, and Tom was being tried in the courts of public opinion.

Sister Agatha fought to keep her spirits up. Maybe Tom's blood had been tested by now. If he'd been drugged, as they suspected, those positive test results would add credence to his own explanation—that of a third person at the scene. That extra footprint and confirmation of a knockout drug in his system would mean that there were at least two irrefutable facts in his favor.

One question, however, continued to gnaw at her. Would she be able to prove his innocence before it was time for her to leave New Mexico?

As if sensing her thoughts, Sister Bernarda pointed to the quote from Matthew that had been embroidered on white linen, framed, and hung on the wall. *With God all things are possible.*

Drawing strength from the words of the apostle, she walked out of the scriptorium and, in silence, followed Sister Bernarda to the chapel. The moment she stepped inside, she saw all the remaining sisters there, kneeling in silent prayer. Brides of Christ, they instinctively reached out to Him in times of trouble, placing their cares in their lover's gentle hands.

Early the next morning, after Morning Prayers and Terce, Pax and Sister Agatha set out to town. Feeling strengthened by the power of prayer, she was ready to tackle the day's challenges.

Twenty minutes later Sister Agatha arrived at the station. As they went inside, Pax headed directly to the bullpen. Seconds afterward, he graciously accepted his first doughnut piece of the day.

Seeing he was in good hands, Sister Agatha smiled and continued down the hall. As she turned the corner, she saw Tom standing there, shaking hands with one of the lieutenants.

Sister Agatha smiled broadly. "You've been released!"

He gave her a weary nod. "Yes, but there's a lot of work to be done before I can put all this behind me and get back to being sheriff again."

Millie, who'd come out of her own office, gestured for them to come inside, then closed the door behind them. Glancing at Sister Agatha, she said, "The approval for the tests came through, and the lab confirmed that the sheriff had been drugged with benzodiazepine, what they call a date-rape type of drug. It's pretty fast acting, and that explains why he passed out and why he can't remember things too clearly. It also supports the sheriff's claim that Robert never attacked him—that the blow to his head came *after* he was out cold."

"Like we figured, I was struck on the head to explain away my unconsciousness. It was supposed to mislead the detectives long enough to reduce the chances of my being tested and having the drug detected," Tom said.

"How was the drug administered, do they know?" Sister Agatha asked, looking at both of them.

"It was in the hot dog relish," Millie said. "We tested the residue from a napkin the sheriff had wadded up and stuck in his pocket."

"So it's now downhill from here?" Sister Agatha asked, looking at Tom. "You'll be in charge of the case again soon?"

"No," Tom answered. "Some people, including the DA, are suggesting that I purposely ingested the drug *after* the crime so I'd have an alibi."

"What about the blow to your head? That would have served

as an alibi, too," Sister Agatha said, "and it would have made taking the drug unnecessary. How do they explain that?"

"They don't even try. My attorney plans on making an appeal, but until that happens, I'm on paid suspension. I'm also forbidden to contact anyone who might be connected to the case, including my fellow officers." He glanced at Millie. "Thanks for everything, but I better get out of here before Captain Chavez shows up and wonders what we've been talking about."

"Tom, didn't you say earlier that Robert had handed you the hot dog?" Sister Agatha asked as they reached the door. Seeing him nod, she glanced at Millie. "So, was Robert drugged, too?"

"They did a tox screen on him, but the victim usually has a whole battery of tests, and some of those take days to complete. Only the sheriff's results are back from the lab," Millie answered. "Initial results on Robert's lab work may be in by the end of today."

"Thankfully, the judge saw all the inconsistencies in the case against me. That's why I'm out now," Tom said.

"What we have to do next is find out who added the contaminated relish to your hot dog," Sister Agatha said, glancing at Tom. She then turned to Millie. "Have you heard if anyone else was drugged that evening? I imagine you would have known by now if anyone else at the park had passed out, right?"

"If anyone else did, nobody's reported it. To me that suggests that only the sheriff was targeted—" A knock sounded just as she placed her hand on the knob. Millie opened it and stepped back as Frank Marquez came striding in.

He took them all in at a glance, then fastened his laser-sharp gaze on Millie. "The sheriff no longer has any jurisdiction over the Garcia murder case. I'd hate to find out that you've been sharing privileged information."

"I've just informed Sister Agatha that Sheriff Green is currently on suspension," Millie said.

It was only a fraction of the truth, and they all knew it. Sister Agatha looked back at Frank. "I also wanted to assure Millie that I'd be passing on any information I uncover."

"Sister Agatha can be an asset," Tom added. "Her special talents will speed your case along."

"Asset or not, you'd be better off staying out of this, Sister," Frank said, meeting her gaze. "A person who commits murder has already shown what he's capable of, and your habit won't give you much protection."

As Marquez left the room, Sister Agatha glanced at Tom. "Walk me out?"

"Sure," he answered.

As soon as they were in the parking area, Tom bent down to pet Pax. "What's on your mind, Sister?"

"Have you remembered any more details about that evening—like maybe your conversation with Robert?" she asked.

"No, not really," he answered, rubbing the back of his neck in a gesture of weariness.

"Try to visualize him for a moment," Sister Agatha insisted. "What do you see?"

"A few extras that probably don't mean a hill of beans," he answered after a moment or two. "I remember his flashy silver and turquoise watch, the flag pin on his lapel—I had one, too. There was a silver pen in his front shirt pocket, along with some kind of pamphlet that stuck out. I remember it had a line of stars along the top edge—probably some campaign literature. He also had a foam cup in his hand, not that cottonwood branch I saw when I woke up later. When I started to lose my balance he jumped back, maybe afraid I was going to fall on him, and spilled some of his punch. I went out fast after that. I don't even remember hitting the ground," he said.

"What about your earlier conversations?"

He shrugged. "A few angry exchanges, accusations, mostly."

Sister Agatha noticed he was having a hard time maintaining eye contact. "Tom, you're not holding back on me, are you?" Even before she'd become a nun, Tom had never been able to look her in the eye for long when he was keeping something from her.

"Don't worry. I know who my friends are," he said in a reassuring tone—but his eyes wandered again.

"Which doesn't answer the question," she insisted, trying once again to meet his gaze. "You're deflecting, not to mention playing with your future."

"I didn't do anything to Robert," he said, this time looking directly at her, his eyes unwavering. "You know that's true."

"Yes, but that wasn't my question," she pressed.

He glanced back to the entrance, where several deputies had just stepped outside. "We'll talk again if I remember something else. Right now, I need to find a ride home." With a nod, he walked toward the officers.

He hadn't asked her for a lift, and that told her all she needed. For whatever reason, there was something Tom wasn't ready to tell her, and that spelled trouble. Glancing down at Pax, Sister Agatha smiled at her faithful friend.

"Let go pay Chuck Moody a visit, boy," she said, climbing on the cycle.

Recognizing Chuck's name, Pax barked happily.

"Nothing ever worries you, does it, my friend?" she said, thinking out loud. "I envy you that."

Sister Agatha headed down the street, then turned and went up the lane that held the newspaper office. She'd find at least some of the answers she needed there.

7

WHEN SISTER AGATHA STEPPED INSIDE THE *CHRONI-cle*'s front office, Chuck was at his computer. His right hand was on the mouse, and his left curled around a half-full plastic soft drink bottle.

"Hey, Sister! What brings you back here so soon?" He stepped to a waist-high refrigerator, pulled out an unopened bottle of cola, and offered it to her. "Here, have one. I bet you can use this about now. The temperature is supposed to hit the high nineties today, but I was outside checking the mailbox a while ago, and it already feels like one hundred."

"It certainly does, particularly coming off the asphalt," she said, wishing, if only for a moment, that she'd joined an order who used modern, short habits and lighter-colored fabric.

"How about you, Pax? I have a dish of water for critters, too." He gestured toward a metal watering dish against a wall.

"Did you all get an office pet?"

"No, not really, but sometimes we have a big gray cat who drops by to say hello. I'm not sure who he belongs to, but the guy looks well fed."

"He's not here now, is he?" She looked around anxiously. "Pax likes to chase them off."

"Nope, don't worry. More often than not he only comes around after dark," Chuck said, taking a swig of his own drink. "So what can I do for you, Sister?" he asked, sitting down at his computer again and swinging around to face her.

"I need your help, but first I want us to come to an agreement similar to ones we've had in the past. I'd like your word that you won't print anything we uncover together until the time's right—my call. Do we have a deal?"

"You bet," he said almost instantly. "Every time you and I team up we both come out ahead. I see no reason to change a winning game."

Game . . . She never would have called it that, but this was no time to quibble. Sister Agatha brought him up to date on the results of the drug test they'd given Sheriff Green. "Detective Marquez will undoubtedly follow up that lead by looking for known drug dealers in our area. I'd like to work it from a different angle. I'm thinking that the killer isn't a pro, though he's got some knowledge of police procedure. The fact that there were so many officers at the park that day—on and off duty—makes me think that our guy's strictly a small-time dealer, or maybe user, who's a complete unknown to law enforcement."

Chuck nodded slowly. "Makes sense to me. Did you suggest that to the police?"

"I didn't think it would do a lot of good. One theory being tossed around is that Tom purposely ingested the drug to give himself an alibi."

"I guess that in their eyes anything's possible. Of course,

they're not nearly as sure as we are that the sheriff's innocent, so they have to find a way, no matter how convoluted, to establish his guilt."

Sister Agatha, noting his use of the word "we," smiled. "So here's the way I see it, Chuck. We're looking for someone who has stayed below the radar but has access to date-rape-type drugs."

"Is there anything else you can think of that might help narrow the search a bit?" he asked.

Sister Agatha thought back to the blow on Tom's head, which was on the left temple. Judging from the angle, whoever had struck Tom with that stout branch had been right-handed and standing more or less in front of him.

"Was Robert Garcia right-handed?"

"Let me take a look at some photos on file," Chuck said. Several moments later, he looked up from the screen. "Yeah, it looks like it."

"The police are assuming that Robert hit Tom, but what this tells us is that Robert's killer is also right-handed."

"That's not much of a clue, Sister," Chuck said. "The majority of the world is right-handed."

"Yes, but that was no tiny branch, for one, and the blow that struck Tom packed a great deal of force. The person we're looking for may have a sore arm, swollen fingers, or scratches on their right hand."

"It's a possibility—unless the person was wearing gloves. Either way, we should take a closer look at Robert's cronies and see what we find," Chuck said.

"The funeral—has a date been set?" she asked him.

"As a matter of fact, yes. It's tomorrow." He checked a small notebook next to the phone. "The family wanted the funeral and burial to take place as soon as possible, and they put some serious pressure on the ME's office. Raul Garcia, the ninety-year-old patriarch of the Garcias, insisted on leaving his assisted living facility and staying at JD's until Robert was buried. The family's very worried about Raul and wants him back at the home, where he'll get the specialized round-the-clock care he needs."

"I'm going to do my best to attend that funeral, Chuck."

"I'll be there, too, covering it for the paper."

"Do me a favor," she said. "If you see anyone with a sore finger or arm, let me know."

"You've got it, Sister. I'll also be taking photos, so if you'd like, you can browse through those later."

"Thanks," she said.

Chuck focused back on the information on his computer screen. "There have been no area arrests dealing with date-rape drugs within the last ninety days, Sister. I can go back farther if you want."

"No, let's try a different approach. Suppose I wanted to find an amateur who occasionally deals low-profile drugs—meaning not anything heavy like cocaine or meth. Who would you suggest I talk to?"

"That's a tough question to answer, Sister. I know of some of the major players, but they're ones that the police know about, too, like the owner of the Alibi Inn."

"That place sounds vaguely familiar."

"It's between here and Corrales, in north Rio Rancho. Once or twice a week, the police arrest someone in their parking lot for dealing."

"That place sounds too high-profile for the type of person we're looking for. Think strictly low-budget and small-time," Sister Agatha said. "Like a high school or college kid who maybe deals on the side."

Chuck considered it for a moment. Suddenly his expression changed from thoughtful to hopeful. "I know who we can ask. His name's Arnie Cruz. He's a professional student at UNM."

"A what?"

"The guy's been going to the university since he was eighteen—and he's at least in his early forties now," Chuck said. "He used to belong to a fraternity, but they eventually kicked him out because he never would graduate. Arnie works during the summer to pay for his classes in the fall. Right now, the university's in summer session, so he's got a full-time job."

"Any idea where? I'd like to catch him when he's getting off work—today, if possible."

"I should go with you. Cruzer—that's what they call him—has authority issues with nuns. He had a bad experience in Catholic school."

"I gather you know him well."

"Well enough. He's one of my university sources, but I should warn you. He can be temperamental."

"Is he dangerous?"

"Cruzer?" Chuck laughed. "No way."

"Then let's take the bike, and you and Pax can squeeze into the sidecar."

"If he doesn't mind, I don't." Chuck picked up his tape recorder and pocket-sized notebook, then patted his pocket. "Cell phone—check. Now I'm ready to roll."

A short time later, they pulled up next to the Bernalillo Community Center. It was close to 1:00 P.M. now, and Sister's stomach growled loudly as she switched off the motorcycle's engine.

Chuck laughed. "Yeah, me, too. Let's go inside. There are always doughnuts or something at the snack bar, or maybe we can raid one of the vending machines."

"What kind of work does Arnie do here?" Sister Agatha asked as they stepped into the lobby.

"Don't call him Arnie when you meet him, Sister," Chuck said. "The only thing he hates more than that is Arnold. He prefers Cruzer—from cruising through life, get it?"

"Got it." Sister Agatha had Pax on his leash and received only a casual glance from the security guard at the front desk. "So what's he do here?" she repeated. She turned a half circle, trying to figure out which direction to go.

"He's an artist and has been teaching disabled kids how to paint. At night, he teaches sculpture to adults with disabilities," Chuck said, motioning her down a long hallway. "I did a piece on his classes, and what struck me most is that they're not really about painting or sculpture—they're about hope."

"He sounds like a good man." She looked through the open door into the gym, where about thirty children were playing volleyball.

"Cruzer's got a good heart, Sister, but he's also a little strange. He could be a lot of things—artist, teacher—but he never sticks with anything."

Sister Agatha looked ahead, then back down the hall in the direction they'd come. "Where's his classroom?"

"I'm not sure. I figured we'd stop by the office and ask." He pointed to a sign that read MAIN OFFICE on the wall at the end of the corridor.

As they approached, the brightly lit room reminded her of a high school office, with a long counter near the entrance, then several smaller workstations beyond. At the far corners were doors leading to internal offices.

No one was behind the big counter, but Sister Agatha immediately recognized the plump young woman seated at the first desk on her right. She'd known Tina Ansel and her family for years. Tina had briefly considered becoming a nun, but her path had taken her in a different direction. She was now the mother of six girls. Tina worked hard at two jobs to make ends meet but never complained. She loved being a mom, as the photos all over her desk testified.

"Hey, Sister Agatha!" Tina greeted her cheerfully. "What brings you to the BCC?"

"We're looking for Mr. Cruz's art class. Do you happen to know where it is?" she asked.

"I think Cruzer took his students outside today, Sister." Tina glanced up at the clock on the wall. "His class will end in another five minutes, and once things get put away, he'll be coming here. Why don't you stick around? Today's payday, and nobody in the summer program ever forgets to pick up their check." She paused, then, giving Sister Agatha a worried look, added, "Nothing's wrong, is it?"

"No, not at all," Sister Agatha assured her quickly.

"Good," she answered, relieved, "because Cruzer's our resident miracle worker, Sister."

"That's quite a title," Sister Agatha said.

"He's earned it. One ten-year-old girl who had her arms crushed in a car accident came in so depressed she'd even stopped eating. Cruzer showed her how to paint by holding the brush in her teeth. That slowly brought her out of her shell, and now she's like a regular kid again. I actually heard her laughing with some of the other art students yesterday in the hall."

Sister Agatha's opinion of Cruzer suddenly went up several notches. Even cruising through life, the man was doing God's work.

"Those cinnamon rolls sure look good," Chuck said and sighed wistfully, seeing the half-full box on an unoccupied desk.

Tina laughed. "You're as subtle as a freight train, Chuck."

She picked up the box and brought it over to Sister Agatha. "You get first choice, Sister. I baked them earlier this morning for the staff, but as usual I made way too much."

"Thank you," Sister Agatha said, picking up a roll.

"You're very welcome," Tina said, then held out the box for Chuck, who promptly took two.

"I need to make copies in the other room," she said. "Enjoy!"

Although there were no class bells, it wasn't long before children's voices filled the outside hall and people began to pass by.

"See him?" Sister Agatha asked, joining Chuck at the doorway.

"There he is. He's got thin red hair and is wearing a tie-dyed shirt. And there he goes. I think he saw your habit." Chuck hurried out into the hall. "I'm going after him. Go out the door we came in and circle around the building, toward the west side— where the employees park. If we're lucky, we'll catch him between us."

Sister Agatha hurried out, Pax at her side, then headed west. Just as she reached the corner, she saw a man fitting Chuck's description of Cruzer coming down the sidewalk.

Cruzer stopped in midstride and stared at her in surprise.

"Hello. You must be Cruzer," she said pleasantly. "I'm Sister Agatha from Our Lady of Hope Monastery."

"Nuns . . . I should have known I couldn't ditch you," he muttered with a scowl. "You guys have always been able to read my mind. Ever since high school. Spooky—real spooky. Is this about that donation I was going to make for Father Rick's chapel project? Things are really tight for me this month—"

Sister Agatha held up one hand. "That's strictly between you and Father Rick."

"Oh, good," he said, visibly relieved.

Seeing Chuck come out the front door, Sister Agatha waved at him.

"Yo, Cruzer," Chuck said, joining them.

"Hey," he muttered as the two greeted each other with fist bumps. "You with Sister A?"

"Yeah, she's the one I told you about, remember? The ex-journalist. Sister Agatha basically saved my life a few years back when I got into trouble with the wrong people."

"I'm impressed. Good for you, Sister A. So what's going down?" he asked, looking back at Chuck.

"We just wanted to ask you a few questions about stuff you might have seen on the Fourth," Chuck said.

He rolled his eyes. "Here we go. This is about the hot dogs again, isn't it?" he asked, looking at Chuck, then back at Sister Agatha.

"Hot dogs?" Sister Agatha asked, more curious than ever. "What do you mean?"

"The deputies and that state cop have been questioning everyone who worked the booths on the Fourth. If I'd known that Mayor Garcia and his bean counters were going to have their eye on every bleeping hot dog . . ." He looked at the ground and shook his head.

"What exactly have they been asking you?" Sister Agatha pressed, keeping her voice as casual as possible.

"They want to know who ordered hot dogs, who was watching the condiments, and if we saw anyone tampering with the food, or maybe just hanging around. Like that." He graced them with a martyred sigh. "So okay. Call the law. I confess. I gave a few hot dogs away. Scout, that homeless guy who hangs around, kept looking at people stuffing their faces, then going back to the trash and looking for food there. After a while I couldn't stand it anymore, so I took him a bag of unopened hot dogs. There were plenty to go around. No one went away hungry. The Garcias in particular stuffed themselves silly, taking away four or five at a time. RJ, the son of the guy who ended up dead, came by three times."

"Is that what you think this is about—hot dogs?" Chuck asked him, surprised.

"Well, isn't it?"

Sister Agatha didn't answer. "Did you talk to him? Scout, that is."

"Talk?" He shook his head. "No, it wasn't like that. I spotted him hanging out behind the trash cans, and Mike Herrera, who was working the concession stand with me, saw him, too. He tossed me the pack of hot dogs and told me we could afford to lose a bag. I went over to where Scout was to hand it to him, but as I got close, he gave me this panicked look and started backing off. I knew he was about to bolt, so I broke eye contract, placed the bag of hot dogs on the trash lid, and walked off. When I looked back, Scout and the hot dogs were gone."

"I'm glad you were both watching out for him," Sister Agatha said.

"Mike and I figured that the town wouldn't miss one bag, but judging from the way the cops have been coming down on everyone, I guessed wrong. Who'd have thought our city would actually try to track down a few hot dogs?" He shook his head. "Look, Sister, all this is penny ante, if you ask me, but I really need the job here at the center. If you turn us in, Mike and I will probably get fired. Mike will be okay, but I need the money. Summer jobs are hard to find this year, and tuition's going up again."

"You help us, and we'll help you," Chuck said, taking over. "We actually need a line on someone who's dealing drugs on the side—date-rape drugs, stuff like that, nothing hard-core. Most likely an amateur. Can you nose around and see what you can find?"

"Anything specific—Rohypnol, GHB, or ketamine?" Cruzer asked.

"Huh?" Chuck asked.

"Sorry. I have fifteen hours in chemistry, and those are three of the most common benzodiazeprines—date-rape drugs."

"Now we're on the same wavelength," Sister Agatha said with a nod.

"So *that's* what this is all about? Someone drugged one of the ladies the other night and tried to get personal? That makes a whole lot more sense than the township getting sore over some hot dogs." He glanced at Sister Agatha, then back at Chuck, and nodded. "Yeah, sure I'll help you." Cruzer paused, then added, "Hey, you don't think Mike had anything to do with drugging some babe's hot dogs, do you? If you do, that's way off base."

"Why's that?" Sister Agatha asked, allowing Cruzer to think they had something other than Robert Garcia's murder in mind.

"Mike's not only got a sweet deal with his rich new wife, but he actually loves the girl. He'd never even think of cheating on her. Besides, his father-in-law, *el mayor*, would come unglued. JD told Mike he'd bury him alive if Mike ever hurt his daughter in any way. He wasn't kidding."

"Could be that one of Mike's friends drugged the hot dogs," Chuck suggested, not correcting any of Cruzer's assumptions. "Or maybe put stuff in the mustard."

"No way. I was standing there almost all the time, and when I wasn't, there were dozens of other people around us keeping watch. The mayor insisted we follow all local ordinances. We had to wear hats or hairnets, those stupid latex gloves, and keep the water at just the right temperature. He made it crystal clear that nobody was going to get sick and blame the Garcia administration."

"Yet you still managed to grab some hot dogs for your welfare operation," Sister Agatha said.

"Slipping away with a bag of hot dogs from the cooler is a lot easier than drugging a hot dog on the production line. Everyone's watching you there, giving you instructions on how much mustard they want, hold the onions, more ketchup, stuff like that. You couldn't fiddle around with the food once it was on the counter, either. Half a dozen people would see you for sure."

"Okay, Cruzer, we believe you," Sister Agatha said. "Will you keep an eye out for anyone who's dealing and pass on any information you get?"

"Sure. I'll do my best to get a name to you in a few days."

As they headed back to the newspaper office, the roar of the chopper would have made conversation impossible even if they hadn't been wearing helmets.

Sister Agatha parked a short time later, and Chuck climbed out of the sidecar. "Sister Agatha, I've been giving this some thought, and I'm going to stay away from you at the funeral tomorrow. Marquez is bound to be there, and it'll be better if he doesn't link us."

"Good thinking—and thanks for your help today, Chuck."

"No problem."

"Thank you, too, for not correcting Cruzer when he misinterpreted why we were interested in the drugs," she added, revving up the engine. "Information like that is better off staying between us for the time being."

"I figured that," he said, petting Pax one last time. "Where are you off to now?"

She hesitated. "It's better if you don't know."

He gave her a somber nod. "Just be careful, Sister. You don't want to end up becoming the killer's next target."

"I'm pretty sure God has other plans for me, Chuck. Don't worry."

8

SISTER AGATHA DROVE DIRECTLY TO TOM'S HOUSE NEXT. It was time for them to speak privately. She was certain that he was holding something back, and that wouldn't do him or his case any good.

As she pulled up, Sister Agatha saw the living room curtain move back slightly and caught a glimpse of Tom standing to one side. Sister Agatha waved at him just as Gloria opened the front door and came out, purse in hand.

"I'm off to the store, Sister, but I should warn you that Tom's behaving like a caged bear today. We had a visit from Detective Marquez, and Tom's mood went downhill after that," she said, slipping inside her car. "One more thing—I heard Detective Marquez say that he'd hang your hide and habit to the wall if he caught you interfering with his investigation."

"Then I'll have to make sure he doesn't catch me," Sister Agatha said with a quick smile.

As Gloria drove away, Tom met Sister Agatha at the front door. "I hope you've brought me some good news," he said, bending down to scratch Pax between the ears.

"Actually, I've come because you and I need to talk. I know you too well, Tom, not to notice you're holding something back," she said, following him into the kitchen side of the great room. "With Gloria out shopping, it's just you and me, so let's stop wasting each other's time. What's going on?"

"I've told you everything that pertains to the murder. You have my word on that."

She leaned back in her chair and gave him a cold glare. "That's not good enough, Tom. There's something else going on beneath the surface, and in murder investigations, things like that often hold important clues. You know that as well as I do. Stop playing games."

She was about to say more when they both heard a car pulling into the driveway. It was followed immediately by the sound of a second approaching vehicle.

Seconds later, Gloria came back into the house, empty-handed except for her purse. Officer Sanchez, a deputy with the sheriff's department, was directly behind her.

"Tom," Gloria called out as she crossed the room. "There's someone here for you."

Gloria took a seat at the kitchen island beside Sister Agatha as Tom greeted Sanchez with a nod. "What brings you here, Deputy?"

"Sheriff, I've owed you one for a long time," the tall, lean uniformed officer said. "That's why I stopped your wife down the street. I wanted her to tell you that I'll be working on your defense off duty, but she suggested I come by and tell you myself," he said. "If you need any legwork done to clear your name, count me in."

"Thank you, Louis," Tom said. "You put your job at risk coming to tell me that, and your loyalty's appreciated."

"There's something else," Sanchez said. "Detective Marquez ordered me to tail you whenever you left the house—particularly if Sister Agatha was with you or had come by recently. Of course, I can't be watching everywhere at once, can I?" he added with a grin.

Tom shook his head. "I appreciate what you're trying to do, Deputy, but follow your orders. The charges against me are false, but if I end up going down, I'm not taking anyone else with me."

"But Sheriff—"

"No. If I need you to help me locate a witness or do some legwork, I'll give you a call. Meanwhile, when you're on duty, follow your supervisor's orders."

"All right, Sheriff. Listen, though—you've got friends in the department who know you're not guilty. We're all working behind the scenes to find out who killed Garcia and set you up." He started to the door, then stopped and glanced back. "If you need anything in the meantime, I won't be far."

After Deputy Sanchez left, Gloria looked at Tom, then at Sister Agatha. The lines on her face revealed her weariness. "Is he for real, or is this a Marquez type of setup? If you do something stupid and interfere with the case, or try to corrupt a witness, Marquez could throw you in jail, right?"

"Yes, he could, but I don't think Sanchez is playing us. I did save his butt once, and I can understand why he might feel that he owes me."

"He might owe Marquez, too," Gloria said.

"I don't think Frank Marquez is out to get anyone," Sister Agatha said. "I've known him since we were in our teens, and he's always been a stand-up guy. From what I've seen so far, I think he just wants to do the job he's been given, close the case, and go back to Santa Fe."

"Probably, but don't underestimate Frank," Tom said. "As a law enforcement officer, he's extremely driven. He's got an impressive conviction record and usually closes his cases—one way or another. I've heard that's the reason Mayor Garcia requested him specifically. JD's hoping Frank will go with the easy answers instead of drawing things out. If that's the way it goes down, then I'm going to be left twisting in the wind."

"You're both police officers. He'll want to make certain you get a fair shake," Sister Agatha said.

"Normally that would be true, but the circumstantial evidence is against me, and when it looks like an officer has gone bad everyone closes ranks," Tom said, shaking his head. "We come down even harder on our own because it makes us all look bad."

Sister Agatha waited, hoping Gloria would leave and go finish her errands, but no one moved. As minutes ticked by, Sister Agatha became acutely aware of the tension between Tom and Gloria. It resonated in the silence between them, breathing with a life of its own.

Knowing Tom wouldn't speak freely now that Gloria had decided to stick around, Sister Agatha stood. "Pax and I better get going."

Tom walked her to the door. "What's next on your agenda?"

"I've got to go back to the monastery and help Sister Bernarda pack up more of our scriptorium equipment."

"Are you shutting down the scriptorium?" Tom asked. "I thought you were still making money off of that."

She'd spoken without thinking and now regretted her lapse. Recovering quickly, she answered, "We've decided to get some of our older computers and other hardware out of the way for now." At least that wasn't a lie.

His eyes narrowed as he gazed at her. "What else is going on over there?"

"I've heard some interesting rumors," Gloria said, coming up behind them.

"Like what?" Sister Agatha asked, her curiosity getting the better of her.

"A few days ago, a white car with a nun at the wheel went past Mrs. Santeiro's house on its way to the monastery. Then, about an hour later, the car drove back out, but that time there were two more nuns inside. At first Mrs. Santeiro figured it was probably all part of a doctor or dentist visit. What she couldn't figure out was where the white car had come from, since she'd never seen it before."

Sister Agatha knew Mrs. Santeiro well. She lived up the road from the monastery, close to the highway. She'd often wondered how the woman ever got anything done, always looking out her front kitchen window.

"A few days later, Mrs. Santeiro went to the monastery to ask Sister Clothilde if she'd be willing to bake some Cloister Cluster Cookies or make that new wonderful fudge recipe of hers—Sweet Habit—for the annual senior center fund-raiser. Sister Bernarda told her that Sister Clothilde was taking care of other responsibilities and their new cook wasn't up to the job," Gloria said. "So what's happened to Sister Clothilde? Did she and some others get transferred out, and will more follow?"

Keeping a secret in a community as small as theirs was nearly impossible, Sister Agatha realized. As her gaze settled on Tom, another much more encouraging thought came to mind. Maybe that would ultimately help Tom out.

"Sure sounds like something's going on," Tom said, his laser-sharp gaze on her.

She considered telling him what was happening, but why add another worry to what he was already shouldering? Once the monastery shut its doors, whether or not the case was closed, she'd still have to leave, and that would mean he'd have one less ally working to clear his name.

"This isn't something I can talk about yet, but as soon as I can I'll fill you both in," she said at last.

He nodded once, his expression hard. He'd never liked surprises.

Gloria shrugged. "Okay, then. I was just curious."

Sister Agatha and Pax were soon on their way back to the monastery. She would spend the rest of her day in quiet solitude. Maybe their familiar rounds of work and prayer would result in inspiration and insight, two things she sorely needed at the moment.

Tomorrow, Robert Garcia would be buried in the old graveyard behind St. Augustine Church, the same cemetery where her own parents and brother had been laid to rest. Although she'd give priority to clearing Tom and focus on the funeral Mass and the service, she'd also make time to visit her family's graves. Once she moved to Colorado and Agnus Dei, she might never be able to do that again.

As a sudden rush of grief washed over her, tears flooded her eyes and spilled down her cheeks. Unable to brush them away because of the helmet's faceplate, she concentrated on the road, forcing back her sorrow.

There was no reason to grieve. She knew better. Earthly remains were all that were buried at the graveyard. Her family's spirits had moved on, soaring to God's heaven, where they would live on, forever unlimited by human boundaries.

It was the truth. Yet the pain remained, and her tears continued to fall.

It was eleven the following morning when Sister Agatha and Sister Bernarda pulled into the parking lot of St. Augustine

Church. Only a few spaces were available, and Sister Bernarda chose the one closest to the cemetery grounds.

"As we turned in, I saw people heading over to the new section of the cemetery. That means we didn't miss the graveside ceremony," Sister Bernarda said.

"We would have been better off had we taken the Harley," Sister Agatha said. "This old wreck cuts out when it reaches thirty miles per hour, and if you ignore that and push it, the whole engine starts shaking. I think it's the carburetor acting up again—and the timing, and the spark plugs."

Sister Bernarda said a quick prayer, then turned the ignition off. The engine ran for another second, then stopped. "At least we got here in one piece. And thank the Lord we didn't announce our tardiness with an ear-splitting backfire."

"Sister Ignatius lit a candle for us," Sister Agatha said by way of an explanation.

"I'm going to join the mourners," Sister Bernarda said, leaving the car, "but seeing you is likely to upset the Garcias. Where do you plan to be?"

"I'll circle around and remain in the shadows. The main reason I'm here is to watch and listen to people talk. We can meet back here at the car later."

"All right, then," Sister Bernarda said and strode off.

Sister Agatha circled around the church and entered the newest section of the cemetery. She chose a spot in the deep shade beneath the elms that stood near the north end of the grounds and prepared to view the proceedings from there. Though out of the way, she still had a clear look at all the mourners gathered around Father Mahoney.

What she intended to do now was remain still and watch people's reactions when they shook Father Mahoney's hand. With luck, she might be able to spot an indication of pain from an injured wrist or arm. Of course, that was a real long shot. As Chuck had pointed out, the killer could have worn gloves.

Sister Agatha's gaze drifted over to Victoria Garcia and her son, RJ, who stood beside her, shifting from side to side. Although there were no signs of grief in the boy's face, there was an unmistakable restlessness. He looked bored, as a matter of fact.

As Father Mahoney read from Psalm 23, RJ tugged at his mother's arm and whispered something to her when she bent down. She shook her head, then stood up straight again. The boy waited for a heartbeat, then, letting go of her hand, walked away. Victoria reached out for him, but the boy wriggled loose and kept going.

Mike Herrera, who'd been behind them, slipped closer to Victoria, whispered something in her ear, then hurried after the boy.

RJ walked as fast as his short legs could manage without breaking into a run. He was halfway to the parking lot when Mike caught up to him. Curious, Sister Agatha walked toward them. Mike and RJ appeared to be arguing. RJ was staring at the ground, angrily kicking at the grass with his shoe. When Mike reached for the boy's arm, RJ jerked free.

Sister Agatha got closer to them and tried to listen in. They were so focused on each other they couldn't see anything else, but their conversation was too low to decipher.

The sudden silence at the graveside service behind her got her attention. Father Mahoney had just ended his prayer. Sister Agatha turned and shifted her focus back to what was happening there. Monty Allen shook hands with the priest, then went to speak to Victoria and the mayor. If any of them had a tender arm or wrist, they didn't show it.

People she recognized from town continued walking past the casket that was resting on a lift above the open grave. Individuals or couples would place a flower on the grave site, then continue. Most looked visibly relieved that the ceremony had ended, and she couldn't decide if it was because of the situation or the ninety-degree temperature.

Sister Agatha edged closer and studied the family members. When Al Russo approached Victoria, she smiled and visibly relaxed. There was nothing inappropriate about their behavior, but the two appeared to have a definite connection.

Almost as if in support of her observation, Al glanced around the graveyard, spotted RJ, and went to where he and Mike stood, still arguing. When Al arrived, Mike threw up his hands in frustration and stalked off. Like two old friends, the boy and Al walked away together, circling the crowd and angling slowly back to where Victoria stood.

Remaining clear of Chuck, who was weaving in and out of the crowd, snapping photos, Sister Agatha worked her way around the mourners. She studied each of the faces she saw, mindful to avoid getting close to either the mayor or his wife.

One small, roundish woman in her late fifties soon caught her attention. She was just coming through the cemetery gate. If she'd intended to attend services, she was late. The woman continued walking toward the grave, then, halfway there, stopped and waited. From the cut of her clothes, she didn't seem to be in the same income bracket as most of those at the funeral. Perhaps she was the boy's teacher, Sister Agatha thought.

Victoria walked purposefully toward the newcomer, exchanged a few words with her, then walked back to join Al and her son, who'd now returned.

As the woman headed back to the parking area, Sister Agatha jogged to catch up to her. Slowing down at the last moment and falling into step beside her, Sister Agatha gave her a tired smile.

"Robert will be missed," Sister Agatha said.

The woman shrugged. "You're Sister Agatha, aren't you?"

"Yes, I am. Have we met?"

"No, but I've heard a lot about you."

"I hope that at least some of it was good," Sister Agatha answered with a sheepish smile.

"It doesn't matter, Sister. I've been told not to talk to you," she said. "I like my job, too, so please don't make any trouble for me." As they reached the church, the woman made a quick left turn and went down the front sidewalk.

"Who told you not to speak to me, and why does that have anything to do with your work?" Sister Agatha asked, though she had a pretty good idea what the answers would be.

"Mrs. Victoria Garcia is my boss, and I can't afford to get her ticked off, Sister. The economy's very bad, and jobs are hard to come by," she said, then glanced back. Assured that the angle was wrong and none of the mourners could see them from here, she relaxed slightly. "I think you worry the Garcias, Sister."

"I do? Why?"

She glanced back again, then looked at Sister Agatha. "Sister, I was raised Catholic, and I don't mind talking to you, but I don't want to take any chances with my livelihood. How about meeting me in the old section of the cemetery? There are a lot more trees and stone monuments over there, so no one's likely to see us talking."

Sister Agatha swallowed hard. That was where her parents and brother were buried. With effort, she forced a smile. "All right. How about east of the mausoleum? Is that okay with you?"

"That's fine." She glanced back to make sure no one had come around the corner, then moved toward her car. "I'm going to drive off just in case, go completely around, and come in from the north."

Sister Agatha went back through the open gate leading into the new cemetery grounds, then walked past several mourners. Seeing Al looking at her with interest—and disapproval—she avoided eye contract and stopped by a statue of the Virgin Mary. Crossing herself, she bowed her head in prayer. After several moments she glanced furtively over at Al, but he'd lost interest in her and was focused on something else.

Sister Agatha found Sister Bernarda in the crowd and signaled her to wait. Hurrying over, she met her near the statue of an angel. "I'm on my way to talk to someone. When I'm finished, I'll see you back in the parking lot."

"No problem," Sister Bernarda answered. "I'll wait for you there."

Crossing what had at one time been a street but was now only an access road for gardeners, Sister Agatha took the path east, entering the old cemetery from a new direction. The route led her to the mausoleum, a gray pseudo-Greek-temple structure probably a hundred years old.

Sister Agatha took a careful look around, but the woman she'd come to meet was nowhere to be seen. After circling the building twice, Sister Agatha began to suspect that she'd been put off by an expert. She'd just decided to go back when she heard hurried footsteps somewhere behind her.

"Sorry I'm late, Sister Agatha. I wanted to make real sure Ms. Victoria wouldn't see me heading here."

"You know my name, but I still don't know yours," Sister Agatha said.

"I'm Crystal Greer, Ms. Victoria's housekeeper and part-time nanny. The reason I was late for the service is that I was back at the house making sure everything was ready for the guests who'd be stopping by after the funeral."

Sister Agatha felt her heart pumping faster. Very few secrets could be kept from a good housekeeper, the person who cleaned up the family's messes.

"I've heard the gossip, Sister, and I know you're trying to find someone else to blame for Mr. Robert's death. You don't want your friend Sheriff Green to face murder charges."

"That's not exactly right—"

Crystal held up one hand, interrupting her. "Sooner or later you're going to find out that Ms. Victoria has what most people would consider a good motive, so that's why I'm here—to tell you to leave her alone and look elsewhere. That woman's a victim, nothing more. She's paid her dues and deserves to get some peace in her life now."

"I understand your loyalty to an employer—"

"No, that's not it," Crystal interrupted again. "Loyalty's a two-way street, and to her I'm just the hired help. I understand the life she's lived, though—more so than most people."

"I don't follow. Tell me what you mean," Sister Agatha pressed in a calm voice. "You can trust me. Whatever you say will stay between us."

Crystal hesitated. "I dislike gossip, but you should know that Mr. Robert was far from the perfect husband."

"You mean he strayed?" she asked.

"No. He had other . . . habits . . . that were far worse." Crystal paused, looking around to make absolutely certain they were still alone. "I'm never at the house in the evenings, but in the mornings, I'd often see that poor woman putting on makeup and trying to hide all the bruises. They were never on her face where people could see. She'd have black and blue marks around her ribs, her stomach, and her upper arms. I saw her come out of the shower one morning, and I thought my heart was going to stop. She had these red, angry-looking welts on her back and right across her breasts, as if he'd used a belt or a strap." She took a shaky breath, then, with a scowl, continued. "Mr. Robert had a very bad temper, but he wasn't stupid. He knew how to hide what he did."

"Did you ever personally see Robert hitting Victoria?" Sister Agatha asked.

"No, but those bruises of hers weren't from bumping into doors or falling down the steps, Sister. I've seen that kind of thing before. When my dad would get drunk, which was often, he'd take out his anger on my mother."

"Was Robert in the habit of getting drunk?"

She hesitated, then shook her head. "That's what I could never understand. He never had more than a small glass of wine at dinner." She paused for a moment, then added, "I think Robert Garcia was just plain mean."

"Why didn't Victoria leave him?"

"Why does anyone take abuse?" she answered. "Fear. It keeps you frozen in place. It takes lots of different forms, too—fear of being all alone in a world that doesn't really care what happens to you, fear of not being able to pay your bills, of failing someone who's counting on you." She shook her head. "Ms. Victoria's greatest fear went beyond all those. One time I heard Mr. Robert tell her that if she wanted to leave, he wouldn't stop her, but the boy would stay with him. If she tried to take RJ, his lawyers would find a slew of witnesses that would testify that she was an unfit mother. By the time they were done with her, she wouldn't qualify to adopt a stray cat."

"How long have you worked for the Garcias?"

"Since after Christmas. The reason I took time to talk to you, Sister Agatha, is because I wanted you to understand that Ms. Victoria didn't hurt Mr. Robert. If she'd wanted to kill him, she would have done it at home the next time he started hitting her and called it self-defense."

Sister Agatha nodded thoughtfully. It was all hearsay, of course, but Crystal's observations certainly opened up a whole new set of possibilities.

Almost as if sensing that Sister Agatha remained unconvinced, she added, "Another reason I know she had nothing to do with Mr. Robert's murder is that, despite the abuse, she liked being the wife of a rich man. She loves her Mercedes and the diamond jewelry he'd buy for her after their fights—once guilt for what he'd done set in. That's also why she never told her friends what was happening. It didn't quite go with the role she liked playing in the community—that of Doña Victoria, the great lady. You get me?"

"She paid dearly for her luxuries," Sister Agatha commented. "Did Victoria ever get herself a gun for protection?"

"No way. She wouldn't even allow one in the house. She hates the danged things. Last spring there were some break-ins in the neighborhood. Mr. Robert was going out of town a lot on business, and I knew she was afraid at night, so I suggested she buy herself a gun. She looked at me as if I'd lost my mind. She told me that she didn't even allow RJ to own a toy pistol."

Sister Agatha considered the possibility that Victoria had been putting on an act—but three months ahead of the death of her husband? That didn't seem likely.

"I better go now," Crystal said at last. "Ms. Victoria asked me to get her clothes ready for tonight's private memorial service at her home."

As Crystal walked back to the main road, Sister Agatha made her way to her family's grave site. Tears filled her eyes as she crouched by her brother Kevin's small granite headstone. She'd spent months at his bedside watching his body being eaten away by cancer. His death, at the end, had been a mercy, yet a part of her had died with him.

Despite the passage of time, she still missed him terribly. He'd been her best friend.

Her parents had followed years later in a car accident. She prayed daily that they'd all found peace on the other side.

On her knees, bent low in prayer, she acknowledged her faults as a sister and a daughter. Even as a journalism professor, Mary Lambert Naughton had never even been close to a perfect example of anything. Sister Agatha still couldn't explain why God had chosen her to enter the religious life. She'd told her novice mistress just that many years ago.

Mother Monica had then reminded her of St. Paul, whom God had chosen, though no one could have considered him a paragon of virtue at the time. She'd advised Sister Agatha to hold to St. Paul's words—"forgetting all that lies behind and straining toward what lies ahead"—as she worked hard to fulfill her vocation. That simple faith-filled counsel had allowed her to forgive herself and continue serving God.

Sister Agatha stood and brushed the grass, leaves, and dust from her habit. *Serviam* . . . the motto of anyone in His service. She walked down the graveled pathway leading back to the church's parking lot. As she approached, she saw that RJ, Robert's son, was still acting up.

"I don't want to go!" he said, trying to pull his hand away from his mother's.

As Victoria bent down to talk to him, RJ jerked his hand free. Al Russo, who was close by, instantly stepped over and put his hand on RJ's shoulder.

RJ looked up, but Sister Agatha noticed that he didn't try to shrug off Al's grip.

"I don't want to go to my uncle's house. I hate it there," he pleaded. "You can't touch *anything,* and all they have on TV is the news."

"Then come stay with me for a while," Al suggested. "What do you say?"

The boy nodded and smiled. "Cool. Thanks," he said, then made a fist and bumped it into Al's in the well-known sign of respect.

"We're all set, then," Al said, mirroring the boy's lopsided grin.

Sister Agatha was struck by the affinity between the two, but before she could give it more thought, Sister Bernarda joined her.

"Chuck said to tell you to drop by his office whenever you're ready. He's got some shots you might like to see."

Taking one last look around, Sister Agatha noticed a woman in a wheelchair making her way slowly across the hard-packed limestone gravel portion of the parking lot. "Do you know who she is?"

"No, I don't," Sister Bernarda answered, following her gaze. "She was out by the grave a while ago."

"Alone?" Seeing Sister Bernarda nod, Sister Agatha continued. "Making her way across the grass would have been hard work."

Sister Bernarda's eyes narrowed as she looked at Sister Agatha. "So what's on your mind?"

"The sheriff was given a knockout drug—a good weapon of choice for a woman with a disability like hers."

"What are you saying—that she appeared *after* the sheriff went down, then took his gun and shot Robert?"

"Or maybe she came up from behind Robert while he was trying to figure out what was wrong with Tom, knocked him aside, then shot him with Tom's gun."

"You're reaching, Sister Agatha. The wheel tracks on the grass would have been obvious." She pointed to the two lines still visible on the ground.

106

"You're right . . . unless the woman can walk short distances on her own." She paused and shook her head. "I'm trying too hard."

"Take things one step at a time," Sister Bernarda advised.

"You're right. Let me find out what her connection to Robert Garcia is first. Wait for me here. I'm going to catch her before she leaves," Sister Agatha said, hurrying across the parking lot.

She was halfway there when a familiar voice called out to her.

"Sister Agatha, do you have a minute?" Father Mahoney said, waving to get her attention.

She stopped, then was forced to wait while a couple stopped to thank him for the service. "Sorry for the delay," he said at last, "but I needed to talk to you about the statues that'll be transferred from your monastery to St. Augustine's chapel."

"Father, Sister Bernarda's in charge of that. She's right back there," she said, pointing.

"Oh, then I'll go talk to her. Thanks for your time."

By the time she reached the parking lot, there was no sign of the woman and only an empty space next to the spot where she'd last seen her. Sister Agatha studied the wheelchair tracks and tried to remember what kind of vehicle had been parked there. Nothing came to mind, except the impression that it had been pale blue.

Sister Agatha asked the few remaining funeral attendees about the wheelchair user, but no one seemed to know who she was. That, of course, raised questions all on its own. Bernalillo was a small community with only a few stores and one post office.

As Sister Agatha headed back to join Sister Bernarda, Chuck Moody, who'd been sitting on a bench under a shade tree, stood and waved to her.

Sister Agatha went to meet him, questions circling in her mind. "I thought we'd agreed that you and I shouldn't be seen together in public," she said, joining him on the bench.

"We're safe enough," he said, his words clipped. "Almost everyone's gone now."

The coldness of his tone alerted her instantly. "What's wrong?"

"I found out that the monastery's probably going to be closing down." He stood up and glared at her. "*Why* didn't you tell me, Sister Agatha? I could have run a story, and maybe donors would have stepped up to help." He ran an exasperated hand through his hair. "What upsets me most is that you don't trust me. I thought you and I were friends."

"We are friends, Chuck, good friends, and I'm sorry, but it wasn't my secret to tell," she said softly. "It isn't final yet, and nobody's supposed to know. Reverend Mother wanted it that way. How did *you* find out?"

"Sister Bernarda slipped up," he said, sitting down dejectedly. "She mentioned how busy you all have been packing. She covered for it almost instantly, of course, telling me that you were just storing old computers. I caught on, though, and used one of your tricks—getting to the truth by making it sound like I already knew all about whatever she was trying to keep secret."

The well-known technique was one she'd taught all her journalism students at the University of New Mexico. It was all in the phrasing. You wouldn't ask, "Did you kill him?" Instead, you'd phrase it in a way more likely to get the answer you needed— "When you killed him, did you wash your hands afterward?"

"I'll give you the highlights, if you agree not to print it until I give you the okay," Sister Agatha said.

"Agreed."

"Let's meet back at your office and talk there. Is that okay with you?"

"Sure."

Sister Agatha stood and, as an afterthought, added, "Did you happen to take any photos of the woman in the wheelchair?"

He shook his head. "I only took photos of people who were at the graveside service, and I didn't see anyone in a wheelchair."

"Okay, thanks. I'll see you later."

As Chuck walked away, Sister Agatha spotted Smitty at the far end of the parking lot unlocking his car. Waving to get his attention, she hurried over to talk to him.

"I'm glad I caught you," Sister Agatha said. "I wanted to ask you if you'd seen Scout since we last spoke."

"No, he's been making himself real scarce lately. I think he's running scared. I left him a sandwich last night, but it was still there this morning."

"That's not good," she said and sighed. "Would you keep leaving food out and call me when he starts picking it up again?"

"Sure. I just hope we don't end up getting him killed," he muttered, sliding onto the front seat of his car.

With his words still resonating in the back of her mind, Sister Agatha watched him drive away. Smitty had voiced a disturbing truth. Murderers required secrecy and seldom looked kindly on any light that could dispel the darkness they left behind. If she somehow managed to get Scout to speak to her, she'd also have to find a way to protect him.

9

AFTER LEAVING SISTER BERNARDA AND THE ANTICHRYS-ler at the monastery, Sister Agatha and Pax took the Harley to meet Chuck at the *Chronicle*.

Taking a seat at one of the cluttered desks, Sister Agatha studied the photos Chuck had taken. He'd printed out a complete set for her. One photo captured her attention almost immediately. It showed Victoria speaking to a statuesque blonde in her late fifties, and it was easy to see from their hardened expressions that the two were not friends.

"Who's this woman with Victoria?" she asked, pointing to the blonde.

"That's Deputy Judy White. Actually, former deputy. She retired a few years ago."

"I'm guessing she was a friend of Robert's, not Victoria's. Is that right?"

"I don't know. All I can tell you is that she and Robert

worked in the evidence room together back in the days when they were both with the department."

"I'm still looking for a motive for Robert's murder, and her background brings up some interesting possibilities. Do you know where I can find her?"

"Sure. She owns Judy's Place, east of the casino turnoff. I hear she's practically always there."

"I remember hearing about that place. Judy's supposedly has the best sandwiches this side of Albuquerque's Central Avenue," Sister Agatha said.

"You should eat there sometime. Her reputation's well deserved."

Sister Agatha thought back to the time when she'd known all the best cafés around—and the ones to avoid. Her life had been so different when she'd been just plain Mary Lambert Naughton. She pushed the thought away almost as quickly as it had formed. As Sister Agatha, she'd found a peace beyond measure . . . but a part of her still missed the little adventures that had defined her back then.

"I did a piece on Judy White when she opened her café. Her mother owned a small restaurant in Los Lunas during the sixties, and that's how they made ends meet when Judy was growing up. The restaurant business was always in Judy's blood, so when she retired, she borrowed against her 401(k) and got things rolling. If the crowded parking lot is any indication, she's prospering right now."

Sister Agatha smiled. "Success usually follows passion and a dream—particularly when those two things are helped along by tons of hard work."

"Then I must be on the right track. I love this paper," he answered with a smile as he looked around.

"You've found your calling, Chuck."

"Speaking of calling, Sister, what's really going on at the monastery?"

She sighed softly. "This past year's been difficult. It's getting increasingly hard to justify the upkeep the old place needs. Now that our income has slipped since our business clients have taken their work overseas, the situation is getting even tougher." She swallowed, determined to keep her voice steady. "It's not cost-effective to run a monastery as large as ours for the benefit of just ten nuns. It makes far more sense to relocate the sisters elsewhere."

"So, that's it? You're leaving?"

"Unless a miracle happens and we get a big job, we'll be closing our doors. The winery next door wants to expand and made us a very generous offer for the monastery and the property around it. The funds from the sale, if it goes through, would be given to the monastery outside Denver that has offered us a home."

"Do you think you might be transferred up north *before* the sheriff is cleared?" Chuck asked, as if reading her mind.

"There's a chance that'll happen, but I'm praying that I'll be able to finish the job I've started."

Chuck looked down at Pax. "He'll be making the move, too, I hope?"

"Yes, Pax is part of our family," she said, standing. "I better get going. I want to give myself plenty of time to talk to Judy, and if she's busy, I intend to wait. Something tells me that she could turn out to be a big help to me," she said, remembering the disdain on Victoria's face.

As she and Pax headed for the Harley, she looked down at the big dog and smiled at him. "You may not be allowed inside the restaurant, boy, but we'll find a shady place where you can wait."

Pax looked at her, unperturbed. For dogs there was no "later" or "tomorrow." There was simply now. There was a lesson in that for her, too. She had to stop worrying about the future. As the Lord had said, "Sufficient unto the day is the evil thereof."

Sister Agatha arrived at the café just west of the main highway junction, a short time later. By then, some serious storm clouds had rolled in from the west, and the wind was picking up, another sign that rain wouldn't be far behind.

As she pulled into the parking space nearest one of the two side entrances, Sister Agatha could see that most of the round, bistro-sized tables inside were occupied—not bad for a late lunch. The tall blonde she'd seen in the photo peered out at her from behind the front counter, apparently having heard the distinctive-sounding Harley engine.

Sister Agatha was climbing off the bike when Judy White came out onto the sidewalk.

"Sister Agatha and Pax! I've heard all about you two, and your flashy motorcycle! I'm Judy, but you must know that by now. I had a feeling you'd be stopping by after I saw you staking out the graveside service."

Sister Agatha's jaw dropped. "I didn't think I was being obvious."

"Hey, I was with the sheriff's department for more years than I care to count," Judy said, chuckling. "After a while, you learn to notice even the little things most people just let slide by." She waved toward the rear of the building. "Why don't we go around the back, and I'll let you and Pax into my office. We're in for a gullywasher soon, and you don't want your canine friend to get soaked. Besides, it's time for *my* lunch. Would you like a sandwich—on the house?"

Remembering her earlier wistfulness, Sister Agatha silently

gave thanks for the unexpected blessing. "A sandwich sounds great. Thanks!"

Judy led the way through a rear storeroom and into the small but carefully laid-out office. File cabinets and a sturdy oak desk fit perfectly within the floor space, and a round window granted a magnificent view of the mountains to the east. Reaching into a tiny refrigerator installed below the right side of the desk, she brought out two bottles of cola and handed Sister Agatha one.

"Would you like to see our menu? We have over two dozen specialty sandwiches."

"I've heard, but no menu is necessary. Just bring me one of your favorites. I'm sure it'll end up being one of mine, too."

Judy returned a few moments later with a plate containing the biggest and thickest sandwich Sister Agatha had ever seen.

"This is our number one customer favorite. It's shredded premium sirloin, sharp cheddar, fresh Hatch green chile, and grilled mushrooms on sourdough." She placed the plate on the desk in front of Sister Agatha.

"We're going to split this, right?" Sister Agatha asked, trying to squelch the sin of gluttony that had suddenly reared its ugly head.

"No, that one's just for you. I've got another sandwich being prepared for me, and some beef slices for the dog, too." Judy stepped out of the room, then returned a moment later with her own platter and something for Pax on a bread plate.

"Thank you very much—from both of us," Sister Agatha said. After saying grace silently, she took a bite of her sandwich. It was unbelievably good, moist, savory, and perfectly spiced with just the right level of chile heat. Judging by this sandwich alone, the café's reputation was well deserved. No heaven would be complete without a sandwich like this on its buffet table.

"Now tell me what I can do for you, Sister," Judy said, taking a large bite of her own sandwich—a steaming hot, freshly grilled, olive-oil-brushed panini sandwich filled with what looked like ham, mushrooms, and red bell peppers. "I have a feeling that you noticed that Victoria and I don't get along."

"I did," she admitted.

"I'm closer to Robert's age than she is, and there was a time when she thought there was something going on between him and me. Of course, he may have led her to believe that on purpose, to make her jealous. He liked playing mind games with people. There was never anything between us, though. I can't stand control freaks."

"I'm trying to get a better feel for who he was, and who his enemies might have been. Can you tell me more about Robert?"

"I worked with him for about eight months, but he and I never really got along. He had to micromanage everything and everyone around him. At the time, he didn't outrank me, and I had more years in the department, so I didn't have to take orders from him."

She paused and took a few more bites. "That man used to call his wife six or seven times a shift to check up on her. From the bits and pieces I'd overhear, I think he believed Victoria was having an affair. He *had* to know where she was every minute and who she was with, even after the baby was born. Over the years, I heard that his control issues got even worse."

"What do you mean?"

"There were rumors that he started slapping Victoria around, but I never noticed any marks on her, so who knows? As for Robert, I hadn't seen him for a long time—since we last worked together, to be exact. He certainly never stopped by here, at least when I was behind the counter."

"Do you know if Robert had enemies in the department?" Sister Agatha asked.

Judy stared down at her plate, lost in thought. "Only one name comes to mind—Deputy Tony Gannon. When some items supposed to be in the evidence room turned up missing, Robert blamed Tony. Tony insisted that it wasn't his fault, that he'd done the initial paperwork. He blamed Robert for failing to enter the data into the system and not properly shelving the items. Robert argued that he'd never received anything from Gannon, nor had he handled the evidence container. They went back and forth like that for a long time."

"What was missing?"

"A couple of handguns taken during a drug bust."

"What do you think happened to the pistols?" Sister Agatha asked, noting the sudden rattle of heavy raindrops on the metal roof.

"They probably got misplaced," she said with a shrug. "My gut instinct is that Robert dropped the ball on that. Whenever Robert argued with his wife—an almost weekly event—he'd be stomping around and fuming for the rest of the shift. If Gannon turned in the handguns on one of those days, it's possible that Robert never even processed the paperwork."

"What happened to Deputy Gannon?" Sister Agatha asked quickly, excited to have found a possible suspect in addition to having had a terrific lunch.

"Nothing was ever proven, so both officers had a letter placed in their files. Eventually, both Robert and Tony left the department for greener pastures. You already know about Robert. Tony was poached by the Austin Police Department for half again the pay as well as a housing allowance."

Sister Agatha's spirits plummeted. For a moment she'd thought she'd found a viable lead, but now it appeared she'd reached another dead end. "What about Robert's security firm? Do you know anything about his business?"

"No, not really. I've never been much interested in rent-a-cops. For that, you'll have to talk to his partner, Monty Allen."

Finished with lunch, Judy went to open the window, which pivoted in the middle, an interesting design feature. The rain had stopped now, leaving a cool, fresh breeze in its wake. "I love the scents that always follow a good storm," she said, inhaling deeply.

"It's a rare enough treat here in New Mexico," Sister Agatha said. "Now that the rain's let up, I better be on my way. Thanks very much for that wonderful lunch."

"You're welcome, Sister Agatha. Come by anytime."

Soon Sister Agatha was on her way north, toward home, with Pax in the sidecar. To avoid the deep puddles that now filled the low spots, she kept the Harley closer to the centerline. The absence of a curb and storm drains made New Mexico roads like this one a mixed bag of hazards during seasonal thunderstorms.

Twenty feet beyond the graveled shoulder was a concrete-lined flood control canal, essential across the metro area during summer downpours. This twenty-foot-wide portion of the system was currently filled to the brim with muddy water and plant debris carried down from the higher ground to the east.

Looking ahead through her water-splattered helmet visor, she saw a hunched, soaked figure walking north along the roadside adjacent to the canal. Something about him looked familiar. As she drew closer she realized that it was Scout.

He must have heard the roar of the Harley above the rush of water, because he turned to look. The second he saw her, Scout took off at a jog.

"Wait," Sister Agatha yelled, then realized that with the helmet muffling her voice, the roar of the cycle's engine, and the sound of water in the ditch, there was virtually no chance of him hearing her.

Before she could decide what to do next, she heard the blare of a car horn behind her. In a heartbeat, a pickup whipped around her, spraying water everywhere. Blinded for a few seconds by the sudden deluge, she backed off the throttle and tapped the brakes, worried she'd drift out of her lane or lose control altogether. The mud-splattered white truck cut in front of her and swerved to the right, onto the shoulder.

Fifty yards ahead, Scout was running for his life. Glancing back over his shoulder, he veered out onto the concrete slope of the raging canal, desperate to avoid the oncoming vehicle.

"Lord, help!" Sister Agatha prayed, helpless to intervene.

As the pickup brushed by him, Scout slipped and fell into the churning stream of water. Swept downstream, he groped in vain for anything to hang on to, but the rushing water carried him relentlessly along, his head barely visible.

For a second the pickup skidded, and she thought it would go into the water as well. Then the driver regained full control and swerved back onto the highway.

As the white truck accelerated away, Sister Agatha tried to read the license plate, but between the mud and the distance it was a futile effort. All she could tell from the color was that it was a New Mexico plate.

Focused solely on saving Scout now, she pressed the motorcycle for more speed. About a mile ahead, the canal intersected the main channel leading west to the river. If Scout got carried that far, he'd be swept against one of the big metal grates and drown. She had to get ahead of him somehow, then grab him as he went by.

People drowned in these ditches every year during flash floods. There was even a special fire department rescue unit that practiced ditch rescues, but they wouldn't be able to get here in time to do any good. Knowing that, she gunned the engine and raced down the road, looking ahead as well as in the rearview mirror for any other vehicle that might be able to stop and help.

Speeding past Scout, she found a spot that would serve her purposes and pulled over to the shoulder of the road. Pax sat up immediately, but without even looking over at him, she gave him the command to stay. He couldn't help her here.

Sister Agatha yanked off her helmet and dropped it on the ground as she hurried over to the concrete apron of the ditch. On her knees in six inches of water, she gazed upstream, trying to spot Scout's bobbing head. That was when she saw a tree branch riding the waves along the edge. Without hesitation, Sister Agatha reached out as it passed by and grabbed the branch.

The stout tree limb was much bigger than it had looked and yanked her forward almost into the stream. She braced herself with her left arm, dug in with her feet, and somehow managed to keep hold of the branch without getting pulled into the raging waters. Using all the strength she had left in her arms, she lifted and pulled the cottonwood branch onto the concrete. Now she had something for Scout to grab—if he was still alert and conscious when he passed by.

Sister Agatha stood, trying to spot him among the debris, and saw that he was much closer than she'd expected, still trying desperately to swim to the edge of the canal. Waving to get his attention, she called out to him.

"Grab hold!" she yelled.

She got down on her knees, anchoring herself the best she could against the outer edge of the concrete, and swung the branch out over the water, trying to avoid touching the surface. Though it was heavy, she had to keep it clear of the water or it would be carried away, out of his reach and useless.

As Scout swept past, he reached up at the last moment and managed to grasp the branch. The sudden impact nearly yanked her off her feet. The swirling waters became a powerful adversary as she fought to pull him to safety.

Her joints ached from the stress, and as her skin was scraped raw, her grip on the branch started to slip. Groaning from the pain, she tightened her fingers and held on, praying for strength as the laws of physics took over. With her as the anchor, the man was swung out of the main stream of water and to the edge of the canal.

Scout reached the upper slope of the concrete seconds later, grabbed the same edge that anchored her feet, and pulled himself up out of the water, choking and gasping from the effort.

As he reached safety, Sister Agatha let go of the branch, at long last allowing it to be swept downstream.

"Are you all right?" she managed, trying to catch her breath.

He didn't answer, but his pale gray eyes met her gaze and held it for a heartbeat.

Sister Agatha saw human recognition there, and for a second Scout almost smiled. Yet that brief, gentle emotion vanished almost as quickly as it had formed.

Scout reached behind his shoulders with bony, bleeding hands, searching in vain for his backpack, which had been lost in the current. When he realized it was gone, fear and confusion took control of him again. He scrambled to his knees, looking around in desperation.

"It's okay. You're safe now," she said softly.

Like a trapped wild animal, he stared vacantly at her, then raced off, heading for the highway. Thankfully, no cars were coming, because Scout didn't think to look. Seconds later, he leaped into the underbrush and disappeared into the bosque.

By the time she managed to stand, he'd disappeared from view. She returned to the Harley, where Pax was waiting for her, and called in the report to the police.

"It's time for us to go home, boy," she said, putting the cell phone away and giving Pax a hug. Sometimes, there was nothing more comforting than having your arms around a big dog like him.

As they headed back, she remembered the gratitude and relief she'd seen in Scout's gaze for a few precious seconds and whispered a prayer of thanks. Instinct, and perhaps more—a stirring of certainty—assured her they'd meet again.

10

THE FOLLOWING MORNING SISTER AGATHA, SISTER BER-
narda and Maria Victoria worked to pack up most of Sister Clothilde's remaining kitchen appliances.

"So we're moving for sure?" Sister Agatha asked.

Sister Bernarda nodded. "It's definite now. The Archbishop
informed Reverend Mother that no additional funding can be
found to counter our budget deficiencies. The sale of our monastery is going through, and we'll be leaving by the middle of this
month."

"That's only seven days away," Sister Agatha said, trying to
swallow back the sudden panic that swept over her.

"We'll take care of the packing while you finish what you
need to do in town," Sister Maria Victoria said. "Sister Ignatius
started a novena for you, too, so that you'll be able to find the
answers you need to clear the sheriff."

Sister Agatha smiled. "Good. I'll need all the help I can get."

She glanced at the packing crates, then added, "Let me finish printing labels for those boxes. Then I'll go."

Before anyone could answer her, Reverend Mother came to the door. "The others will handle that work, child," she told Sister Agatha. "You're needed elsewhere. The sheriff and his family have supported our monastery for many years. Let's do all we can for him while there's still time."

The message was clear. Sheriff Tom Green would be her priority now, second only to her duty to God. "I'll get started, Mother," she said, bowing her head and hurrying down the hall.

As she stepped outside, she glanced back at the old building with tear-filled eyes. She'd say a final good-bye to Bernalillo and Our Lady of Hope by making sure justice was served. She couldn't think of a more fitting way to end her days here.

Seeing Pax stretched out on the porch, sunning himself, she motioned to the motorcycle. "Come on, boy. We'll be working overtime till we find answers."

Five minutes later, she was speeding south in the Harley, Pax in the sidecar. Today she'd pay Monty Allen, Robert Garcia's partner, a visit. She didn't expect things to go smoothly. Like the Garcias, he was probably opposed to any effort on her part to clear Tom Green. The challenge would be finding a way to get him to answer at least some of her questions.

The business was located on Bernalillo's southern margins, and it took her twenty minutes to reach the low metal warehouse that housed Garcia and Allen Security Systems Corp. So far, all she really knew about Monty was that he was a friend of the Garcias and might be running for county sheriff as a write-in candidate.

As she stepped inside the reception area, a pretty, dark-haired woman in her early twenties greeted her with a friendly smile and hello. On her glass-surfaced desk was a red baseball cap, one of the promotional gimmicks used by Robert Garcia's campaign.

Sister Agatha introduced herself and Pax, but before she could even state her business, Monty Allen came into the room. He was dressed in casual pants and a knit shirt with the company logo embroidered on its pocket.

"I hope you're here to tell me that Tom Green is ready to withdraw from the race," he said, his smile as phony as it was fleeting.

The brash words took her aback. "If you have questions about the election, I suggest you speak directly to Sheriff Green," she said, employing her best Catholic-school nun voice. "I'm not anyone's political spokesperson, Mr. Allen."

"Somehow, I doubt that," he said acerbically.

She refused to take the bait, suspecting he was trying to get her angry enough to give him something he could use against Tom. "I came here this morning to talk to you. Since my presence wasn't a total surprise, and you're still here," she said, gesturing to the surveillance camera mounted on the wall, "I'm going to assume that you're willing to give me some of your time."

He gestured to the door he'd come through. "After you—and feel free to bring your dog," he added, his phony smile plastered back in place.

After a short walk down a wide hall, they entered a spacious office. He invited her to take a seat, then made himself comfortable behind a huge, horseshoe-shaped mahogany desk.

"So what brings you here, Sister Agatha? I don't suppose the monastery requires the services of the best security firm in the Southwest?" He laughed loudly as if he'd found the outrageous question hysterically funny.

"We're far more worried about other people's security, Mr. Allen, and that's why I'm here," she said as Pax lay by her feet.

"I know precisely what brought you to my door, Sister Agatha," he snapped, this time without any trace of humor. "You're trying to get Sheriff Green off the hook."

"Off the hook implies deception and dishonesty. That's not what this is all about. I'm after the truth. That's all."

He shook his head. "What you're trying to do is uncover a truth that doesn't exist," he said, leaning forward and resting his elbows on the desk. "The evidence speaks for itself. There's no reason to question the sheriff's guilt."

"If he's guilty, as you believe, my investigation will only seal the case against him. If he's innocent, then it'll help the police catch the real killer. What harm could there be in that?"

"In the process of investigating a straightforward case, you may also end up uncovering things no one wants brought to light." He gazed at her consideringly for several moments. "The Garcias are a powerful family, Sister, and powerful families usually have more than their share of secrets—ones they'll do just about anything to protect. You may not be afraid of them, but if you keep pushing this, you'll find that people in this town are— and with good reason. Your little investigation may end up doing far more harm than good."

His message was clear. She'd have to be very careful who she was seen talking to from now on. She could end up placing other people—anyone who tried to help her—in the line of fire.

"Are you afraid that my coming here will place *you* in jeopardy?" she asked.

"I can take care of myself, Sister, and the Garcias know I'm loyal to them."

"Do you feel secure enough to answer a few of my questions?"

"Of course. Shoot."

That had been too easy . . . maybe he intended to ask her for something in return. She focused on the matter at hand. A partial win was better than no win at all. "Did Robert make enemies while he worked here, or did the firm?"

"Robert and I sued a couple of deadbeat clients," he said with a shrug, "but no one's tried to murder *me* over that, so I think you're on the wrong track."

"Think harder. Robert must have made enemies. It's the price of being a successful businessman," she pressed.

"Let me tell you how things work around here. People who've experienced thefts or security issues, or think they run that risk, contact us. We come in, identify potential problems, and safeguard them against any future trouble. We don't accuse or arrest anyone."

"Everyone liked Robert and no one had any reason to wish him harm, is that what you're telling me?" Sister Agatha said with a clear touch of sarcasm.

"No, not quite. People just find it more profitable to be friends with the Garcias."

"So Robert had the best friends money can buy. Do you include yourself in that?"

"Don't expect a reaction from me," he said, laughing. "At this stage in my career, I rarely fall for amateur interrogation tactics."

"Try one honest answer, then, and it'll stay between us. Are you afraid of the Garcias?"

"No, I'm not, but I'll tell you this—it's a lot smarter to stay on their good side. If you went to them and offered to drop the investigation, I'm almost certain that you'd see a lot of the monastery's current problems disappear. They take good care of their friends."

"What problems are you talking about?" Sister Agatha asked, wondering how much he knew.

"I know the monastery will be closing its doors for good soon."

She stared at him. "How could you possibly know that?"

He smiled slowly. "Luz del Cielo Winery has offered JD Garcia a limited partnership if he'll finance the monastery's conversion to a modern bed-and-breakfast."

There was a knock at the door, and his secretary came in. Moving quickly, she placed some papers in front of him.

He glanced down and wrote some notes on the margins.

As Sister Agatha glanced at his handwriting, she suddenly realized he'd written the note that had been left for them in the Antichrysler. Knowing that her observation didn't constitute proof, she decided not to pursue that for now.

Once his assistant left, closing the door behind her, Sister Agatha answered him. "Robert deserves to have his real killer brought to justice. Maybe that'll be worth something to the Garcias someday."

"That'll all depend on how much harm you do between now and then."

"Help me minimize that. Tell me who Robert's enemies were," she insisted.

"Anyone who is anyone has enemies, Sister. That's a fact of life. Even so, most people know power when they see it, and respect that. The attack on Robert was made by someone who didn't care that Robert was a Garcia—that tends to indicate a personal stake. Maybe it was someone who wanted to see him out of the way, like his political rival."

They'd gone full circle now. She stood, then asked one final question. "Had Robert won the race for sheriff, what would have happened to this company?"

"I would have run day-to-day operations, and Robert's share of the profits would have been placed in trust until he was no longer in public office." Monty squared his shoulders as he rose and faced her. "I've done my best to help you today, Sister. Now I'd like you to return the favor."

She'd been expecting this. "What do you need from me?"

"Talk to Green. Convince him to withdraw from the race. He'll be facing trial sooner or later, and our community needs a sheriff who doesn't have a cloud like that hanging over his head."

"That'll mean you'll run unopposed," she observed.

"Probably, but I can do a good job for this county. I've also got the backing of the Garcias. They've even encouraged me to use the promotional baseball caps that Robert gave to his supporters."

Sister Agatha glanced behind him and saw another of the red caps on top of the filing cabinet. "TFC, Time for Change. That was his slogan, right?"

"Would you care for one?" he asked, only half joking.

"I don't think it'll go with my habit," she answered with a thin smile.

"Your choice," he answered, then held the door open for her. "Do we have an agreement? Will you speak to the sheriff?"

"I'll pass your message along to him. That's the best I can do."

"Good enough. If he has half the integrity you think he does, Green'll understand that this county deserves more than what he can offer under the present circumstances."

As Sister Agatha walked out with Pax, she mulled over what she'd learned. She hadn't received the answers she'd hoped to get, but Allen had certainly opened new avenues for her to consider.

Twenty minutes later, as she drove through the monastery's gates, Sister Agatha saw Sister Bernarda gathering flowers. This time of year, fresh bouquets were always placed on each grave inside the monastery's cemetery. Her chest tightened as she realized once again how much they'd be leaving behind.

"The roses are doing exceptionally well this year because of the rains," Sister Bernarda said when Sister Agatha joined her.

Sister Agatha didn't reply as she helped place flowers by each headstone.

"Is everything all right?" Sister Bernarda asked, once they were on their way back to the parlor.

Sister Agatha shook her head. "Every time I think I've found a promising lead, it fizzles out on me. Instead of getting answers, I just keep finding more questions. All things considered, I'm not sure I've made any progress at all lately."

"Maybe you should focus on today's Divine Office," Sister Bernarda said, referring to the readings and prayers that centered their day. "One in particular, actually, from James. 'Patience hath a perfect work,'" she quoted.

Sister Agatha sighed. "I know that patience is a virtue, Sister, but I've got to hurry—"

"That's vanity speaking, Sister Agatha," Sister Bernarda said in a quiet and resolute voice. "*You* don't have to do anything except get out of God's way and let Him do the work. Remember this morning's reading from Philippians? That's one of my all-time favorite quotes—'For it is God who worketh in you, both to will and to accomplish, according to His good will.'" She paused. "So stop telling God how you think things should work out and quit making demands. Open your heart and listen to Him first, then act."

The simple truth behind Sister Bernarda's advice touched her heart. "You're so right, Sister."

Before she could say more, the Maria bell announced Vespers.

11

THE FOLLOWING MORNING, AFTER THE END OF THE
Great Silence, Sister Agatha went directly to the parlor.
With Sister de Lourdes already in Denver and Sister Jo,
who'd only had a brief stay at Our Lady, transferred to a teaching
order in Albuquerque, Sister Bernarda hadn't had a break from
her portress duties in days. She hadn't even been able to go for
private prayer in the chapel.

This morning Sister Agatha had agreed to take over for a
half hour so Sister Bernarda could spend quiet time in adoration.
It was in those moments that the soul affirmed its total depen-
dence on God. Now, in the midst of all the troubles they were
facing, times of contemplation in chapel had become a necessary
lifeline.

The phone rang shortly after eight thirty, and Sister Agatha
picked it up. She recognized the caller's voice even before he
identified himself.

"Sister Agatha, you and I need to talk. This is Frank Marquez."

"Is something wrong?" she asked quickly.

"You tell me. We had an agreement. You were going to pass on whatever you uncovered, but even though you've been working the case for two days now, I haven't heard a word. I hope you don't expect me to believe that you've uncovered absolutely nothing."

"If I'd found out something definite, I would have called you, Frank. All I've really got at this point is gut feelings based on rumors."

"Rumors can sometimes lead to facts, and gut feelings to suspects. How about meeting me at the Java Shack, the coffee shop across from the station, at around ten thirty?"

She'd heard of the place, of course. It was supposed to sell some very upscale coffee. Young professionals and upper-class business owners flocked to it. It surprised her that Marquez had suggested the place. Almost all the officers she knew preferred coffee that didn't require an entire hour's wages.

"Don't worry, I'm buying," he said.

"I'll be there," she answered cheerfully.

Sister Agatha placed the phone down and had just started dusting the parlor's desk when she heard the sounds of happy barking outside. Standing by the window, she saw Pax making the most of the cool morning temperatures. Two quails with their question-mark bonnets were walking along the top of the wall while Pax lunged and jumped, trying in vain to reach them. Animals and children . . . even the simplest things could renew their zest for life.

As her thoughts wandered, she thought of Robert's son, RJ. Sister Agatha wondered how Robert's death would affect the boy over time. Would he draw closer to his mother, or not? Now that Robert's cruelty was no longer a part of their lives, would RJ and

Victoria drift apart? Without a common threat, the need to band together was no longer there—at least not to the same extent—and the boy seemed primed to rebel already.

By the time Sister Bernarda came into the parlor, Sister Agatha had made up her mind to go speak to Victoria. Regardless of what Crystal, the housekeeper, had said, an abused wife always had a strong motive for wanting to ease her suffering—one way or the other.

"I'm ready to take over, Your Charity," Sister Bernarda said. "Thanks for taking care of things here so I could have time in chapel."

"Anytime, Sister—and I mean that."

Sister Agatha and Pax left the monastery five minutes later. Unsure whether Victoria was still staying at her brother-in-law's house, she passed by Victoria's home first, since it was on her way.

Seeing a car there, Sister Agatha drove up the long driveway and parked. A few moments later she and Pax, on a short lead, passed through the turquoise blue gate leading into the walled courtyard, then walked up to the heavy carved door. Pax remained at heel, seated on the flagstone step as she rang the doorbell.

As she waited, Sister Agatha studied her surroundings. This wasn't a particularly large house, but it was well appointed—a modern frame-and-stucco version of the classic Southwest adobe home. The private courtyard was filled with colorful desert shrubs and indigenous flowers that flourished in the dry climate. Carefully positioned sandstone boulders accented the enclosure. The effect was cool and soothing.

When there was no answer, Sister Agatha rang the bell again. A minute later, she heard running footsteps, and the door was opened.

"Sister Agatha, I'm surprised to see you!" Victoria said, still catching her breath. "I was expecting the parcel express man."

Sister Agatha wasn't sure how to respond. Did that mean that she wouldn't have answered had she known?

"Come in," she said, waving her inside. "The dog, too." She walked to the doorway leading to the den, then stopped and glanced back at Sister Agatha. "Since you're here, how about giving me a hand in RJ's room? My housekeeper's running an errand, and I could sure use an extra pair of hands. I'm trying to hang up a poster I know RJ will just love. It's a surprise for when he gets back from day camp."

"I'd be happy to help."

Sister Agatha followed her down the hall, and soon they entered what could only be described as a little boy's dream room. From floor to ceiling, it was filled with everything baseball. There were posters of Major League players on every wall, autographed team photos, a full-sized cardboard cutout of an apparently famous player swinging a bat, and half a dozen pennants of the local minor league team, the Albuquerque Isotopes. There was even a huge teddy bear on the shelf, dressed up in a pin-striped baseball uniform and cap. A new-looking baseball glove sat beside it, along with an autographed ball inside a plastic case. In the opposite corner stood a wooden bat that had to have been at least as tall as Robert Jr. Beside that was a well-used plastic bat and ball, more suitable for a child just learning the fundamentals.

"I want to hang the poster just to the right of his bed. We got RJ's favorite player, Mitch the Missile, to sign it for him."

"We?"

"Al Russo helped. I think you've met him. Al figured that RJ needed a little boost right now." Victoria handed her a big rolled-up poster, then reached onto the top of a large dresser for several push tacks.

"How's this?" Sister Agatha said, unrolling the poster half-way and holding it up against the wall.

"Could you move it about six inches to your left and lower the right side about an inch?"

Sister Agatha made the adjustment, then eyeballed the top edge, trying to get it level.

"Close enough. Just hold it there so I can put two tacks into the top," Victoria said, coming up from behind her.

"I imagine your son is taking his father's death really hard right now," Sister Agatha said, stepping to the side enough so Victoria could put the tacks in place.

"My son and I will get through this. It won't be easy, but we'll manage," she answered.

Together, they unrolled the remaining portion of the poster, and Victoria placed four more tacks in place.

Victoria then stood back to survey their work. "That'll do it for now. If RJ wants it elsewhere, it won't take long to pull it free." She glanced at Sister Agatha. "Thanks for the help, Sister. Now what can I do for you?"

"I came hoping for a chance to speak to you alone."

"We're not actually alone, but we won't be overheard," Victoria said. "My sister-in-law, Alyssa, kept us company last night. She's staying in the guest bedroom. You don't have to worry about our privacy, though. Alyssa took one of her pills, so she'll be out till noon, at least."

Victoria led the way back to the big, open front room and offered Sister Agatha a seat on a comfortable-looking sofa. "So what brings you here?"

Sister Agatha decided to get right to the point. "I've heard some disturbing stories about the way your husband treated you," Sister Agatha said gently. "Including physical abuse," she added.

"I loved Robert, Sister Agatha. Why else would I have stayed with him? He had a temper, ask anyone, but he was a great provider. I never lacked for anything, and, more importantly, neither did my son. Sure, Robert had his faults, and getting too rough with the people he loved was one of them—but he had a good side, too. He always made sure my son and I had the best of everything." She stood, her eyes cold and focused. "I think you should leave now," she said, walking to the front door and holding it open.

"I'm sorry if I offended you," Sister Agatha said, seeing the woman's hand shaking.

"Just go," Victoria said, pointing down the walk.

Sister Agatha walked back to the motorcycle with Pax and reached for her helmet. "Seems I touched a nerve, boy," she commented. "Or did it seem to you that she was just putting on an act? I'm not convinced her indignation was as sincere as she wanted us to believe."

Pax looked at her and cocked his head, almost as if pondering the question.

Sister Agatha reached out and patted him on the head. "Never mind. Sidecar ride, get in!" He jumped in immediately and sat up so he could see around the cockpit's small windshield.

Easing back onto the saddle, Sister Agatha considered the various impressions she'd gotten during her short visit while they were still fresh in her mind. Though she hadn't been there long, one curious fact had come to the surface. Victoria had repeatedly referred to RJ as "my" son, not "our" son.

Although it might have simply been an act of independence, or defiance, Sister Agatha intended to look into that some more. She'd start by comparing how long Robert and Victoria had been married with RJ's age. If Victoria had been carrying someone else's child, that could certainly explain Robert's resentment— though it still didn't justify his abusive behavior.

She was just about to put on her helmet when Frank Marquez, now driving an unmarked sedan, pulled up beside her. "Interesting that I should run into you here, Sister."

"I might have said the same thing if you hadn't beaten me to the punch," Sister Agatha said with a sheepish smile.

"You coming or going?"

"Just leaving," she said.

"Then we'll talk more about this later," he said. "Right now *I* need to talk to Mrs. Garcia."

Sister Agatha then put on her helmet and started the engine, watching as Frank climbed out of his car and walked through the courtyard gate. She would have loved to ask him what had brought him here . . . and maybe she would, later.

Driving slowly down the street, she noticed a woman wearing jeans and a T-shirt working in the yard of the house next door. On impulse, Sister Agatha decided to go talk to her. A snoopy neighbor could be worth his or her weight in gold.

As she drove up the adjacent circular driveway, the woman heard the Harley, waved, and walked over to greet her. "Sister Agatha, I presume?" she asked with a smile. She was tall and very thin, and her silver hair was styled in a simple pageboy. Sister Agatha guessed that she was in her midsixties.

"That's me," Sister Agatha answered, taking off her helmet so they could see each other face-to-face. "Have we met?"

"No. My nephew works in the mayor's office, and he once described you to me. My name's Kathy Duran." She shook hands, then, cocking her head, invited Sister Agatha and Pax into the house. "Let's get out of the heat for a bit. It's time for my break. Gardening keeps my blood pressure down, but I have to take it in increments, especially this time of year."

The conventional pitched-roof, ranch-style home was decorated in warm earth tones. The peeled log furniture appeared to be handmade, with carved Western images of cattle and rearing horses adding detail to the simple but functional style.

"Those are just for decoration," she said, pointing to two large, antique-looking enamel coffeepots on the kitchen's center island. "I don't drink coffee or tea, but I have apple and orange juice if you'd care for something to drink."

"Apple juice would be nice," Sister Agatha said. She wasn't particularly thirsty but had learned over the years that the simple act of sharing a refreshment with someone often worked wonders. People relaxed, and conversations flowed more freely.

"Now tell me what brought you here. I heard the motorcycle and saw you visiting with Victoria a while ago." She stood at the kitchen island, a heavy wooden table fitted with drawers and cabinets. "I also noticed that you didn't stay long. I imagine your visit didn't go well, particularly since Alyssa's there."

"You've got me curious. Why would you say that?" Sister Agatha asked.

"Alyssa wouldn't risk getting her husband angry by talking to you," Kathy replied matter-of-factly.

"No one would have had to know," Sister Agatha protested.

Kathy smiled. "Ours is a small town. We all know each other's business."

Knowing the truth when she heard it, Sister Agatha nodded but said nothing.

"In that family, men run things, too," Kathy said in a slow, thoughtful tone. "The women . . . well, they're more like window dressing, if you ask me. Trophy wives. Although Alyssa and Victoria are different in a lot of ways, they have one thing in common. They live under their husband's thumbs. I don't waste time feeling sorry for them. When your toys are more important to you than your freedom . . ."

"Some women don't mind taking a backseat to their husbands. It spares them the responsibility of making their own decisions—and relieves them of all accountability," Sister Agatha said.

"Sister, both of those women are gluttons for punishment—especially Victoria. I've seen a few of her fights with Robert, and heard even more. One time she ran out the back door, crying like a baby. Robert grabbed her by the arm, twisted it behind her back, and practically threw her back inside the house. I called the sheriff's department, of course."

"What happened?"

"After about a half hour, a deputy finally came out, but nothing was done from what I could tell. The next day I was out watering the tomatoes when I saw Victoria in the backyard wearing shorts and one of those tank tops, sunning herself on a lounger. Even though there's a fence between us, I could see the huge bruises on her arms and shoulders. Of course, when she went to town later, she covered all those up with a long-sleeved blouse."

Sister Agatha shook her head slowly. "I can't understand why she never tried to get help."

"And create a scandal?" Kathy shook her head. "That's not the way things work, not for the Garcia women, at least."

"How did the family get their money, do you know?"

"I understand that JD and Robert's grandfather made a bundle selling black market gasoline and ration coupons across the West during World War II. He then used that money to buy legitimate businesses. Since then, each generation has done better than the last.

"Prospering is a matter of pride to the Garcias. Their men don't bother with the rules, and they compete against each other almost as hard as they do against outsiders. Take a look at JD and Robert. They both married beautiful women, though neither man is much to look at. I'm sure that deep down they know their wives married them for their money, and maybe that's why they treat them like . . . crap," Kathy said at last, then shrugged. "But that's just my opinion."

"Do you think it's possible Victoria really loved Robert, despite the way he treated her?" Sister Agatha asked.

"Stranger things have happened, I suppose. I can tell you one thing for sure, though. She's not acting like a grieving widow now." Kathy paused and took a deep, shaky breath. "Believe me, I'd know those signs better than almost anyone else. When my husband of forty-five years died last year, I was devastated. I sat in his favorite chair in our living room and stared at the wall for hours. I prayed I'd die, too. It wasn't until my daughter and her husband moved in with me for a while that I was able to climb out of that dark place and find a reason to go on.

"After the death of someone you truly care about, you're never the same." Kathy swallowed hard, then continued. "I don't see any of that happening to Victoria. Instead, when I look at her, I see a young mother who finally has the backbone to stand up for herself."

"What do you mean?"

"Yesterday afternoon I was out on my balcony, reading. The Garcias were out on Victoria's back patio when Robert Jr. hurt himself on something and started crying. Victoria immediately tried to comfort the boy, but JD pulled her away from him, kind of rough, saying that she was going to turn the kid into a crybaby. JD shook the boy and told him to go to his room and not come out until he could act like a man instead of a sissy girl. It took her a second or two to get herself together, but as soon as the boy went inside, Victoria turned on JD. She told him *never* to disrespect her in front of her son. JD laughed and told her to remember her place. She'd married a Garcia, but her son was the genuine article. He had standards to meet, and no man in his family was going to grow up whining like a woman."

"How did she take that?" Sister Agatha asked.

"Victoria got in his face and, in a voice loud enough to be heard all the way down the street, told him no blanking Garcia would ever tell her what to do again. She said she had Robert's life insurance and that was all she and her son needed now. They'd be taken care of without any more of the blanking Garcia money, so if he didn't like the way she was raising RJ, he could get out and not bother coming back."

Since the Garcias didn't seem to do anything halfway, Sister Agatha was sure that the life insurance Victoria had mentioned was substantial. "Living next to them, did you get the impression that Robert Jr. and his dad were close?" Sister Agatha asked Kathy.

"That's a tough one to answer," Kathy said after a pause. "I think RJ was a little intimidated by his father, but he was proud of him, too. At least that's the impression I got at the games."

"What games?"

"You know, the church league. Robert plays—played—on the church's softball team. I'd go to watch my son-in-law, who's one heck of a second baseman, and I can tell you that RJ and Victoria would cheer louder than anyone else there whenever Robert got a hit."

Sister Agatha smiled. "That part of their lives sounds normal, at least."

Kathy glanced at her watch. "You'll have to excuse me, Sister, I have to get ready to leave. I need to be at the community center in a half hour. I teach knitting classes two days a week."

Noting the time and aware that she was supposed to meet Frank at the Java Shack soon, Sister Agatha thanked Kathy and headed to town. Forced to choose a parking spot three buildings away in order to provide tree shade for Pax, she left him by the bike and ordered him to wait. With that command, Pax was free to move about as long as he remained in close proximity to the Harley.

As she went through the doors, the scent of coffee and fresh rolls, and other wonderful smells, like cinnamon, filled the air. Spotting movement out of the corner of her eye, she turned and saw Frank wave from one of the round parquet-topped wooden tables. He stood as she joined him.

"I'm sorry I'm a few minutes late," she said.

"Not a problem. It gave me a chance to enjoy my coffee and think."

"I'm surprised to see you here. You were always a no-frills type of guy."

"Guess I've been spoiled by twenty-first-century innovations. I grew up drinking wimpy coffee boiled over a campfire. Now the beans are roasted and pressurized by thousand-dollar stainless-steel monster machines, and I feel cheated unless I get coffee that'll keep me awake for three full days," he said, pointing to the steaming cup.

"Boiled coffee eats up the walls of your stomach," she said, then, with a smile, added, "I guess we all have our vices."

"Even you?" Seeing her nod, he said, "A nun with vices? 'Fess up. What's yours?"

"Chocolate. White chocolate in particular. It's my weakness."

"Hold that thought." He went to the counter and ordered a white chocolate iced mocha java with extra whipped cream. Moments later, he placed it in front of her, complete with straw. "Give that a try."

After thanking him, she sipped the cool drink. "I've died and gone to heaven," she sighed with a happy smile.

Marquez laughed. "Okay, Sister, now that you've been properly bribed, it's time for some straight talk. I read the report you called in about the hit-and-run attempt on a transient known as Scout. I understand you pulled him out of the flood canal, but that's the only official news I've received dealing with your investigation. I want to know what else you've got."

She gave him details of what she suspected Scout might have seen and why she thought the killer had targeted him. She concluded with a quick overview of her other inquiries, including her suspicion that Victoria had scored big with Robert's life insurance policy. "I'd really love to know how much that payoff's going to be," she finished.

"Toward the high end of seven figures," he responded.

"That's a lot of motive," she said, then, after a beat, added, "but considering what her housekeeper told me about her dislike for guns, maybe I should be looking elsewhere."

"It's too soon to discount her as a suspect. Victoria Garcia doesn't have a secure alibi for the time of death—and the housekeeper might be lying on her behalf."

"Good points," she said. "Next on my agenda is taking a closer look at Al Russo."

"You think he's a serious player?"

"I don't know, but his name sure comes up a lot. He also seems pretty close to the family for an outsider."

"I know he worked the picnic crowd, campaigning, on the Fourth. He also shared some hot dogs with a few of the teens from a local youth program, Second Chance. I understand he sponsors several boys—all one-time offenders who were given community service as probation. That program seems to be doing a good job keeping the kids out of trouble, too," he said.

"So he can account for his time?" Sister Agatha asked.

"Not for every single minute, no, but under the circumstances

I would have been far more concerned if he could. That's the kind of thing a suspect does if he has something to hide."

"There's something else I wanted you to know," she said, then told him about the monastery's closing. "So I'm going to be pushing myself hard to find answers quickly, Frank. I don't have a choice."

"Just be careful not to jump to conclusions. Speed is the enemy in a police investigation. That's what I've told the Garcias, too. They want instant answers, and that's not the way things work."

"Speaking of the Garcias, I'm glad you're not afraid to be seen with me," she said and went on to tell him about the pressure she'd heard the family was exerting on community members.

"They're not happy with me, either. My supervisor in Santa Fe got a call from Mayor Garcia. Somebody apparently told him that Tom and I spent two weeks at Quantico last year taking a special law enforcement seminar. JD claimed that was a clear conflict of interest and I should be taken off the case."

"But you're still in charge?"

"You bet. My chief knows that I've always played it straight with him and that I would have said something if there had been a conflict of any kind." He finished his coffee. "Thanks for the info on this Scout character, Daniel Perea. I'll approach him carefully if we cross paths." He stood. "I better get going, Sister."

"Me, too," she said, finishing the last drop of coffee, then using her finger to wipe a smattering of leftover whipped cream from the side of the paper cup. "Thanks again for the treat."

They reached the door together, and Marquez held it open, then followed her out. "Let's do this again soon, Sister. Exchanging information doesn't have to be an unpleasant process."

Seeing her as she stepped out onto the sidewalk, Pax, still half a block away, stood and barked, his tail wagging. Sister Agatha smiled. "Come, boy."

As Pax joined her, she watched Marquez walk toward his police car. Frank had just stepped off the sidewalk when another vehicle suddenly pulled in right behind his unit, blocking him. Mayor Garcia got out, then stepped between Marquez and the driver's side door, preventing him from getting in.

Sister Agatha stood frozen to the spot, watching, her hand on the dog's collar.

"Are you goldbricking with the village snoop, or just scraping the bottom of the barrel looking for help? I thought you could do this job on your own, Marquez," JD said, challenging him.

Marquez's gaze locked with JD's. "Guess they had it right in Santa Fe, Mr. Mayor. You *are* as stupid as you look. If I were you I'd be careful about interfering with a police investigation. It's bad politics," Frank said in a deadly monotone.

"It's *you* who better start doing your job. Close this case!"

"Move back," Marquez ordered.

"A word of warning. Unless you're looking forward to a change in careers, don't screw with me," JD growled, then stepped back.

"Don't *ever* threaten me," Marquez said, his voice barely a whisper.

"Look at it as helpful advice."

As Frank turned sideways and reached for the door handle, JD shoved him in the back.

In the blink of an eye, Frank regained his balance and whirled around. Grabbing JD's forearm and wrist, he slammed him backward into the car door. He then applied pressure to a spot on the back of the mayor's hand until JD groaned in pain and sagged to his knees.

"Oops. I see tears in your eyes, Mr. Mayor. Allergies?" Marquez whispered and stepped back, letting go of the man's hand.

JD straightened up quickly. "Allergies, yeah," he said in a

voice loud enough to carry. Stepping away hastily, he hurried into the café without looking back.

"See you soon, Sister," Frank said pleasantly, then climbed into his car.

As Frank drove away, Sister Agatha kept her hand on Pax, whose body had tensed considerably. "Relax, Pax. The mayor could use a bite or two, but you're not a police dog anymore. Live up to your name, my friend."

She continued to speak softly to him, and the dog relaxed by the time they reached the motorcycle. She was just fastening the strap on her helmet when Jay Jaramillo pulled up next to her in his plumber's van and waved.

Sister Agatha greeted him with a quick hello. She knew Jay well, having seen him often at the church's rectory doing work for Father Mahoney.

"Ya going to the game tonight, Sister?" he called out. "We're playing the Presbyterians. Those suckers are tough, and we need a cheering section full of people who know how to pray big-time."

Remembering that Robert had played in the church's league, she smiled and nodded. When people were having fun, they lowered their guard. Tonight's game might be the perfect time to do some more snooping.

"I'll be there," she said. "Count on it!"

12

IT WAS ALMOST SEVEN THIRTY IN THE EVENING WHEN SISTER
Agatha pulled up to the baseball field adjacent to the high
school. At least two dozen vehicles were parked against the
fence. About a hundred fans were in the three sets of bleachers,
one behind each dugout and one back of home plate.

Teams from the different churches in town had formed a
slow-pitch softball league and played each other at least twice
during the summer. From what she'd heard, there was a long-
standing rivalry between First Presbyterian and St. Augustine.
Yet even when these two teams were competing, the games remained good-natured fun—most of the time.

She walked along the fence with Pax toward the bleachers on
the first base side, where the St. Augustine dugout was located
tonight. Sister Agatha soon spotted Father Mahoney standing
with a bat in his hand. The teams didn't have complete uniforms,
only matching caps and short-sleeved T-shirts with the name of

their church on the front and a number on the back. Father Rick, a big, muscular former professional wrestler, was talking to Smitty, who was the Presbyterian team's pitcher. The rest of the Presbyterian team was out on the field, their coach warming up the infield, hitting ground balls for them to catch and throw to first.

Smitty walked to the pitcher's mound as Sister Agatha and Pax took a seat in the bottom row of bleachers next to Frances Williams, Father Mahoney's housekeeper. The view was perfect, with the top of the fence even with the roof of the dugout below them.

"Hey, Sister!" Frances greeted. In her late sixties, Frances was endowed with boundless energy.

As Father Mahoney went up to bat, both of them cheered. "Yell louder," Frances told her. "Father Rick's a great infielder—when the ball's hit within reach—but he can't run worth a hoot, and when he's at the plate, he doesn't have a prayer beating the throw unless he hits it well out of the infield. Maybe if he hears us cheering, he'll connect and send one over the fence. With those arms and shoulders, he's got more power than anyone else on the team."

They both cheered as enthusiastically as possible, and Father Mahoney hit the ball hard. Unfortunately, it popped almost straight up. The ball went so high it was hard to follow, but that didn't seem to bother the defense. Smitty made the catch about halfway between the mound and home plate. Frances sat back and sighed as Father Rick jogged back to the dugout.

"He really does try," Frances said. "He had one of the high school kids helping him with his base running and getting the jump on the ball. It's a good thing they're playing slow pitch. He's so *slow.*"

The woman on the other side of Frances chuckled. "My husband is the one with the potbelly in center field. I love him, but, frankly, none of them are very good. If they win more than two games a season, it's a good year. Of course, they just play for fun," she said. "Well, mostly," she corrected. "A few of the players are hard-core competitive, and they can get a little carried away at times."

The woman smiled as Sister Agatha introduced herself. "I already knew who you are. You and that dog are practically famous around here, Sister," she said, then, extending her hand, added, "I'm Brenda Hayes."

As the softball game continued, Sister Agatha noticed how many people in the bleachers, and not just above the St. Augustine dugout, were wearing red ball caps with the Garcia slogan—TFC, Time for Change. Even Brenda was wearing one.

"I noticed your Garcia campaign cap," Sister Agatha commented with a pleasant smile.

"It's Monty Allen's campaign now," she said somberly. "Keeping the caps and the slogan was a great way to honor Robert, don't you think? He was a really good Catholic, Sister," she added. "He never missed Mass."

There was a loud crack and a cheer, and Sister Agatha turned back to watch. One of the Catholic players had hit the ball deep into right center field, and the crowd was on its feet. The right fielder raced over, leaped, and made a spectacular grab up against the fence—the third out, which ended the inning.

Cheers went up from the Presbyterian fans, and the spectators around her, including Frances, groaned.

Brenda glanced over at Sister Agatha, her attention diverted during the break as the Catholic team once again took the field. "The worst thing I think anyone could have said about Robert is that he was a poor sport at times. His problem was that he loved beer *and* softball, and he didn't usually wait until the game was over to have a drink. Whenever we were losing—which was most of the time—he'd have one beer right after the other. Then came the arguing and shoving, just like in professional baseball. His teammates would back him up—loyalty and all that—but it sure got ugly a few times. He was ejected from the game twice this year already, and I heard the team got a warning about his behavior from the league directors."

"All that at church league games?" Sister Agatha asked, finding it hard to believe what she was hearing.

"You bet, Sister. Calvary Baptist won't even play us anymore. They don't drink at all, you know?"

As Sister Agatha made a mental note to ask Smitty about Robert's history on the softball diamond, the team on the field began warming up, throwing the ball around. While the Presbyterian coach spoke to the umpire about something, Sister Agatha stood and looked around. She needed to find someone else to question before the next batter came up to the plate.

Sister Agatha was moving along the bleachers when someone behind her yelled, "Look out!"

The ball hit her on the shoulder, pushing her sideways. She fell onto the bleachers, ripping her sleeve as she slammed her elbows and knees on the wooden bench.

Cries of concern erupted from all around her, even from across the diamond and the other bleachers. Untwisting her habit, she sat up slowly, rubbing the sore spot, and concern quickly turned to cheers and applause.

"Sister Agatha, are you okay?" Frances asked, hurrying over.

"I'm fine—but where did that ball come from?" she muttered, still trying to make sense out of what had happened. "Nobody was at bat, were they?"

Mike Herrera, who'd been playing second base, was now standing in front of the dugout, looking up. "Sorry, Sister. I was making a warm-up throw to first, and the ball just took off on me." He gave her a little smile, but the gesture didn't reach his eyes. "Good thing I missed your head. You need to keep your eye on the game, or it can get downright dangerous out here."

As Sister Agatha looked at him, she knew she'd just been given a warning. In the thick of the fight, anyone could get hurt.

Feeling someone touch her arm, Sister Agatha jumped.

"It's okay, Sister. It's just me," Frances said. "Your habit tore loose at the seam, but it shouldn't be too hard to repair. Let's you and I go back to the rectory, and I can help you with that and maybe put some ice on that shoulder of yours. In the meantime, we can pin it up," she said, reaching into her purse for some safety pins. "There you go. Not pretty, but it'll do. Good thing I always carry safety pins around. They've come in handy many times, I'll tell you."

Less than ten minutes later, after a short motorcycle ride, Sister Agatha and Pax entered the rectory. Frances, who'd made all the traffic lights, handed her an ice pack made from a freezer bag as they went through the kitchen door.

Although the ache had already subsided, Sister Agatha placed the ice bag on the sore spot.

Frances motioned them into the study. At the table was a needle and a spool of thread. "You can undress in Father's office and fix that torn seam yourself in private, or you can keep that ice on your shoulder and I'll do my best to sew it up," she said. "I'm not a very good seamstress, mind you, but I can make it stay in place."

"It's okay. I'll fix it. That softball just winged me anyway. I'd rather you look after Pax and give him some water. Though the sun's almost down, it's still hot outside."

"Here in the desert the temperature can drop forty degrees or more at night, but today it seems to be taking its time."

Sister Agatha undressed in Father's office, first taking off her belt, the cincture. Its three knots symbolized their vows—poverty, chastity, and obedience. She then slipped out of her cross-form serge habit, remaining in her long cotton slip. The bruise on her shoulder was visible but only a little tender now, so she ignored the injury and mended her sleeve. As she worked on the repair, she gave some more thought to everything she'd learned. If nothing else, it had been a very interesting day.

A short time later, she met with Frances in the kitchen and was greeted with a glass of iced tea. Pax was stretched out on the cold tile floor.

"How's the shoulder?" Frances asked, taking the plastic bag Sister Agatha handed her.

"Just a bruise. I'm glad it was a softball."

"Me, too."

"Frances, what can you tell me about Robert Garcia?" she asked, making herself comfortable at the kitchen table.

"I *knew* you were going to ask me that. Everyone knows that you've been looking into the case and giving the Garcias fits," she said, chuckling. "Sister, you get yourself in more trouble—" She stopped speaking abruptly, her eyes growing wide. "Wait one darned minute. When Mike Herrera cut loose with that wild throw . . . that *was* an accident, wasn't it?"

"I'm sure it was," Sister Agatha said confidently, wanting to give him the benefit of the doubt—publicly, at least. "But getting back to Robert . . ."

"Outside his public image, I barely knew him, Sister, so I can't tell you much. I know he always came to ten o'clock Mass on Sundays, 'cause that's the service I attend. He also contributed generously when we needed funds to repair the roof. He was a good man as far as I know—well, other than when he was stirring up trouble at a softball game." She paused, then, after several moments, added, "I've always wondered what things were really like at home for his family."

"What makes you say that?"

"Have you ever met Isabel Cordova, Sister?"

Sister Agatha thought about it, then shook her head. "I don't think so."

"She used to work as a housekeeper and nanny for Victoria and Robert. Isabel lived with her mother, next door to me, and that's how I got to know her. Isabel's dream was to run Del Sol Stables—the Garcia clan's horse farm. The problem was that Isabel didn't have the experience and training to do much more than muck out the stalls. Then one day, out of the blue, she became the Garcias' stable manager."

"What changed?"

"Beats me, but from what I've heard, she gets paid a lot more than the old stable manager, Dusty Brown, ever did. Isabel was also given some land adjacent to the horse farm and enough cash to be able to build her own house there. These days, Izzie drives a fancy truck and flashes a lot of silver and turquoise jewelry."

"Did the old stable manager stay with the Garcias?"

"Dusty's still there, but I'm told that's only until he finds a new job."

"It sounds like the Garcias paid her off . . . but for what?" Sister Agatha mused. "Was she having an affair with Robert, or was it something else?"

"Definitely *not* an affair. Isabel's interests don't include men, so it has to be for other reasons. There's been lots of speculation about this, but Isabel's not talking."

"Thanks for the tip, Frances."

"Don't make me regret it, Sister. You stay out of trouble, you hear?" Frances said, walking her and Pax to the door.

Taking the long way home, Sister Agatha made it a point to go past Del Sol Stables. It was nearly 9:00 P.M., and the sun had set a half hour ago, but there were still half a dozen trucks parked there.

Sister Agatha drove up the long driveway and parked near the stable, a long line of stalls on both sides of an enormous barn. Past the far end of the building, on the other side, was a large circular corral. A man was busy there working a young horse on a lunge rein. Pax, eyes focused on the large animal trotting in a circle, strained at the leash.

"Don't you dare act up. You hear me, Pax?"

The dog never looked at her.

"Pax!"

The dog turned around, looked at her, and whined.

"No chasing *anything*," she said, knowing that Pax loved to go after whatever ran from him. Horses, more often than not, were a huge temptation.

Rather than risk interrupting the trainer, Sister Agatha turned away from the arena and headed across soft ground toward an adobe-style casita near the stables. The hand-carved sign over the door read OFFICE.

As she drew near, a young woman coming out of the doorway smiled. "Hello, Sister. I'm Natalie Granger. Can I help you?"

"I'm looking for Isabel Cordova—the stable manager?"

"She's not here right now. She usually quits early, but sometimes she returns in the evening to work her mare. Do you want to wait and see if she comes by, or can someone else help you?"

"How about Dusty Brown? Is he here?"

"Dusty's always here," she said with a smile. "Right now he's helping one of the grooms with a Clydesdale we're stabling for a client. Come on. I'll take you there."

Natalie led the way through the stable. At the end, near one of the stalls, was an enormous horse. He dwarfed the two men grooming him.

"Sister's here to see you, Dusty," Natalie said, looking at the man holding up one of the animal's legs.

"That's the biggest horse I've ever seen," Sister Agatha whispered.

"Hugo's eighteen hands—that's six feet at the shoulder. He weighs close to twenty-five hundred pounds," Dusty told her as he showed the groom how to polish the hooves. "Give me another minute, Sister, and I'll be right with you. This guy's a handful when he wants to be."

Sister Agatha stayed well back. Anything that large demanded—and received—her respect. Even Pax was sitting very still and not making a sound.

Once assured that the groom could handle his large charge, Dusty came to meet her.

"I'm Dusty, Sister," he said, wiping his hand on a rag and offering to shake hands. "How can I help you?"

"Can we talk privately for a few moments?"

"Of course." The old cowboy was in his early seventies. His roughened complexion and wrinkled hands attested to long hours in the sun and a lifetime of hard work. Yet, though he stooped a little at the shoulders, he moved with the confidence and fluidity of a much younger man.

As they entered a small office at the end of the barn, opposite an empty stall, he waved to an empty chair. "Make yourself at home. I've heard what you're up to, Sister, and I'll be glad to help you in any way I can," he said, closing the door behind them. "The Garcias think they own this town, but they don't. Money buys power—but not loyalty."

"You're no fan of the Garcias, I take it?"

He took a seat across from her behind an old, worn wooden desk. "Time was when I respected that family, but they took advantage of me. I was hired to manage this stable and take care of their animals in exchange for a base salary and the opportunity to build my own home and arena on that west side property over there."

He cocked his head in the direction of Isabel's house, then lapsed into a long silence as he stared across the room.

"What happened?" Sister Agatha prodded.

"I was a fool. There was no written contract or agreement, just a handshake between Robert and me. That used to be more than enough around these parts, and it never occurred to me to doubt the word of a Garcia." He shook his head slowly. "Then one day out of the blue Robert brought Isabel Cordova in and gave her my job. That girl had no experience whatsoever, but Robert stuck with her. He told me to answer any questions she had. And the section of land I was going to get—that's where her new house is being built."

"You should have taken Mr. Garcia to court. Didn't Robert at least have the decency to offer you a different parcel of land?"

"Yeah, he did that. It was some mountain property so steep you'd have to build on stilts or take out half the hillside. It was a terrible place to raise horses, too, even if you could sink a well. I got cheated—pure and simple. I'm selling it as soon as I can find a buyer. It's not exactly the type of location that people go wild for. No water, no well, and only one bad road into the property."

"I'm so sorry—but why are you still working for the Garcias?"

"I couldn't afford to just walk out. At my age, jobs can be hard to find. Experience still counts for something, though, and

I've found a new position. I'm leaving at the end of this week and heading to Scottsdale. I'll be giving trail rides at a high-end dude ranch." He rubbed the stubble on his chin. "That job's a lifesaver for me. Isabel will be named the new owner of Del Sol by the end of this year, and there was no way I would have stuck around after that."

"Did Robert give you a reason why Isabel got your job?" Sister Agatha asked.

He shook his head. "Robert never explained himself—on anything—but I managed to put it together. A buddy of mine, Paul Mathis, has a landscaping business, and Robert's one of his customers. Paul told me he was working on Robert and Victoria's sprinkler system one morning when he overheard them having a real knock-down, drag-out. He stays out of family disputes, so he just kept working. Then a cast-iron bookend came flying out the window, shattering the glass into a million pieces. He heard Victoria scream, so he rushed inside through the back door to see if he could help, or maybe call the police." He paused, taking a deep breath. "Paul found Victoria in the kitchen, completely hysterical, broken things all over the place. Isabel was sitting on the tile floor, bleeding like a stuck pig from a gash on the back of her head."

"What happened? Did Isabel get caught up in the cross fire?" Sister Agatha asked.

"That's what Paul figured. According to him, Robert calmed everyone down, called a doctor friend of his, and got Izzie sewed up. A few days after that, Izzie came over here, all bandaged up. When I asked her who'd hit her with the bookend, Robert or Victoria, she told me to mind my own business."

"Interesting," Sister Agatha said thoughtfully.

"Yeah, particularly when you take into account that it all happened around the same time that Robert announced his plans to run for sheriff. The way I see it, he obviously didn't want the incident made public, so he paid Isabel off."

He shook his head, then, in a voice filled with disgust, added, "Iz struck the mother lode when she got slammed in the head that day. All things considered, I wouldn't rule out the possibility that she stepped in the way on purpose, figuring there'd be dollar signs in it."

Sister Agatha stood and followed him to the door. "I wish you the best of luck, Dusty," she said, "and thank you for helping me tonight."

Before she could grab the door handle, the man she'd seen grooming Hugo earlier came rushing in. "We've got a horse with colic—Isabel's mare. I've called the vet."

"Better call Isabel, too, Ben." Dusty hurried past Sister Agatha. "I've got to deal with this emergency, Sister."

Sister Agatha walked out with Pax. When she reached the cycle, she saw a large midnight blue truck parked beside it.

Pax had just jumped into the sidecar when a tall, thin woman in her midthirties stepped out from the far side of the pickup.

"The minute I saw the motorcycle, I knew you were here asking questions," she said in a soft voice. "Don't make trouble, Sister Agatha. I've done nothing wrong."

"So it's true—how you got this job. What really happened that day at the Garcias'?" Sister Agatha asked. "I'm not the police. You can trust me."

"Sister, I now have everything I've ever wanted. That's what comes from making the most out of each and every opportunity—and keeping my mouth shut."

"The path you've chosen will never bring you peace of mind. It carries a price—whether or not you realize it."

"Everything carries a price, Sister, but I like where I am."

"I already know most of the story, but I'd like to hear your side of it," Sister Agatha insisted.

"My luck's finally changed, Sister, and I'm not going to let you ruin things for me. There's nothing here for you. Go home."

Sister Agatha was about to answer when Isabel's phone rang. She flipped it open, listened for a moment, then hung up. "My horse needs me. I've got to go. I suggest you do the same."

Sister Agatha, her hand on Pax's head, watched the woman rush away at a jog. "You can't trust any deal you make with the devil, Pax."

13

THE NEXT MORNING SISTER AGATHA LEFT THE MONAS-
tery early. Seeing packing boxes everywhere saddened her
terribly, and she was glad for a reason to leave. Our Lady
of Hope felt more like an abandoned building these days than
the home they'd loved.

Her first stop was at Paul Mathis Landscaping, which opened
at 7:00 A.M. One of Paul's drivers had given her his schedule, and
it seemed he was a busy man this time of year. Rather than have
him wait for her somewhere, she decided to catch up to him.
Sister Agatha managed to miss him at the wholesale nursery but
finally found him at the community center.

As she approached him, Paul was adjusting emitters on a
drip system that supplied a newly added xeriscaped section of the
grounds.

Sister Agatha told him why she'd come. "Whatever you tell
me will stay in confidence," she assured him. "I'm simply after

some background information." She looked back at Pax, who'd been put on stay beneath a Navajo willow in the shade. He watched but didn't move.

"I knew to expect you. Dusty and I spoke last night," Paul said as he continued working. "Generally, I don't care what goes on with my clients. In fact, I don't *want* to know," he added emphatically. "Thing is, folks sometimes forget I'm there. That's why, every once in a while, I end up seeing or overhearing stuff that's supposed to be private."

His words made her think of Scout. The forgotten people who were generally ignored by the majority sometimes had the most information to share—if they would.

"I worked on their property every Saturday morning," Paul continued, "and it seems like every time I was there, Victoria and Robert were having a fight. Sometimes Mrs. Garcia would start throwing stuff at Mr. Garcia. Then there would be a slap, like he was hitting her, and she'd start crying, or their fight would just get louder. A few times Mr. Russo showed up to calm them both down."

"Who called him, do you know?"

"Men don't call for help, and the housekeeper knew better than to interfere. I think it was probably Mrs. Garcia."

Sister Agatha nodded. It made sense.

Paul moved toward the next plant, then checked the drip rate from the emitter. Lowering his voice, he continued. "Mr. Russo had a thing for Mrs. Garcia, too. One time I heard him tell her to get a divorce, that he'd take care of her. She thanked him, sounding really surprised, but told him that she could defend herself if it ever got too ugly." He pulled off the emitter, let the water run for a few seconds, then attached a new, smaller one he'd taken from his jacket pocket.

"She was willing to put up with it, Sister Agatha, so who

knows? A part of her might have enjoyed it. I've given up trying to figure people out."

Al Russo's personal interest in Victoria raised a lot of questions, but she decided not to pursue it directly. Paul was at ease, and she wanted to keep him that way.

"You said you were there once a week. In the past month or so, how often has Mr. Russo been there?" she asked as he pulled some weeds from around the next plant they approached.

"The last three times I was there, Mr. Russo showed up right after the fight got started. Once he'd show up, the arguing would stop—every time."

"Afterward, would he stick around for long?"

"Sometimes he would, depending on if Mr. Garcia left or stayed at the house, and how upset RJ was. I saw Mr. Russo take the little boy outside for batting practice on the lawn lots of times. All that yelling and screaming was obviously doing a number on the kid. Interestingly enough, I never saw RJ play with his dad. Maybe that's why the boy's so crazy about Mr. Russo and Mr. Herrera."

"Mike Herrera?" she asked.

"Yeah. From what I've seen, RJ seems to prefer Mr. Russo, but he still liked playing catch with Herrera."

"So Mike would come over to see RJ from time to time?"

"Yeah, but that was mostly back in the spring. He'd come to take Mrs. Garcia out for practice. Then afterward, when the boy came home from school, the two would play catch."

"Wait—practice? What were Mike and Victoria practicing—country-western dancing, golf, tennis?"

"Naw. He was teaching Mrs. Garcia how to shoot."

"Really?" she asked, totally surprised by the news. "I'd heard that Victoria hated firearms and wouldn't even allow one in the house."

"I was standing just a few feet away one time when I heard them talking about sight picture, trigger control, and line of fire—what else could it have been? There had been talk of break-ins in the area, too, around that time, and I remember Mrs. Garcia saying that she needed to be able to protect RJ if they had an intruder. Mr. Garcia was doing a lot of business travel back then."

"What kind of weapon did she have, rifle or pistol?"

"I never saw it, so you'd have to ask them."

Sister Agatha thanked Paul, then returned to where she'd left Pax and the cycle. "Every time I think I've got a handle on this case, Pax, something I knew nothing about comes up. I'm beginning to think we've just begun to scratch the surface."

Responding to her frustrated tone, Pax looked at her soulfully. Sister Agatha bent down to give him a hug.

Then, Sister Agatha and Pax started over to Tom Green's home. She had more questions for him—and this time she wouldn't accept his evasions.

Throughout the ride, she thought of everything she'd recently learned about Victoria, including the news that she'd taken firearms lessons. Victoria certainly had a motive for killing Robert, and, to top it off, she didn't seem to have an alibi for the time of death. The woman, right now, was at the top of her list of suspects.

There was also Monty Allen. The security firm was his livelihood, and he now had unlimited control. He had also obviously been interested in the position of sheriff, or he wouldn't have been running as the write-in candidate.

Mike Herrera, too, was in a position to have seen Robert Garcia's true nature. Had he acted to protect Victoria . . . or maybe RJ? The same could apply to Al Russo, especially factoring in his fondness for the boy. On the other hand, Al's career had been tied to Robert's success, so it wasn't likely he would have murdered his meal ticket.

When she pulled into Sheriff Green's driveway, Sister Agatha saw Gloria already outside.

"That motorcycle's sure distinctive," Gloria said, coming up to greet Sister Agatha. "I heard it coming all the way down the lane." She headed to her car and slipped inside. "I'm on my way out for a bit, but Tom's in the kitchen. Go on in."

Sister Agatha stopped beside Gloria's driver's side door. "How are you two doing? A crisis like this could break any marriage, Gloria. Don't make any hasty decisions. You two need each other more than ever now."

Gloria shook her head. "You're wrong, Sister. Everything has a beginning, a middle, and an end. When the dust settles, we'll go our separate ways. We each deserve a new start."

"It doesn't have to be like that. Have you tried—"

Gloria held up one hand. "Stop. I don't want to hear about this anymore. Just help Tom clear his name so we can both go on with our lives."

"I'm working on it, but I could sure use some help. Tell me, how well did you know Robert?"

"Not very. We never socialized with him and his wife. I'd never admit this to anyone else, but there was bad blood between him and Tom. Robert had to leave the sheriff's department under less than ideal circumstances, and though Tom's never discussed it with me I think he had a big part to play in that."

"He won't give me any details either," Sister Agatha said. Tom wouldn't violate the department's confidentiality, but to clear him she'd need every bit of information she could get.

Tom came out before Gloria could reply. "If you two are going to chitchat, come inside. It isn't a good idea to stay out here in the open."

Seeing the sheriff, Pax stood up and immediately began straining at the leash to get Tom's attention.

Smiling, Tom came over to pet him, then glanced at Gloria. "Going shopping again?"

Sister Agatha couldn't help but notice the dark edge of sarcasm in his voice.

Gloria didn't look directly at him. "I'll be gone for a few hours," she said, then pulled out of the driveway.

Tom watched Gloria drive down the street, then turned and gestured for Sister Agatha to follow him into the house. "Let's talk."

Sitting on Tom's comfortable leather couch, Sister Agatha filled him in on what she'd learned about Victoria, including news that Victoria had learned how to shoot. "What caliber weapon was used to kill Robert?"

"A nine millimeter, but that's a very common caliber," he said. "You might follow things up by asking Millie to check and see if Victoria purchased a handgun recently. You may get lucky, but if it wasn't a licensed dealer purchase, it's very possible there won't be any record of it. Gun show purchases aren't registered, and neither are private sales."

"All right," Sister Agatha said, making a mental note of that. "Now I need you to tell me all about you and Robert. You can start with why he left the department. I need specifics, Tom."

Tom hesitated.

"It wasn't just to go into business, was it?"

Tom didn't answer.

"I can check on the dates—when he left the department and when his firm opened. My guess is that some time passed between those two events. I'm thinking you forced him to resign."

"Robert didn't go into business right away," Tom said, sidestepping her question.

"Time's ticking. Are you going to tell me why he left the department, or should I start asking other officers?"

He glared at her. "I can't discuss department business with you, Sister. Those matters are sealed for a reason."

"Robert's dead. What purpose could it serve now to keep his background a secret?"

He took a deep breath and seemed to consider his options. "Robert Garcia and I had more than our share of problems. Some of those are public knowledge," he said. "The only thing I can do is suggest that you talk to Leon Jones, Robert's neighbor on the east side. Leon's recently retired, so he's usually at home."

Sister Agatha studied Tom's body language as he stared at a framed photo of him and Gloria that was hanging on the wall. Unconsciously or not, he was also fiddling with his wedding ring. Realizing that she was studying him, he dropped his hands and glanced away, his lips stretched in a thin, taut line.

"I've known you for a long time, Tom. You're holding out on me, and not just with departmental business. You *know* I'm on your side, and if there's one person you can trust, it's me. You said you'd talk to me—"

"I've told you all I can," he said, then stood and jammed his hands into his pockets. "Just one more bit of advice. Detective Frank Marquez is a good man. He's tough but fair. If you get in over your head, call him. Frank'll find a way to help you."

"He's got problems of his own right now," Sister Agatha said, then told him about the incident with the mayor outside the coffee shop.

Tom laughed. "Don't worry about Frank. When the heat's on, he just gets stronger."

"Tom, I want you to think hard about what you're doing. If what you're holding back is pertinent to the case, it'll surface sooner or later, and the damage may be even harder to control by then," Sister Agatha said, heading to the door. "Don't let whatever you're keeping secret blindside me—or Frank. We're going all out for you, and you're not helping—yourself or us."

Leaving Tom's, Sister Agatha set out to go visit Leon Jones. As she glanced at Pax, she saw him enjoying the blast of cool air that swept around them on the bike. It was the perfect morning, with the sun shining in a cloudless sky. If things had been different, she would have enjoyed the ride as much as Pax.

As she turned down the street where Victoria lived, she saw someone pulling into the Garcia driveway. She backed off on the throttle to reduce the obvious sound of the Harley, then watched as she drove past. Mike Herrera emerged from a shiny luxury sedan and glanced in her direction. The red-and-white-painted Harley and sidecar, coupled with a nun in a black habit and a big white dog, wasn't exactly subtle.

Making a spur-of-the-moment decision, Sister Agatha turned around in the road and headed back. As she drove up, she saw that Mike had waited for her. He was leaning back against the driver's side door, arms crossed in front of his chest. "Hey, Sister, what's up?"

She took off her helmet and held it on her lap. "Hello, Mike. I'm glad you waited. I've been wanting to ask you a question. I understand that you taught Victoria how to shoot a pistol," she said, hoping he'd confirm her guess on the type of weapon.

His face darkened, and he balled his hands into fists. With effort, he relaxed them again. "I *told* Victoria to watch what she said around the help. She's lucky no one's ever blackmailed her."

"What has she done that would make her a target for extortion?"

"Victoria?" He suddenly burst out laughing. "You don't know her very well, or you wouldn't be asking."

"You obviously do. So why don't you tell me?"

"People think Robert controlled Victoria, but that's not the way it really was. Victoria held the reins, and she loved pushing his buttons. She knew exactly how to set him off."

"Interesting viewpoint. Tell me more."

"She'd go shopping, max out all the credit cards, then 'forget' to pay the bills on time. Then she'd make sure that Robert found out about it. Their credit rating was like a roller coaster, and that made Robert nuts. During the campaign rallies, she'd always stand in the background acting the part of the dutiful, faithful wife, smiling at everything he said, but Victoria knew how to get under his skin, and she liked making him crazy. The shooting lessons she had me give her are a good example of that. When Robert started traveling a lot, trying to expand his business out of state, she decided she wanted to learn to shoot a pistol. She *knew* Robert would eventually find out, and after that he'd never be able to raise a hand to her without wondering if he'd get shot later that night as he slept."

"Maybe she was the one who killed him," Sister Agatha said.

"No way. Victoria had no need to kill him. She knew how to play him." He pushed away from the car and stood up straight. "Besides, she never actually owned a gun. She just borrowed one of mine. She kept it for a few weeks during the time a residential burglar was working the area. After the cops caught the guy, she gave it back to me. She didn't want a pistol around her house. She was afraid RJ would get hold of it."

"What caliber was it?"

"A nine-millimeter Walther P38. It was an old World War II German semiauto I'd carried back in the days when I was dealing drugs. But don't bother looking for it. I'm still on parole, and I'm not allowed to have a weapon, so I got rid of it."

"When?"

"Months before Robert got shot, if that's what you're really asking."

"Can you *prove* that you got rid of that gun before the murder?"

He shook his head. "I sold it one night to a guy outside a bar for two twenties and a beer. He didn't know me and I didn't know him. I realize that you're looking for a suspect other than your friend Sheriff Green, but I had nothing to do with what happened to Robert," he said.

"If you say so," she said with a skeptical smile.

"Look at it logically. I have too much to lose and nothing to gain. I'm a Garcia now, and I don't want to rock that boat. I get a lot of toys just by playing it cool," he said, gesturing to his new car. "Victoria wouldn't have shot Robert, either. She'd be more inclined to twist the knife somebody else had placed in his gut."

"You may be sure about yourself, but you can't speak for Victoria. You don't know what she might have done if pushed hard enough," she said, mostly to see his reaction.

"Oh yeah, I'm positive. Victoria and Robert had a strange relationship, but they were two of a kind. Nothing was more important to Robert than status, power, and wealth. Victoria was perfect for him because she loved being the wife of a man people respected—and feared. She paid her dues for sure, but she got exactly what she wanted and needed—status." He said nothing for several long moments, then, in a thoughtful, quiet voice, added, "Oh yeah, Sister, I know exactly how she thinks."

"Because you're doing the same thing yourself?" Sister Agatha pressed. "You also married into the Garcia family. From small to tall, is that the way it is?"

"Yeah. Like that. As I said, Victoria and I understand each other."

"There's more to it than that. Your eyes give you away, Mike. You're in love with her," she said, playing a hunch to see how he'd react.

He shrugged. "So what? It doesn't alter anything. Neither of us wants to change our current arrangement."

"Which is?"

"We're friends who keep each other's secrets."

Sensing she'd gotten all she would from him, Sister Agatha raised her helmet to her head. "Okay, Mike, thanks for clearing things up a bit."

"Sister, let me make a deal with you. If you keep quiet about that pistol, I'll do my best to find out who really shot Robert. Providing it turns out to be someone outside the Garcia family, I'll pass that information along to you just as soon as I have it."

She lowered her helmet again. "What makes you think you can find out and I can't?"

"I know a lot of people, Sister, and we move in *way* different circles. You'd be surprised what someone like me can dig up."

She had no doubt that Mike could be a valuable source, yet withholding information about that pistol might end up costing Tom in the long run.

"Look at it this way, Sister," he said, as if he'd read her mind. "Even if I could find the gun again and turn it over to the police, what would it prove? That it wasn't the weapon that killed Robert? He was killed with the sheriff's own pistol, and everyone knows that. I could have gotten another gun, and so could Victoria. Bottom line is that I'd be putting my own freedom on the line for no reason at all."

She considered it, then nodded. "All right. See what you can find out and get back to me."

14

SISTER AGATHA WENT ALL THE WAY AROUND THE BLOCK, in case Mike was watching or listening for the bike, and approached Leon Jones's home from the opposite direction. As she drove up the long driveway, a gray-haired man in his mid-sixties wearing jeans and a pullover shirt looked up. Stopping work trimming the hedge that separated his property from the Garcias, he waved at her.

She stopped the Harley, turned off the ignition, and flipped up her helmet visor.

"You have to be Sister Agatha. I saw you the other day and figured you'd be stopping by sooner or later. I'm Leon Jones," he said, putting the hedge clippers down and wiping his brow. "You've got great timing, Sister. I was just about to take a break."

He led the way inside the spacious Territorial-style house. The living room had the feeling of a cool, shady parlor, full of overstuffed furniture, but the large kitchen was bright and airy, with Mexican tile counters and backsplash. He pulled out two Cokes from the old-style white fridge and placed one in front of her. "These are imported from Mexico. They're sweetened with sugar instead of corn syrup—just the way I like them. In the bottle okay with you?"

"Sure, that's fine." She remembered how young Sister Jo had raved about Mexican Cokes.

Leon used a "church key" to remove the caps, which weren't twist-off, and handed her one of the icy bottles.

"So you're here wanting to know about that row I had with Robert several years ago, right? I actually had to get a restraining order against that lowlife, and he was a deputy at the time!"

"I've heard that Mr. Garcia could get violent," she said with a nod. "What happened between you?"

"Our neighborhood association rules are clear. You're allowed to prune a neighbor's plants back if their branches extend over onto your yard, but you can't do anything that would kill the plant—in this case, a cottonwood. I'd asked Robert to give me a hand with the tree trimming several times, but he never got around to it. I was worried those cottonwood branches would come crashing down on my car during the next windstorm. You know how brittle they can be. So I finally decided to do the job myself."

He took a long sip of the Coke, then continued. "It was bad timing on my part. He'd been arguing with Victoria that day. When he saw me on the ladder, he accused me of spying on him and his wife. I told him he was nuts, and that's when he pulled me off the ladder."

"Were you okay?" she asked, leaning forward.

"He nearly broke my arm, and all over a stupid tree. That was just the beginning, though." Leon paused, shaking his head. "I filed assault charges, and the judge ended up granting me a restraining order. Robert was supposed to stay off my property and not come within fifty feet of me. Well, that order just made him crazier."

"He came after you again?"

Leon nodded. "At first he was just trying to intimidate me. Whenever I went to the store, gas station, or anywhere in my car, he'd follow. He'd tailgate, even bumping into me at stop signs— just enough to shake me up. I tried using the camera on my cell phone, but I had my hands full driving most of the time. It was clear to me that he had a screw loose, and what's worse, he was in his patrol car and carrying a gun."

Sister Agatha nodded but didn't interrupt.

"One day I finally had enough. I remembered that Smitty had told me that he'd installed new surveillance cameras in his parking lot, so I decided to set Robert up. He was tailgating me as usual, so I deliberately pulled into Smitty's parking lot. Robert blocked me in so I couldn't get back out, something he'd done before at other places. Knowing the cameras were rolling, I went over and asked him to move his car. When he laughed at me, I brought out my cell phone, took a photo of him, then started to call Sheriff Green. That's when he really went nuts. Robert jumped out of his car, knocked the cell phone out of my hand, and stomped on it. Then he grabbed my arm and swung me around, slamming me face-first into his car. When Robert started punching me in the kidneys, Smitty heard me yelling and came out. If Smitty hadn't been there, Robert would have put me in the hospital for sure."

"Why wasn't he charged with assault?" Sister Agatha knew that could have led to a felony conviction, and a man with a record wouldn't have been able to run for sheriff.

Leon sighed loudly. "My print shop depended heavily on city business, and the sheriff didn't want a scandal, so we cut a deal.

Sheriff Green gave me his word that he'd handle the matter, and he did. I never had a problem with Robert again."

"When Sheriff Green gives his word, you can count on it."

"I agree with you, and I talk from experience," he answered, then, giving her a long look, continued. "Detective Marquez came to talk to me about Robert yesterday. I think he thought *I* may have killed him."

Sister Agatha didn't respond.

"Were you wondering the same thing?" He didn't wait for her answer. "The day Robert was killed, I was in the center of the park, playing my fiddle with the Good Gravy Band. We signaled for the start of the fireworks by playing the National Anthem, then performed five Sousa marches in a row. Everyone saw me. I was in the front row, sitting right beside the piccolo."

"It sounds like you had a wonderful time," Sister Agatha said, hoping to defuse the defensiveness she heard in his tone.

"The Fourth's my favorite holiday," he said, sounding much happier. "I love the parade, the picnics, and the fireworks, too." He paused, then went on in a thoughtful voice. "I remember seeing Robert and feeling sorry for him. He was missing the point—it was a holiday. A day to honor your country and have fun, but he was doing neither. He was busy campaigning and giving out political flyers. I figure he must have had hundreds in that large envelope he was lugging around tucked under his arm. Despite his casual clothing, it was obvious he didn't intend to give it a rest, even on his nation's birthday."

"Envelope?"

"Yeah, one of those large manila ones with the string fasteners. The reason I noticed it was because of his son. RJ loves Mitch Landreth—Mitch the Missile, you know—star pitcher for the 'Topes. He was there in the afternoon, signing autographs before he left for the ballpark. RJ wouldn't leave Mitch's side, even after the autograph. Finally Robert came over and hauled the kid away." He shook his head slowly.

"RJ must not have been too happy about that," she commented, hoping to keep him talking.

"You've got that right. I was sitting under a tree, working on my second hot dog, when I heard Robert tell RJ to hand over that autographed roster Mitch had signed, that he'd keep it safe for him. RJ didn't want to give it up, but Robert grabbed it away and started to put it in that big envelope. RJ reached for the envelope, and that got his dad *really* ticked off. He shoved the kid to the ground on his butt, then folded up the roster and jammed it into his shirt pocket. RJ was in tears by then. Robert just made it worse, yanking his son to his feet and telling him to quit acting like a girl."

Leon scowled; then his expression turned to sheer loathing as he added, "He didn't have a clue on how to raise a kid."

Sister Agatha leaned back in her chair and fingered her rosary beads, her thoughts on what she'd just learned. "Robert may have had lots of money, but he sure wasn't a happy man."

Leon gave her a wry smile. "Maybe so, but money can usually make you comfortable in your misery."

She smiled but said nothing for several long moments. At last she spoke. "Tell me, what actually happened to Robert after you turned him in to Sheriff Green?"

"I don't know firsthand. All I can tell you is what I heard through the grapevine. Robert was advised to resign or risk an internal affairs investigation that would have undoubtedly gotten him charged and fired. When I found out that . . . what . . . five years later, he was running for sheriff, you could have knocked me over with a feather. Had he been elected, I would have sold my house and moved out of town for good."

"Do you think he could have actually won?" Sister Agatha

asked, wondering if someone else Robert had terrorized had decided to settle matters in his—or her—own way.

"Sheriff Green's a good man, and most of us are very happy with the way he's run his department. Robert would have kept throwing his money around and convinced some of the people, but the majority would have backed Sheriff Green. I'm pretty sure of that."

"I guess we'll never know now," Sister Agatha said pensively.

After saying good-bye to Leon, Sister Agatha and Pax set out once again, going the back way to avoid passing by Victoria Garcia's home a second time. What she needed most of all now was the opportunity to think, to assemble details in her mind and see what kind of picture emerged.

Close to the bosque and the river beyond, she decided to take a drive down the shady ditch bank road. As she passed a parked city pickup—one of a small fleet of vehicles that maintained the road and irrigation system—she waved to the driver. He was looking away at the moment, busy with something on the seat, and didn't glance up, even though the motorcycle and sidecar usually attracted attention.

Sister Agatha drove slowly, not wanting to generate any dust or excessive noise. Several residences lined the bosque—a quiet, peaceful location close to nature. It was easy to think here, among the willows and flowers of the wooded area and surrounded by the musky scent of the river beyond.

In the tranquility of that setting she allowed her thoughts free rein. There was so much that still wasn't adding up right, starting with Tom. Though Tom Green *knew* he could trust her, he was still holding something back. It just made no sense . . . unless he was protecting someone else. But who?

At the heart of all her unanswered questions was Robert himself—a former deputy with an explosive temper. She knew how he'd treated his wife, but there were probably others out there he'd intimidated, too. It seemed doubtful that Leon had been the only other person he'd ever threatened.

She then thought about Mike Herrera, another unknown in the equation. He had a connection to the Garcias in more ways than one, and he'd worked the food line that day at the park. Had he somehow drugged Tom so that the actual frame-up could be carried out with greater ease by his unnamed partner?

She then considered what she knew about Victoria. She liked younger men—or maybe it was just men in general. Stepping out on Robert could have been her way of getting back at the man who'd abused her.

That round of speculation brought her thoughts back to Tom and what he was holding back. Recalling Leon telling her about the envelope Robert had carried around on the Fourth, she now wondered if that was somehow the key.

From what she remembered, it hadn't been on the list of items found at the scene. Logic assured her that if Robert hadn't handed it to someone else prior to his murder, that envelope must have had some value to the killer. As she considered that possibility, she remembered that Tom had been very eager to see the list of everything found at the crime scene, but he'd never mentioned seeing any envelope . . .

Sister Agatha continued down the ditch bank at fifteen miles per hour, looking ahead for the next road leading away from the river. Behind, in her side mirror, she could see the white city truck closing the gap between them slowly. Knowing the access road was just ahead, she maintained her leisurely pace. She'd be out of his way soon enough.

As she reached the small bridge that crossed the ditch, she saw someone sitting on one of the big logs that comprised part of the traffic barrier. Beside it was a narrow opening in the fence with a log in the way that only people on foot or horseback could negotiate to enter the bosque. She slowed to turn left, toward town, and suddenly realized that the person sitting on the log was Scout.

She waved to get his attention, and, seeing her, Scout walked out to the edge of the road. This time he didn't run away. Praying he wouldn't change his mind, she slowed and pulled over to the right side of the road, braking to a stop about fifty feet from him.

Suddenly she heard an engine roar and, as she turned her head, saw the white city truck accelerating. It was moving so fast, it was losing traction and peeling out in the gravel and dirt. She placed a hand on Pax and prayed as the truck with the city logo on the side whipped past her, leaving a cloud of dust in its wake. In a heartbeat, the pickup swerved, heading straight toward Scout.

"Look out!" she yelled, but by then Scout was already running down the road.

Realizing he had no chance of outracing the pickup, he dove headfirst over the fence into some brush, then bounced about ten feet. Scrambling to his feet, he took off through the waist-high shrubs, zigzagging his way in the direction of the river.

The truck, unable to follow, came to a sliding stop. There were two quick, loud pops, like gunshots; then the driver took off again down the road.

Sister Agatha, her heart pounding like a drum, saw Scout veer to his right, putting more distance between himself and the shooter, who'd come to a stop again. The pickup started to turn around, but Scout had vanished into the bosque.

Instantly aware that she was now the closest target to an armed man moving in her direction, Sister Agatha whipped the Harley around and raced away from the ditch road. As she glanced back in the side mirror, she saw the city truck hurtling back up the road, racing past the spot where she'd been only seconds earlier.

Knowing that Scout was still in danger, Sister Agatha reached for her cell phone and quickly dialed the sheriff's department. In a matter of minutes she heard the wail of a siren. A car must have been nearby. When she looked back toward the bosque, the white city truck was no longer visible.

It was midafternoon by the time the sheriff's department's search for Scout and the gunman came to an end. To her own great disappointment, she hadn't been much help. She hadn't seen the license plate number, nor looked closely enough at the driver to get more than a vague impression of a short-haired man behind the wheel. Things had happened too fast.

After making her statement, Sister Agatha had remained at the station, hoping to learn something new about the city truck. After all, there were only a limited number of those around. Her hopes were dashed when Millie came into the office where she'd been invited to take a seat.

"I've got some news on that truck," Millie said. "It was stolen earlier today from Al Russo's driveway. The mayor used it to visit a construction site yesterday evening and dropped it off at Al's, asking him as a favor to return it to the city yard this morning. Al didn't notice it was missing until it was time for him to drive to his office."

"Why didn't he report it missing right away? You just got the news, right?" Sister Agatha wondered aloud.

"He reported it to the city motor pool, and they filed a report with us a couple of hours ago. The problem was that Al assumed that the mayor had sent someone else to pick it up. Al had apparently made a fuss about not being anyone's errand boy, since he had morning meetings of his own. For that reason the motor pool decided to follow things up with the mayor before reporting it to us, but JD was in a meeting in Albuquerque. Rather than make a police report and embarrass him, they waited."

"I was hoping that this lead would actually go someplace," Sister Agatha said with a soft sigh. "The thief got lucky. Circumstances bought him some valuable time."

Millie gave her a sympathetic tap on the shoulder. "Sister, it looks like you could use something cold to drink. Why don't you and I take a few minutes off?"

Sister Agatha knew Millie well enough to instantly recognize the change in her tone. Although it had been made to appear like a casual invitation, it was anything but that.

As soon as they reached the break room, Millie glanced inside, then, shaking her head, took Sister Agatha down the hall. She led her all the way to the small office situated next to the evidence room and closed the door.

"We've got new information on the case, and I wanted to pass it along," Millie said, keeping her voice low. "It appears that *both* Robert and Sheriff Green were drugged with benzodiazepines, though Robert didn't have quite as much in his system as the sheriff did. A tox screen was done using organ and tissue samples taken from the deceased. Doug Sanchez, the sheriff's attorney, insisted on the test. He'd initially hoped to find too much alcohol in Robert's system—something that would precipitate aggression and support the claim of self-defense—but this is even better for Sheriff Green. It strongly suggests a third person was involved."

"Right. The drug was in the relish, yet no one else was drugged, apparently, so that means only those two men were targeted," Sister Agatha said, thinking out loud. "Only one answer makes sense and clears up all the apparent inconsistencies.

A third person wanted both men out cold so he, or she, could stage the scene and frame the sheriff."

"It works, but you'll still need to find a way to prove it. Lawyers can argue that the sheriff purposely ingested the drug. As part of our investigation, we've already spoken to Mike Herrera and Arnold Cruz—Cruzer—who served the hot dogs that day, but we've got nothing."

Sister Agatha thought about Mike Herrera and Cruzer. Mike had given her all he was going to for now, but Cruzer . . . now that he'd had time to think about things, perhaps he'd remembered something else that might turn out to be helpful.

After leaving the station, Sister Agatha stopped by Tom's home. No cars were there, however, and no one answered her knock. Hoping that Tom was only out on a short errand, she drove around for a bit, then returned. The driveway was still empty. She then called him on the cell phone, but all she got was voice mail.

It was long past dinner at the monastery when she decided to stop at the community center on her way home. She wasn't sure which days Cruzer taught, but she did remember something about evening classes for adults.

Hearing an unexpected clicking noise coming from the sidecar, Sister Agatha pulled off to the side and checked the tire. A big piece of gravel had wedged in the tread. All in all, a simple fix. She dug it out with a screwdriver she took from the cockpit, then remounted.

"I bet you're hungry, too, by now, Pax," she said to the dog, who'd been incredibly patient all day. "Don't worry. We'll eat when we return home, and it won't be long now."

Pax snorted and gave her a haughty look.

"Hang on just a little while longer," she said, switching on the ignition again. "We've got work to do. Others are counting on us."

15

SISTER AGATHA ARRIVED AT THE COMMUNITY CENTER A short time later. The parking lot was full, and from the sign in front and the sound of big band music, she knew immediately it was senior dance night.

She drove around to the far side of the building, found a space, and parked. She could hear the music and laughter coming from inside and smiled. Life went on no matter how grim things appeared to be at times, and the realization soothed her.

As Sister Agatha walked along the sidewalk toward the front of the building, Pax at her side, a flicker of movement on her right caught her attention.

"Pssst!"

As Sister Agatha glanced around, the hair on Pax's neck and back rose and he growled.

Sister Agatha snapped the leash. "Quiet."

"Psst! Over here," came a soft voice.

Scout, wearing his familiar cap and handkerchief, stepped out from behind a juniper.

Sister Agatha smiled, walking slowly over to join him in the building's shadow. "I'm so glad we've run into each other again. Are you all right? I was so worried when I heard those shots to-day!" she said quickly.

He shrugged.

She looked behind him and saw an opened trash bag on the ground beside the large Dumpster. Sister Agatha watched as he started to rummage through it.

"Let me go inside and get you some food," Sister Agatha said.

"No." He fished out a half-eaten burrito, then finished it in two bites. "See? They waste good food. Do you want me to find something for you and your dog?"

"No, that's okay," she said quietly, wishing he'd let her help.

"You helped Scout. Now tell me how Scout can help you."

"I need to know what you saw on the evening of the Fourth, the day of the fireworks, over by the swings," she said.

Wiping his hand on his pants, he nodded. "The sheriff yelled at that other man. Called him lots of bad words. Then the sheriff fell down, like he was dead. The other man looked at him, then fell down, too."

"Did anyone else come up to them?"

"There were two people," he said, "wearing caps like mine, but red. The tall one saw me, but I can run faster. He couldn't catch Scout. Now he's looking for me. He wants Scout dead."

"What about the other person with the cap? What did he do?"

"He watched the other one, but didn't chase me."

"Were they together, then?" Sister Agatha asked.

"I don't think so. The short one was following the tall one, hiding like me."

"Scout, come with me and tell the deputies what you saw. They can keep you safe."

He shook his head. "No. *You* tell them. People . . . they think Scout should be more like them, but I see they're not happy. They worry all the time. Scout's free."

Before she could say anything else, he hurried away with the bag, disappearing around the far corner of the building.

She ran after him, having to restrain Pax a bit. When they reached the rear of the building, Scout had vanished.

Pax pulled at the leash, wanting to give chase, undoubtedly picking up the scent. Sister Agatha snapped him back until he sat next to her. "I know, I can smell him, too, but he's helped us all he can, Pax. Let him be."

Like most of the homeless, Scout was a whisper in the night, a rustle in the wind. Freedom came in many guises. Scout had found his in movement and in the long shadows that shielded him from the world he'd left behind.

Lost in thought, Sister Agatha went in the front entrance and soon learned that no classes were being held that night. As she returned to the motorcycle, a new idea formed in her mind. With luck, Chuck would still be at the newspaper office, working on the morning edition of the *Chronicle*.

Instead of heading home, Sister Agatha drove quickly to the small downtown office building not far from the sheriff's department. She smiled as she pulled up, seeing Chuck's beat-up sedan parked next to the entrance. Taking Pax, she knocked on the door. A few seconds passed; then there was the click of a lock, and Chuck poked his head out.

"Hey, Sister! Pax! Thought I'd heard the Harley. You two working late tonight?"

"You bet, and I need your help. Can I see the photos you took at the park on the Fourth one more time, Chuck?" she asked.

"You got it! Come on in."

Once she was seated at a table, he placed the file in front of her. Then, before she could look inside, he pulled a large submarine sandwich out of a paper bag and set it on the desk.

"How about splitting this with me, Sister? I'm not hungry enough for a footlong tonight."

"By all means let's not let it go to waste," she said with a smile. "I'll split my half with Pax, if that's okay with you," she added, and the dog barked.

While they were eating, she got Chuck caught up on the latest. Then, after they'd finished, Sister Agatha began to study all the photos that included Robert Garcia.

As Leon had mentioned, several of the photos showed Robert carrying a large manila envelope tucked under one arm. In a few others, he had the envelope in his hand. Upon closer inspection, they were able to determine that there was no writing or label on it.

"When was the last photo of Garcia taken?" she asked.

He turned around in his desk chair to the computer, brought up his file, then checked the thumbnail images of his shots. Within a few seconds, he looked over. "Eight forty-seven. It was getting dark—notice the lighting? My camera was using the flash by then."

"In that last shot, does he still have the envelope?"

"Sure does, under his arm," he said, enlarging it and then pointing. "He's also holding something in a napkin. A hot dog, I think."

"Thanks, Chuck," she said. "I think I know someone who might be able to tell us what was in that envelope, and I intend to pay him a visit first thing tomorrow."

"Where are you off to now?" Chuck asked, walking her out to the motorcycle.

"Home," she answered, motioning for Pax to jump into the cockpit of the sidecar. "It's been a very long day."

Enjoying the coolness of the desert evening temperatures, which could go from three digits to the fifties by midnight, she opted to take the long way home. Turning on a side street that joined the highway, she drove slowly, taking in the view. The moon was just coming up, and the entire valley was bathed in its glow.

As she approached the newly remodeled Purple Sage Motel, a couple was coming out of one of the rooms. Sister Agatha smiled, remembering her old college days, being head over heels in love, and the pleasure she'd always found in her lover's arms. When she'd taken her vows, one of her regrets had been knowing that no one would ever hold her like that again. She slowed as the couple kissed under the glow of a parking lot light. Taking in that romantic moment, Sister Agatha sighed.

Apparently hearing the motorcycle, the woman ended the kiss and turned to look toward the street.

Sister Agatha waved, then suddenly realized who it was— and, more importantly, who it wasn't.

Gloria Green stood rock still, a horrified expression on her face. "Wait!" she yelled an instant later.

Her heart sinking, and wishing she could be almost any-where else in the world at the moment, Sister Agatha turned the Harley and cruised back slowly toward the sheriff's wife. Sister Agatha looked at the man, who was climbing into a dark blue pickup with the local high school's parking lot sticker on the bumper. She didn't recognize him. Her heart suddenly went out to Tom, and she wondered if he already knew. Of all the secrets she wished she'd never uncovered, this would top the list for a very long time.

As the man drove away, Sister Agatha pulled up beside Glo-ria, who was now standing beside her car.

"You and I need to talk, Sister Agatha. Not everything's the way it seems on the surface."

"You're *not* having an affair?" she managed in a croak, hoping against hope.

"Oh yes, that part's true. Follow me if you want to know the rest of the story."

"All right," Sister Agatha said, wishing she could take a pass. Instinct assured her that what she'd learn tonight would only serve to strengthen the case against Tom.

Sister Agatha followed Gloria back through town, driving toward the south and west until they arrived at a small adobe casita adjacent to the ditch bank. Even in the moonlight, she could see that someone with a green thumb had spent a lot of time working in the garden.

"This is my sister Jill's place, but she's on vacation," Gloria said, meeting Sister Agatha at the front door. "No one will bother us here."

Moments later they sat in the small kitchen. Gloria, her hand shaking slightly, poured herself a glass of wine and offered Sister Agatha one, but the nun declined.

"You saw me with Coach Brady, Sister Agatha, and you know what was going on. My question is, what will you do now?"

"I honestly don't know, Gloria. My head's still reeling. Why on earth would you do something like this—particularly now?"

"Tom and I are over. I told you that two days ago. I'm only staying at the house because of what's happened. I was actually planning on moving in here with Jill on the fifth."

"What could be so wrong with your marriage that it drove you into another man's arms?" Sister Agatha asked, still in shock.

"Things kept getting worse and worse between us. I tried to

fix it, I really did, but sometimes you just have to end the unhappiness and let go."

"Don't either of you care anymore?" Sister Agatha asked, trying to make sense out of what seemed incomprehensible.

"I still care about Tom, but I want more from a marriage than Tom's capable of giving me. Tom's career is *always* number one, and at best the kids and I come in second." She shook her head slowly. "Kyle's my future. I matter more to him than anything else. I'll never have to fight for stolen minutes of his time."

Sister Agatha stared at Gloria. "But you have two sons . . . Think of your family and what this could do to them," she managed, then continued. "You need to find what brought you and Tom together in the first place, the love, the caring. It may have been brushed aside for other concerns over the years, but it's still there. All you have to do is reconnect and make it strong again."

"You're wrong about that. Tom's married to his job, Sister Agatha. I can't change that fact. The boys are the only reason we've stayed together as long as we have."

"Gloria, Tom *does* love you. I've seen it on his face time and time again. How can you not know that?"

"Tom puts his heart in his work, and there's very little left over for us at the end of the day. Nothing's going to change that."

Sister Agatha, needing comfort, reached for the rosary attached to her cincture. "When was the last time you tried talking to Tom about the way you feel?"

"That's part of the problem. Tom and I don't talk. We haven't for a long time, and ever since he started his campaign, we barely even see him. Kyle needs and wants a family. The job's not his passion—I am. He loves the boys, too, and they adore him."

"How long have you been seeing Coach Brady?"

"You mean how long have I been having an affair?" Seeing

Sister Agatha nod, she continued. "We'd meet often for coffee and to talk, but things didn't get serious until school ended. It wasn't planned, Sister Agatha, it just happened. Of course, by now I expected to be here at Jill's with the kids, at least until we found a place of our own." She stared vacantly at her wine. "Tom and I are currently living under the same roof for appearance's sake only. I *will* be leaving him as soon as possible."

"When were you planning on telling Tom about Coach Brady?"

"I wasn't. There's no point to it," she said. "He has his life, and I have mine. Our marriage . . . has been over for a long time." Her voice broke, but she swallowed quickly and continued more steadily. "I've made my peace with that."

Something in Gloria's voice caught her attention. "You're still in love with Tom."

Gloria's eyes filled with tears, but she shook her head. "No. What we had died, and we can't bring it back. It's too late." She took an unsteady breath. "Kyle not only loves me, he's my best friend. I need him just as he needs me."

"It's not too late for you to reconnect with Tom. Your heart's still his. I hear it in your voice and see it in your eyes. Gloria, think of your boys. They need their father."

"I *am* thinking of them. They need more than a part-time dad. And I want a husband who *wants* to be there for us, not one who needs to be tricked into taking time off. Ending our marriage is the best thing for everyone. Tom, too, needs a different kind of wife, someone who'll understand his dedication to his profession because she's the same way about her career. A police officer, or someone more like you."

Sister Agatha shook her head. "You couldn't be more wrong. Tom needs your dedication to family to balance his own life. He confronts the lowest levels of depravity every day. It's your love and that of the boys that helps him retain his own humanity. He may not always show love in the way you think he should, but he's showing it in the way that makes sense to him." Sister Agatha leaned forward, resting her elbows on the table, and held Gloria's gaze. "He was a deputy when you got married. You've known all along what drives him. If you want more from Tom, you have to confront those needs head-on—not by walking away."

Gloria took an unsteady breath. "It's too late now. He'll never understand why I turned to Kyle."

"Tom will take you back—if you ask him," Sister Agatha said without hesitation. "He loves you, just as you do him." Maybe she was still a romantic, but she wanted nothing to do with the modern thinking that so easily discarded what could be mended without so much as a backward glance. "Listen to your heart, Gloria. Shut up and listen like you've never listened before. Love is a gift, but it has strings attached. To hold on to it, you have to forgive the failings of another as well as your own."

"Maybe Tom and I do deserve another chance . . ."

Sister Agatha smiled. "Go talk to him. I'll be praying for both of you. God is always on the side of love. He is Love."

Like hope, love was an intrinsic part of mankind's spirit. It was woven in the very fabric of each human being. In that light, even a frail, damaged heart could find healing.

As Sister Agatha drove back to the monastery, she found herself looking forward to the calm simplicity of the life she'd chosen . . . that had chosen her.

After Morning Prayers, Sister Agatha went outside to the cloistered side of the garden and sat in the shadow of the statue of the Blessed Mother. She needed a few moments to gather her thoughts before setting out today.

Mornings were always peaceful at Our Lady of Hope. Though she'd miss these special moments here in their desert monastery, faith in her Lord assured her that there would be many other special moments waiting at their new home.

Reverend Mother, who'd gone to place flowers on the sisters' graves, came out the graveyard gate and joined Sister Agatha.

"This new world . . . so few vocations . . . so much is changing," Reverend Mother said, sitting beside her on the bench.

"*He* remains the same," Sister Agatha said, for her own benefit as well as Mother's.

Mother gave her a grateful smile. "And that's a comfort."

Reverend Mother stood, and so did Sister Agatha. Together they walked back up the pathway toward the cloister door.

"Tell the sheriff that we're all praying he'll have the answers he needs at his fingertips soon," Mother said, going into the cloister.

As Reverend Mother disappeared into the building, a new sense of determination filled Sister Agatha. Today she'd force Tom to tell her what he was holding back. She'd get answers even if she had to threaten to walk away from the case.

Sister Agatha continued to the monastery's parking area. Before she'd even whistled for Pax, the dog raced up.

"Let's go, boy."

When she arrived at the Greens' home, Gloria's car was nowhere to be seen. With a heavy heart, Sister Agatha walked to the front door and knocked.

Tom opened it, a set of keys in his hand, then looked up and down the street. "Did you see Gloria around?"

"No, why?"

He pursed his lips. "She left angry and forgot her house keys."

"What happened?" she asked, stepping into the living room.

He shrugged. "Don't worry about it now. It'll work itself out."

She gave him a hard look. "Not everything does, Tom, unless you try—really hard."

"What's that supposed to mean?" he demanded.

"You figure it out," she snapped, then, sitting on the couch, shifted to face him. "I'm through playing games with you, Tom. You haven't been open with me since day one. You're my friend, and that's what has kept me working day and night to help you out. Now it's time for you to start trusting me—with everything. Time is critical. The only way we're going to make progress is if we work together." She paused and added, "No matter how capable you are, you won't be able to get out of this alone, and pride's going to be a lousy companion in jail."

He looked surprised but said nothing.

Sister Agatha waited, letting him mull it over.

"You're right, I've been holding back—but what I've been hiding doesn't have anything to do with Robert's murder."

She saw the way his gaze strayed to the photo of Gloria and the boys on one of the end tables. "You're protecting your family, aren't you? *That's* what this is about."

He nodded slowly. "They mean everything to me, though I guess I haven't shown it much lately, at least in the ways that count most to them. I was so busy with the job, and the election," he said, rubbing the back of his neck with one hand. "I've made lots of mistakes, and so has Gloria, but I think we could have worked it out if others hadn't been so quick to take advantage of the situation."

He paused and stood by the side of the window, looking outside. "Damage control—that's all I'm trying to do now. It's too late for anything else."

"Are you saying that Gloria's tied to the murder somehow?" She paused as a new thought formed in her mind. "The envelope that Robert was carrying . . . the one you neglected to tell me about. What was in it?"

"Sit back. It's a long story, and not a pretty one."

"Go on," she said.

"You're probably not aware of this, spending so much of your time at the monastery, but the political race between Robert and me was getting nastier by the day. The polls were saying that we were running neck to neck, and the pressure was on. Then an enemy of Robert's surfaced—one determined to bring him down."

"Someone here in town?" Sister Agatha asked. She already had an entire list of possibilities.

"No, she's from Albuquerque. The woman, Sherry Haines, apparently contacted Robert and told him that she was going to ruin his life, like he'd ruined hers. After that, she got in touch with me."

Sister Agatha sat up, her attention completely on Tom. "What's her story?"

"Robert was coming home from someplace, probably a bar, and he was so drunk he could barely walk, much less drive. He pulled out in front of Miss Haines, and she had to swerve to avoid a head-on crash. It was winter, the road was icy, and she lost control and rolled her car. Her injuries were serious, and she was trapped inside. Robert stopped, took a look, then panicked and left the scene. Forty minutes went by before another driver spotted the car and called the paramedics. That lapse in time cost her dearly, too. She lost the use of her legs and right hand and had to go on disability. Right now she's living at Partners in Assisted Living."

"Where did the accident take place?"

"Way west of here, between Bloomfield and Cuba. Apparently, since there were no other witnesses and no physical contact between the vehicles, Robert thought he'd gotten away with it."

"How did she find him?"

"At first, she had no idea who he was or where he lived. She never expected to find him, but then last week, she saw a photo of Robert at a campaign rally on the Internet. The first thing she did was call him and tell him that her second call would be to me. She wanted to ruin him in the most painful and public way possible."

"That must have hit Robert like a bolt of lightning."

"Yeah, but he knew how to cover his butt—in fact, he specialized in it. He called to tell me that the woman had made it all up and asked to meet face-to-face so we could talk. I agreed to a time and place—the park, while the crowd watched the fireworks."

"Were you expecting him to withdraw from the race?" she asked.

"Expecting is too strong a word, though it would have been a logical move. There was no way his campaign could have survived a scandal like that. Once the press heard her story, and a photo of her in her wheelchair hit the TV screen . . ."

Sister Agatha considered it, then spoke. "From what you said, the cars never made contact, and the DWI claim would have been impossible to prove now. The case would have most likely been thrown out of court."

"True, but facts wouldn't have killed Robert at the polls—innuendo would have. Think of the political races in recent years. Careers were ended on speculation alone."

"So what happened next?"

"Robert did what he did best—find a way to turn things in his favor. He came to me with a deal. If I helped him by convincing people the woman was a crank, he wouldn't reveal what he had in the manila envelope." His lips clenched into a thin white line.

He paused for several moments until curiosity made her prod him. "What was in there?"

"Photos of Gloria and Coach Brady. Some of them had been taken with a telephoto lens, but it was clear who they were and what they were doing. When I saw the photos, all I wanted was to rip Robert's head off. I might have done just that, too, but suddenly I felt sick. Everything started spinning, and I knew I was going to pass out. At first I thought I was having a heart attack. I remember Robert stepping away from me. He said something, but I couldn't make it out. Next thing I remember is waking up on the grass with Millie and some paramedics crouched next to me."

Sister Agatha shook her head slowly. "Tom, I can understand your anger after seeing those photos, but surely you don't expect me to believe that you had no idea your wife was having an affair. You're a police officer trained to look for nuances and inconsistencies in behavior."

He took a deep breath, then let it out slowly. "My job is round-the-clock, and with the campaign, I barely had time to think. Gloria's job was the house and the kids. I was taking care of my end, and I expected her to take care of hers," he said, then, in a strained, reluctant tone of voice, added, "I wasn't paying attention."

"So what you're saying is that you ignored your wife and family. Gloria needed you to be her husband, but all she got was a part-time roommate—if that," she said, refusing to sugarcoat it. "Don't you dare pass all the blame on to her."

"I know I'm partly to blame. I get that," he snapped, "but this is larger than Gloria and me. I don't want our kids to see those photos—and I have no idea where they are now."

He gazed at some indeterminate spot across the room. "A dad is larger than life in his own kids' eyes. That look they give you at times can make you feel like you can conquer the world. I don't think I could stand to lose that," he said. "A part of me would die if all I could see in their eyes when they looked at Gloria and me was disgust."

The fact that he was also worried about what their sons would think of Gloria spoke volumes. "You still love Gloria."

"Yeah, I still love her, and despite everything, I'm sure Gloria still loves me. We share too much . . . history."

"Then fight to save your marriage. Everyone makes mistakes. You made yours and she made hers. Don't allow the past to stand between you."

"I want her back, and I intend to fight to fix things with my family—but first I've got to get out of this mess," he said, then took a deep breath.

"What do you think happened to those photos? They weren't around when the deputy showed up, right?"

"No, or my attorney would have heard about it from Marquez by now. I've given this a lot of thought. Either the killer took them or they were grabbed up by the first person on the scene—Al Russo, as far as I know. Of course, someone else could have come by after the killer left and before Russo showed up."

"Al Russo didn't turn in an envelope or even mention the existence of one to the police," Sister Agatha said. "He was Robert's campaign manager—do you think he knew about the photos?"

Tom considered it for a moment, then shrugged. "Maybe so, but he wouldn't have wanted people to see Robert as a blackmailer. If he found them, I'm sure they've been destroyed by now."

"If the killer found the envelope, of course, that opens up other possibilities."

"Like what? I haven't been contacted, so, unlike it was with Robert, it doesn't look like blackmail's going to be his angle. As of right now, I have no idea what, if anything, he intends to do with those photos."

"Maybe he looked them over and threw them out, knowing they would have linked him to the scene," Sister Agatha suggested.

"That's one possible answer. That individual would have probably surmised that I'd be unlikely to mention them to Marquez or anyone else. Those photos would only have established an even stronger motive for me to have killed Robert," he said. "Not knowing what happened to the photos really worries me. If they show up somewhere along the way, they'll end up doing the kind of damage I'll never be able to set right. I'll still be able to prove I'm innocent of killing Robert—I truly believe that—but the harm they'll do to our boys . . ."

Sister Agatha thought about Tom's kids and how they'd react if those photos were made public. The damage that would do wouldn't be easily erased. As often happened, the innocent would pay the highest price of all.

16

AFTER MORNING PRAYERS THE FOLLOWING DAY, SISTER Agatha was summoned into Reverend Mother's office. The starkness of the once cozy room hit her hard. A cardboard box was on the floor beneath the window, and Mother's familiar desk had been replaced with a small vinyl-topped card table. The only other items were two folding metal chairs, a telephone, and the wooden cross on the otherwise bare white walls.

"I wanted you to know that Sister Maria Victoria and Sister Ignatius will be leaving for Colorado this morning," Mother said. "That'll leave only four of us here. Sister Eugenia, who refuses to go until I do, Sister Bernarda, and you."

"Mother," she managed, but no more words came.

Reverend Mother looked at the spot where the small statue of the Blessed Mother had been. "Our own time to leave is fast approaching, too. Have you made any progress helping the sheriff?"

Sister Agatha gave her a quick update. "I'm working as fast as I can, Mother."

"If our time to go arrives before you're finished with the case, you'll have to remain behind. You can meet the rest of us up at Agnus Dei once the case is closed."

Sister Agatha felt torn between relief that she'd be able to complete what she'd started and undeniable sadness at the prospect of remaining alone at the monastery. These halls she'd shared with the sisters would feel unspeakably empty without them.

As she left Mother's office, Sister Agatha silently prayed for guidance. Although she'd been given the gift of time, she still had no idea what the next step in the investigation should be.

"Can you give me a hint, Lord? What should I do next?"

Though no answer came, she knew one thing. The answers weren't to be found here at the monastery.

Sister Agatha headed into town with Pax a short time later, formulating a plan along the way. She'd start by trying to get more information about Sherry Haines, the woman who'd accused Robert Garcia of abandoning her along the side of the road. Sherry Haines hadn't killed Robert—there'd been no wheelchair marks anywhere around the body—but it was possible she'd been in communication with others besides Tom and Robert. That could have started a chain of events that had led to Robert's death.

Monty Allen, for example, wouldn't have wanted her story to appear in the papers or on television. Maybe he'd murdered Robert to save the firm from the kind of publicity that would have threatened his livelihood. It was a stretch, but then again, stranger things had happened.

As she parked outside the newspaper office, Chuck rushed outside to meet her. "You heard what happened, right?"

The wild excitement on Chuck's face made her stomach tighten. "No, I guess not. What's going on?"

"Hang on to your hat . . . or veil. Something with a really bad odor hit the fan this morning." He took her to his desk and picked up a copy of the *Voice*, an Albuquerque tabloid-inspired weekly. "Front page, no less," he said, handing it to her.

Sister Agatha glanced at the cover. The photo was grainy, with Coach Brady's face deliberately blacked out, but even if she hadn't been able to make out the subject, the headline and caption removed all doubt.

GREEN—WITH JEALOUSY?

NEW MOTIVE?

"Gloria Green just blew it for her husband," Chuck said. "This'll cinch the D.A.'s case."

"This looks bad for Tom's wife, but how's this going to hurt Tom? Coach Brady's not dead—Robert is," she said, wondering if he'd somehow made the connection between the envelope Robert had carried and Tom.

"Sister, don't you know who owns the *Voice*?" Seeing her blank expression, he added, "TFC Corp. Recognize the initials? Garcia's campaign logo was the same as that of his corporation. The Garcias own the *Voice*. A case will be made against Sheriff Green saying he'd known Robert was going to print the photos to embarrass him publicly, and the two had argued. Then, in a rage, Tom killed him. You get it, don't you? I mean, it won't be long before people link those photos to the envelope Robert carried with him that day."

Sister Agatha sat down and studied the photos. She had no doubt that these were the ones Robert had shown Tom. "Why would the killer, or whoever removed that envelope from the scene, release the photos now?"

"There's a woman claiming that she was a victim of Robert's

drunk driving—Sherry Haines. She went to the press with her story, and things have been buzzing ever since. That story hasn't reached the newsstand yet, but it will in a matter of hours. Maybe the Garcias, or someone sympathetic to them, decided they needed something to counter it with the public," Chuck speculated. "The edition with those photos just came out."

She nodded. "That would serve to protect the Garcias by turning the scrutiny and suspicion back onto Tom. It would also help discredit the evidence that supports Tom's version of the story—like the fact that both of the men were drugged."

She carefully considered everything she'd learned, but something about the timing still bothered her. It was more important than ever that she find and speak to Sherry Haines. "Do you know where Partners in Assisted Living is located?"

His eyes narrowed as he gazed at her. "Sister, you've got a lead, and I want in."

"I'll tell you all about it, I promise, but first I need to confirm a few things. Will you give me twenty-four hours?"

"In newspaper terms, that's a lifetime, but okay," Chuck said, looking up the address for her.

"Thanks, Chuck. Oh, about Coach Brady—please forget I mentioned his name, okay?"

"Yeah, okay. In this town he could lose his job over the gossip if people found out that he was the guy in the photos," Chuck answered. "Mum's the word."

The drive into Albuquerque took longer than she'd expected, traveling down the old highway and off the main streets. Forty minutes later, Sister Agatha and Pax arrived at the rehabilitation center. Pax was wearing his orange service dog vest as they walked up to the front desk. There, a stately, silver-haired woman greeted them with a warm smile.

"Hello, Sister. I'm Mrs. Goldman. What brings you here this morning?"

"I'm Sister Agatha, and I'd like to speak to Sherry Haines about Robert Garcia," she said.

"She's in therapy right now," the woman replied after checking her computer screen. "Would you like to wait?"

"Yes, I would."

"Then have a seat and make yourself at home. I'll let her know you're here. Ms. Haines has had a lot of company already this morning, so she may be too tired. If she is, you may have to come back later."

"All right," Sister Agatha agreed. "Does she normally have a lot of visitors?"

"No, but I understand that after she gave her story to one reporter, all the others somehow found out about it, too. They haven't stopped coming by since." After answering another phone call, Mrs. Goldman looked at Sister Agatha and smiled. "Sorry for the delay. I'll let Sherry know you're here."

Mrs. Goldman walked down the hall, then returned a few moments later. "Sherry said that she'll meet you when she's finished, Sister. Would you like some coffee while you wait?" she asked, pouring herself a cup.

"No, thanks." Sister Agatha watched doctors and nurses hurrying to and fro in the long hallway. After a gurney with a young patient was wheeled past, she glanced back at Mrs. Goldman. "This has got to be a very demanding job. I imagine you see a lot of tragedy."

"Yes, but I also get to see the best in people. That's why I volunteer here. I see it as a mitzvah."

"I'm sorry. A what?"

"It means fulfilling the commandment through an act of kindness. It's at the center of Jewish beliefs."

"Our doctrines aren't so different, are they? We're told from the beginning to love one another, and it wasn't a request," Sister Agatha said.

"Exactly. We try to honor God by doing His work, and that's what a mitzvah is all about. It's a way of pleasing God."

Sister Agatha watched as the woman stood, then went down the hall to help one of the nurses guide a patient with prosthetic lower limbs.

Mrs. Goldman's simple words had touched her deeply. Under the pressure of recent events, she'd forgotten that honoring God didn't mean achieving grand results. The little kindnesses that made the world a better place glorified God in the best way of all.

Sister Agatha heard a door open, then watched as a familiar-looking woman in a wheelchair came down the hall toward her.

"Here's Sherry, Sister," Mrs. Goldman said, introducing them.

When Pax placed his giant paw on the woman's lap, Sister Agatha started to correct him, but Sherry shook her head.

"It's fine. I love dogs," she said, petting him with her uninjured hand. "So tell me, Sister, what can I do for you?"

Looking for a better place to talk, Sister Agatha suggested they go into the courtyard. At Sherry's invitation, she pushed the wheelchair outside. They found a secluded, shady spot under a patio roof, and Pax, as if sensing he was needed, placed his massive head on Sherry's lap.

Sherry smiled. "Once I'm able to get my own place again, I'm going to see about sharing my life with a service dog."

"They make wonderful companions," Sister Agatha agreed.

"But you didn't come here to talk about service dogs," Sherry said, an unmistakable weariness in her voice. "Did Sheriff Green send you? I've kept up with the news, and I understand he's facing some serious trouble."

"Yes, he is," Sister Agatha said.

"That was part of the reason I decided to release my story to the press now. I want people to know that Robert Garcia deserved no one's sympathy. If Sheriff Green killed him, he did the world a service."

"Sheriff Green is innocent. He didn't kill anyone."

"Then maybe my story will help him. I gave out several interviews this morning, and by this evening people will know that Robert Garcia wasn't worthy of running for dogcatcher, let alone sheriff."

"When did you first talk to a reporter, and who was it?" Sister Agatha asked, trying to determine if she'd unknowingly gone to someone associated with the Garcias. That would explain the speed of the preemptive attack.

"I sent an e-mail to the Albuquerque paper two days ago. Last night, I had several reporters call me—none associated with that paper. I guess they spy on each other."

Sister Agatha nodded, remembering all too well how that game was played. If someone sympathetic to the Garcias had discovered that e-mail or heard about the lead, it was highly likely that he or she had called Al Russo, Robert's front man.

Al had been loyal to Robert. He'd also done his best to ameliorate some of the harm Robert had done, particularly to his own wife, Victoria, and his son, RJ. Yet, despite knowing that his client was abusive, Russo had still worked hard to get him elected. Money, it seemed, could buy a lot of loyalty, particularly in a tight economy—but just how far did that loyalty extend?

"I can't hurt Robert Garcia now except to destroy his memory, and that's what I want to do," Sherry said.

"You may end up destroying someone else—an innocent—in the process. That's the problem with revenge."

"What do you mean?"

"The Garcias will put a spin on your interview using their own print sources. By the time they're through, Sheriff Green will be seen as someone so desperate to save himself he was willing to bury his deceased opponent's family under a mountain of innuendo."

"I'll make sure people know that it was *my* decision to come forward. I want Robert Garcia's memory to be as ruined as my hand—and livelihood," she said, gesturing with a glance at her right hand, which was clubbed and stiff. "The reason I chose to come forward now is because the last operation didn't do as promised—allow me to grip things. No matter how hard I try, my fingers still don't cooperate. I used to make my living as an artist, a painter. I'd do portraits in oil. Those days are over now. I've got nothing—not even a way to support myself."

Sister Agatha's heart went out to her. "I'm so sorry," she said. "If there's anything I can do to help, all you have to do is ask."

Sherry shook her head. "I always believed that if I could unmask the man responsible for what happened to me, I'd find peace. But you know what? That didn't happen. I can't hurt a dead man—but he's still hurting me."

"No, he can't touch you anymore," Sister Agatha argued, compassion washing over her in giant waves.

"Painting was my life, and a part of my heart. I needed it as much as I needed air to breathe. Now I can't even hold a brush."

Sister Agatha watched her cover her injured hand with her other one. She could feel her sadness and despair as keenly as if they were her own. She prayed to find the right words to comfort her, but, instead, she remembered Cruzer.

"There's someone I'd like you to meet," Sister Agatha said, then, leaving Pax with Sherry, went to use the phone.

Sister Agatha called Chuck, got Cruzer's cell phone number, then dialed it. Cruzer answered on the first ring.

"I'm still working on things, Sister Agatha," he said, anticipating her question. "Ya gotta go slowly sometimes."

"I'm calling on another matter. I'd like to ask a favor of you," she said, then explained.

"I'm free this morning, so how about if I head over there now?" he said without hesitation.

She hadn't been sure what kind of response she'd get from him. Cruzer's reaction had exceeded all her hopes.

She returned to where Sherry waited and saw Pax's gentleness slowly bringing her out of her shell. The dog had such a special touch. With that long sigh of his, and that massive paw, he'd given her something positive to focus on.

They moved to the recreation room, which contained craft areas, a TV, and table games. As they waited, Sister Agatha told Sherry a little about Arnie Cruz. "Cruzer's used to working around handicaps and shares your passion for art. Maybe there's something you can teach each other."

"Sister, are you matchmaking?" she asked, laughing.

Sister Agatha just smiled.

It took him thirty minutes, but Cruzer arrived carrying an over-sized bag filled with various art supplies. Sister Agatha introduced them, then stepped back and prayed.

Cruzer's enthusiasm was contagious, and the two soon began discussing pigments and Southwest art. As Sister Agatha watched, he showed Sherry several brush holds designed for people with grip problems or missing digits. Refusing to take no for an answer, and strengthening her grip with his own, Cruzer placed the brush in her hand.

Sister Agatha smiled, then, moving as silently as only a nun could, left unnoticed with Pax.

"That's what I call a mitzvah, Sister Agatha," Mrs. Goldman said as they passed her desk on the way out. "You helped God by making things better for someone else."

"Thank you, Mrs. Goldman," Sister Agatha whispered. "Every once in a while I do get things right."

17

AFTER LEAVING THE REHAB CENTER, SISTER AGATHA drove to the offices of the *Voice*. She wanted to get all the information she could about those photos of Gloria and the coach. Hopefully she'd uncover something that would point her to whomever had taken them. If they'd been e-mailed, the address might lead her to the person who'd stolen the envelope from the crime scene.

As she walked into the cramped offices of the *Voice*, a remodeled former auto shop on a side street in western Bernalillo, the room beyond the empty front desk became completely quiet. She glanced around, but people quickly averted their gazes or turned their backs. Although she asked, everyone pretended not to hear her and no one offered to help.

After a moment, Sister Agatha took a seat in one of the chairs inside the reception area and, with Pax beside her, prepared to wait them out for as long as necessary.

About ten minutes later a short, dark-haired young woman hurried inside and, with scarcely a glance at anyone in the rooms beyond, took a seat behind the desk and shoved her purse into a drawer.

"You're late, Sutherland. I'm docking you a half hour," came a voice from the room beyond.

"Whatever," the woman muttered.

Accessing her desktop computer, Miss Sutherland—Sister Agatha noticed that she wore no wedding ring—lifted her mouse pad and glanced at a piece of paper glued there. She then typed in what Sister Agatha surmised was her password. "I'll be with you in a minute, Sister," she said without glancing up.

"No, I'll handle this," a curt voice interrupted. A man in his midthirties wearing a bolo tie, a Western shirt, and jeans walked out from behind the counter and past the front desk.

"I'm Travis Holbrook, Sister, the editor. Are you sure you're in the right place?"

"I must be, or you wouldn't have pretended I wasn't here for the past twenty minutes. Fortunately, Mr. Holbrook, you're just the person I wanted to talk to. I need to see the original photos taken of Sheriff Green's wife," she said firmly, hoping her tone would pre-empt any argument.

"The originals? Why? We have plenty of newsstand copies. Take one."

She shook her head. "I need to see the originals you received from your informant, and I'd also like to know how you got hold of them—e-mail or otherwise."

"Our sources are our own, Sister. I understand you were a reporter once, so you should know better than to ask."

"The story's already out, and all I want is to see the original photos and find out how they were sent. It's not like I'm asking for the name of your source."

214

"It's close, but I'll save you some grief. The photos were e-mailed anonymously from a proxy server, so they're impossible to trace. Our contacts usually prefer to protect their identities, especially when a public figure is involved."

"When did you receive them?"

"We haven't been sitting on them, if that's your real question, but I'm not going to get any more specific than that. I know too much about you, Sister, and I don't trust you."

"Excuse me?"

"You heard me. You're working to free the sheriff, and I have no intention of lifting even one finger to help him. Tom Green arrested my boy for vandalism last year. It was only a high school prank, but Green made a big deal out of it, and now my kid's got a record. It'll be erased when he's eighteen, but no thanks to Green. If you're looking for someone to help you save that lousy bum's neck, you came to the wrong place. He's a self-righteous jerk who deserves whatever he gets."

It was obvious that Holbrook had a personal score to settle. It wasn't the first time she'd seen journalistic "ethics" twisted to accommodate personal concerns, and it wouldn't be the last.

Still, she couldn't let it go without a fight. "He's innocent. Shouldn't that matter to a person with your responsibility to the community?" she demanded.

"He may not be guilty of this particular crime, Sister, but that man's far from innocent. He's got plenty of baggage behind him. Count on it." He paused, then, in a softer voice, added, "Take my advice, Sister. Cut your losses. Your interference in what should have been an open-and-shut case is going to cost both you and the sheriff dearly."

"What do you mean?"

"Check the editorial page tomorrow. Then run for cover, 'cause a lot of nasty stuff is going to rain down for sure."

Sister Agatha kept Pax at heel close beside her as she left the building. As usual, Pax had sensed her tension and had responded by going into guard dog mode.

"Relax, boy. You're no longer a police dog. You're our peace-loving companion."

Pax's soulful brown eyes gazed questioningly at her, and she bent down to pet him. He could be the most loving companion in the world or a ferocious protector. The way things were shaping up, she had a feeling she'd be needing both.

Sister Agatha drove north, toward the monastery, needing time to think. Everything was coming at her at once, and too much information could be as confusing as not enough.

Hearing her cell phone ring, she pulled to the side, removed her helmet, and answered the call.

"Sister, it's me, Chuck. Can you come by my office? I've just received something from the *Voice* that I think you'll want to see. A buddy of mine works there, and he overheard some of your face-to-face with Holbrook. Considering he hates Holbrook, he decided to do you a favor. He sent me an advance copy of the editorial that's scheduled to come out tomorrow."

"I'm on my way." Judging from the warning Holbrook had given her, she knew to expect the worst.

When they arrived at Chuck's office, Pax immediately lay down on the cool tile floor.

"Sister, this is nasty stuff, so brace yourself," Chuck said, turning his computer screen around.

As she read the editorial, she understood why Chuck had been disturbed. The header read, SEPARATION OF CHURCH AND STATE. The article below that filled her with anger. "This is an outrageous lie," she said. "The monastery is *not* closing because of some supposed impropriety between Tom and me. Yes, it's true that Tom and I have a history—but it's *ancient* history. Whenever we've attended church and city government functions together, we've gone there officially. We were *not* using excuses to meet. This is pure garbage."

"You could sue, but it'll be tied up in the courts for years, and if you notice the wording, it's mostly vague innuendo, not outright claims. In my opinion, you won't have much of a case."

"I'm more worried about the damage it's going to do to Tom," she said.

"Half-truths are always more dangerous than outright lies, which are easy to disprove. You'll have to weather the fallout. The Garcia camp wants to put that final nail in Sheriff Green's coffin because it will deflect attention away from the unflattering truths that are now surfacing about Robert Garcia."

"This is going to make things even tougher for Reverend Mother." Sister Agatha thought of how much weight Mother had lost in the past few months. Under the unrelenting pressure, her health had suffered badly. "I have to warn her. I may not be able to stop this article, but I can make sure our defenses are in place."

"I have an idea that may help you. I'll print an article that reminds people of all the cases you've solved and the good you've done for our community. It'll counter that trash, at least somewhat."

"I appreciate it, Chuck. That'll help. There's another way to head this off at the pass, too," she added in a low, thoughtful voice. Seeing Chuck looking expectantly at her, she shook her head. "I need to think some things through first before I do or say anything else." She'd also have to decide whether or not to keep Reverend Mother in the dark for now. Forgiveness would be easier to get than permission.

"Do you have a laptop I could borrow for a few hours, Chuck?"

Chuck gave her a puzzled look but nodded. "Sure. Take mine," he said, giving her a state-of-the-art laptop about as thick as a slice of bread. It was far superior to the larger ones they had at the monastery. "You'll need my password to start it up. It's 8W1D44AMinus."

"I'll never remember that. Can I write it down?"

"Yes, but you'll have to memorize it as soon as possible, then swallow the paper."

"Seriously?" she asked, giving him a cockeyed look.

"No, just kidding."

Sister Agatha wrote it down, then showed Chuck the paper. "Is that right?"

"Yes, except it's the word 'minus,' not the math symbol," he said, smiling. "I mixed nonsense with sense."

"Thanks. I appreciate this, and I'll take good care of your computer. See you later," she said, then hurried out with Pax.

Instead of driving to the monastery, Sister Agatha drove to Judy's Place, near the casino, and parked in the back directly beside the loading dock.

A head appeared in front of the round window; then, seconds later, Judy stepped out. "Just in time, Sister. I need an excuse to get away from the mountain of paperwork on my desk."

Sister Agatha smiled as Judy bent down to pet Pax. Her easygoing personality was exactly what Sister Agatha was counting on now.

"I've come to ask you a favor—a *big* favor," Sister Agatha said.

"You're hungry and would like one of everything on the menu?"

Sister Agatha laughed. "That's going to seem like a picnic in comparison," she answered, following Judy inside.

Judy gestured for her to take a seat in the cozy office. "You've got me curious. What's on your mind?"

"First, let me fill you in on what's been happening."

As Sister Agatha told her about the photos of Gloria that had appeared in the *Voice*, Judy nodded.

"I've seen them. One of my customers left a copy of that rag behind. It's crap and slander in equal parts," Judy said. "Gloria Green should sue them for invasion of privacy or something."

"Judy, it's absolutely imperative that I find out who took those photos, or if not that, then who supplied them to the *Voice*. Problem is, they won't cooperate with me." She told Judy about her visit to the *Voice* and the hostility she'd experienced, but she didn't mention tomorrow's editorial.

"I wish I could help you, Sister, but I don't know anyone who works there."

"A newspaper's need for advertisers hasn't changed since my days as a reporter. If anything, it's more important now with circulation down and paper costs going up," Sister Agatha said.

"So you want me to go in as an advertiser and see what I can get?" Judy sat back and smiled. "The problem is that advertising is a totally different department, and I'm not sure I could get anything you could use."

"I've got a better idea. You go in playing the part of the eager but long-winded client while I tackle things from a different direction. Can I borrow one of your staff uniforms?"

"Sure. I always keep a few on hand in various sizes in case we need to change tops or bottoms during a shift. Spills happen. What do you plan to do with it?" Judy asked, pointing to four sets of tops and bottoms hung on hooks behind the door.

"Wear it, of course," Sister Agatha said with a smile. "Then you and I can go over there together. I'll be your assistant. How's that?"

Judy laughed. "So you're going to leave your habit here and go secular?" Seeing Sister Agatha nod, she added, "But, Sister, what if they recognize you?"

"What color is my hair? Is it long or short?"

"Uh. Dirty blond? Light brown? Your eyebrows are brown. But I have no idea about the length," she said, then smiled. "I'm starting to get your point."

"People generally don't look past the habit, and with a bit of makeup, I'm willing to bet that even the people who know me won't notice."

"Okay, let's assume we're there and your disguise works out. What happens next?"

"I saw where the receptionist keeps her password. I'll drop a mountain of paperwork on the floor right by her desk, and while she's helping me gather up the mess, I'll sneak a look. Later, after you're shown into the advertising exec's office, I'll excuse myself and hack into their computers using Wi-Fi," she said, pointing to the laptop she had with her.

"It's been a while since I've been part of a sting." Judy smiled slowly. "I'm in."

"Great. One last thing. Well, two. We'll need to take your car, and secondly, Pax is a dead giveaway. May I leave him here?"

"Sure. I'll have some water brought in for him—and a large beef bone, if you're okay with that."

Hearing the word "bone," Pax sat up and barked. Sister Agatha laughed. "I'm okay with it, and Pax is thrilled," she said, taking the simple uniform Judy handed her.

"This looks about your size," Judy said.

Sister Agatha went into the staff bathroom adjacent to Judy's office, slipped out of her habit and cotton slip, then folded them neatly. It felt decidedly odd trying on street clothes. She pulled up the dark slacks, then buttoned up the crisp white blouse. At least the colors were familiar, and the fit generous enough to be comfortable.

There were no mirrors at the monastery. That was considered vanity. As she studied her image she swallowed back a wild surge of panic. Without her familiar habit to define her, she felt vulnerable . . . and alone.

Dropping to her knees, she whispered a heartfelt prayer for help. Courage was called for now, but all she felt was fear—of making a mistake, of the unknown.

"Sister, you okay?" Judy asked, knocking on the bathroom door.

"I'm fine," Sister Agatha answered. Standing, she took one last look in the mirror.

It had been a long time since she'd given her own short hair more than a passing thought. Cropped with Maria Victoria's scissors, the cut was practical but completely uneven. Fluffing it out with one hand, then giving up, she stepped out of the bathroom and into Judy's office.

"You're right. No one will know you," Judy said with a surprised look on her face. "It's a new you."

"No, it's the same old me in a different wrapping," Sister Agatha corrected with a wry smile.

"Your hair . . . Let me even it out a bit." Judy held out a chair. "Sit."

"Bark, bark!" Sister Agatha answered, then laughed.

Trusting Judy, Sister Agatha sat back while she snipped and styled. Judy then reached into her purse, brought out some powder and lipstick, and applied them to Sister Agatha carefully. "Okay. *Now* you're ready," she said, then quickly added, "No, wait. One more thing will make it perfect."

Judy hurried out of the office, then returned with a name tag, which she promptly pinned on Sister Agatha's left breast pocket. "Okay. Now let's go to the full-length mirror in the employees' restroom, and you can take a look at yourself."

Taking a deep, steadying breath, Sister Agatha walked up to the mirror and stared in wonder at the reflection before her. "It's like looking at . . . the distant past—with a few more wrinkles," she said, then, pulling up the name tag so she could read it, burst out laughing. It read MARY. "How did you know?"

"Know what? That's a sample sent by our uniform vendor."

"Mary *was* my former name."

"We'll take that as a sign, then," Judy said with a smile. "You ready to go?"

"One more thing. I'll need to carry some business papers—a stack large enough to make a real mess when I drop them."

"How about the last three months' worth of suggestions from the suggestion box, all in one file folder? You drop those, and the memo-sized papers will fly everywhere."

"Sounds perfect!"

Leaving Pax chewing on a knuckle bone in Judy's office, they set out. "You have a very nice car," Sister Agatha said, silently noting the differences between this small luxury sedan and the Antichrysler.

"It took me three years to save up the money I needed to buy it outright," Judy said. "It's not as fancy as some, but the back folds down and I can carry almost anything I need. Most important of all, it's not a truck," she added. "I *hate* pickups. They remind me too much of my ex."

Thinking of Tom and Gloria, Sister Agatha felt a touch of sorrow for this world she'd left behind. "Marriages these days . . . every other couple seems to be breaking up, even the Catholics."

"In my old profession—law enforcement—marriages were all too often a casualty of war. It wasn't just the long hours, late nights, and the risks we all took. It was what the work took out of us. To keep what we saw daily from destroying us completely, most of us became hardened. Optimism isn't for the battle-scarred."

Sister Agatha didn't argue. All she could do now was pray that Tom and Gloria *would* find their way back to each other. Where love existed, hope wasn't a cheat. "Sometimes, things are worth saving even if it means going that extra mile, and more." She hadn't meant to speak the thought out loud, but life didn't come with a delete key, and she couldn't take it back now.

"You're thinking of Tom Green and his wife, aren't you?" Judy observed, then, without waiting for an answer, continued. "Even if they put things back together again, that crack will always be there, you know."

"I disagree. Remember what St. Paul said about forgetting the things left behind. Looking to the future together is the key. It *can* be done, but you have to really want it. When people go after a goal with all their hearts, they generally find a way to achieve it."

"That kind of optimism belongs to the young. When you get older, you realize that chasing a dream comes with consequences. The more you put your heart into something, the more vulnerable you become—and the harder it'll be to put yourself back together if things don't go the way you'd hoped. The young can mend a broken heart by telling themselves that it'll never happen to them again. The older you get, the more you realize that the only way to avoid that is to stop taking risks."

"Certain things are worth the trials. Real love . . . we idealize it and convince ourselves that it's endowed with a perfection all its own, but that's not the way life works. That gentle emotion often gets buried under the tombstone weight of bad choices. Yet love can still defeat whatever stands in its way if given half a chance, but without patience, the battle's lost before it even starts."

Judy remained silent for several minutes, then asked, "Why didn't it work out between you and Tom? I've always heard that what you had back in college was very strong."

"There was always something missing between us. I couldn't define it, not until I became a Bride of Christ. Then I found a love that went much deeper than any I'd ever known before. I knew He was my answer," she said, pointing upward.

"But to never have kids . . . that's got to leave a hole in your heart. Mine are grown, but they're everything to me."

"That's the biggest sacrifice all the sisters are called to make, but He gives us another gift in return. I've found a center—an anchor—that sustains me no matter what. Even now, in the middle of changes I never thought I'd face, it keeps me grounded. I know who I serve, and I can feel His love within me." She took a deep breath and let it out again. "I know it sounds lofty and idealistic, but what I've told you is as real to me as each sunrise. Besides, what I have can't be taken away from me. How many people can say that with absolute conviction?"

"I've never found the kind of love you're talking about. I envy you."

"You've found your own special place in this life. Judy's Place is your dream—one you turned into a reality."

Judy nodded and smiled. "You're right about that."

A short time later, they arrived at the *Voice*. The woman behind the front desk, Miss Sutherland, was leafing through a women's magazine and talking on a cell phone as Sister Agatha and Judy approached.

According to plan, as Judy asked to see the advertising

manager, Sister Agatha dropped her folder, sending little bits of paper flying all across the office.

"I'm so sorry!" Sister Agatha said, reaching for the ones that had floated onto the woman's desk.

"Let me help you," the receptionist said to her with a sigh. "Call you back in five," she told the person she'd left on the phone, then ended the call.

As Miss Sutherland bent down to retrieve the papers scattered on the floor, Sister Agatha made a show of leaning over the top of the desk to reach several pieces on the far end. Glancing back to make sure that the receptionist's attention was diverted, and seeing Judy step between them, Sister Agatha quickly lifted the mouse pad. Memorizing the password—1voice2—she gathered up the papers.

"Sorry about all that," Sister Agatha said as Miss Sutherland handed her the stack she'd gathered.

"That's okay, Mary. I'm a klutz, too," Miss Sutherland said.

Not giving her a chance to focus on Sister Agatha's face, Judy forced the woman's attention back to her. "What's your advertising manager's name?"

"Joe Montoya. Let me ring his office for you."

Soon they were shown to a small suite at the end of the hall. There, they were greeted by a harried-looking man who offered them a chair. As he began detailing advertising options, Sister Agatha quietly excused herself, leaving Montoya in Judy's care.

Alone, she hurried to the restroom and locked the door behind her. Hoping that Miss Sutherland had gone back to her telephone conversation and wouldn't notice, Sister Agatha logged on, using her password.

A quick search took her to the right image files, and she retrieved the entire folder, loading them onto Chuck's hard drive.

His laptop was fast, and she was done in three minutes. Exiting the *Voice's* local network, she shut down the laptop.

Moments after she returned to Montoya's office, Judy stood. "Thanks for the information, Joe. You've given me a lot to think about. I'll go over my options on the different packages you offered me and let you know what I decide."

"A business like yours can benefit from advertising in our publication. Your regulars already know what you have to offer, but we can really bring up your walk-in and first-time customer numbers. Our newspaper caters to a generation on the go. We target the type of people who frequent small restaurants that cater to local tastes, like yours."

"I agree. My assistant and I will do some number crunching, then get back to you."

Montoya shook hands with both of them and saw them to the door. As they walked down the hallway, Travis Holbrook was coming out of one of the offices. He stepped back to let them pass, his gaze focusing on Sister Agatha.

Her heart hammering, Sister Agatha forced herself not to alter her pace and continued down the hall with Judy.

"That was a profitable meeting," Judy said, loudly enough for him to hear easily. "I think the *Voice* is the best place for our advertising dollars."

The second they reached Judy's car, Sister Agatha breathed again. "I thought we'd be busted for sure when Holbrook came out of that office," she said.

"I think he was trying to place you," Judy said. "That's why I ad-libbed that line about advertising bucks. I figured a conversation like that would be the last thing he'd equate with a nun."

"It worked, too. I glanced back right before we reached the door, and his attention was already on something else. Thanks for the misdirection."

Driving back north through Bernalillo, Judy relaxed behind the wheel. "So, did you get what you needed?"

"I think so. The images were together in a file, so I downloaded the entire folder, or whatever you call it, into the laptop. Now, with God's help, I'll finally get some answers."

18

S ISTER AGATHA WAS ALREADY WIDE-AWAKE BY THE TIME the Maria bell rang at 4:30 A.M. She hadn't slept much, thinking about the duty she'd have to carry out this morning. Today, and, in fact, as soon as possible, she'd have to tell Reverend Mother about the planned editorial in the *Voice*.

The Great Silence wasn't broken, except in grave emergencies, until after Morning Prayers, shortly after eight. It was then that Sister Agatha went to speak to Reverend Mother.

As she stepped inside Mother's office, she could see that it had been a while since Reverend Mother had enjoyed a full night's sleep, too. Though the day was just beginning, she looked nearly exhausted. Sister Agatha would have given anything not to have to burden her with the news she brought, but there was no turning back.

Figuring that in this case quick was better than slow, Sister Agatha didn't draw it out. After she'd finished, she added, "Mother, they make their living twisting things, and this was their way of selling newspapers. That's all it is."

"But there's something so vicious about an editorial like that. We'll sue!"

"Mother, please don't let this upset you. The fact is, we're leaving our home, so they can't really hurt us no matter how hard they try."

"Child, it's what we'll be leaving behind for the archdiocese that worries me. They've had their share of trouble over the years. Another scandal . . ."

"Nothing that anyone can say or do can harm us or His Church, Mother. The foundation that sustains us is beyond the world's reach. Our Lord's at the center of everything we are, and He's already proven that nothing can destroy what belongs to the Father and to Him."

Reverend Mother blinked back tears. "You're right, child. It's my own lack of faith . . ."

"No, Mother, what you lack is *sleep*," Sister Agatha said with a gentle smile.

"That, too," Mother admitted with a sigh. "Are you getting any closer to finding Robert Garcia's killer?"

"I believe I am, even though the devil tries to block me at every turn."

"Evil won't be able to overwhelm you if you try hard to see Christ in everyone you meet. You'll be surprised how this rule transforms everything and helps you." She gazed at the empty spot where the statue of the Blessed Mother had been. "We need to trust in God's goodness, now more than ever. Hope is rooted in that."

"Thank you, Mother," Sister Agatha said, then knelt to receive a blessing.

After leaving Mother's office, Sister Agatha set out to town with Pax. The cool morning felt heavenly. "Lord, help me make the most out of all the opportunities you send our way today."

When she pulled into the *Chronicle*'s parking area a short time later, she found Chuck just getting out of his beat-up old car.

"Good morning, Sister. Did you hear the good news?" he asked, a big smile on his face.

"What good news is that? May the Lord forgive me, but did the *Voice* burn down last night?"

"Not that good, but, according to my friend, their editor, Holbrook, decided not to run that editorial. There was a staff meeting with lawyers, and they decided that while they never identified the sheriff's wife by name in that photo and the sheriff's a public figure, *you* were about to be slandered, and you could sue."

"That *is* great news! Maybe the Garcias decided they'd look even worse if they attacked a nun." She breathed a sigh of relief. "Did Sherry Haines's story run? We don't have a TV at the monastery, so I wasn't able to check things out."

He nodded. "Two Albuquerque stations and the Albuquerque paper ran it last night, but they were careful to protect themselves, too. They had excerpts from Haines's interview, then clearly stated that Garcia's involvement couldn't be confirmed, though the description that she had given the officers after the accident matched Robert Garcia," he said. "They ran the artist's rendition of her description beside one of his campaign photos. Talk about a match."

"Interesting. It looks like the situation evened itself out again, don't you think?"

Chuck shrugged. "Opinions aren't likely to change very much, because both parties in this have taken hits."

"It's the killer who needs to start taking some hits," Sister Agatha replied.

"So, because you're here early, I'm figuring you pulled off something big yesterday afternoon. Am I right? Do you have a big story for me?"

Sister Agatha smiled. "I don't know how big it is, but I've got something," she said. She handed him his computer and filled him in on what she'd done, leaving Judy's name out of it.

It didn't take long for Chuck to download the file. "Holbrook was right, Sister. If this is the way it came in, the e-mail is impossible to trace."

Chuck opened a new file and showcased the photos, which were thumbnail images. "I can enlarge any of them."

"Start with number one, and we'll work our way down," Sister Agatha said.

"Good shot of Coach Brady," Chuck said with a nod after a moment. "No wonder the *Voice* distorted the image of his face. After winning the state basketball championship last winter, Coach is more popular in this community than . . . well, I can't think of anyone even close, except maybe Father Rick."

"Yeah, and they were out to hurt Tom Green, not get sued or run out of town. From these uncropped photos, it's clear they were taken from a city street—public territory. See the street sign?" She pointed it out.

"The photographer, whoever he was, took a lot of care shooting these," Chuck said. "Even though the ones reprinted in the *Voice* were grainy because of the cheap materials and processes they use—not to mention the fact that they've been enlarged to quadruple their size—the originals are clear. Look, you can even see the pattern of the curtains in the motel room."

"They didn't run this one in the paper, but Gloria takes a good photo even in profile. What's that reflected on the window behind her?" Sister Agatha pointed to the screen. "There's some kind of figure in that dark spot."

"Let me lighten up the photo," Chuck said, clicking the mouse and manipulating the sharpness of the image. "It's someone holding a camera—"

"It's the photographer's reflection! Lighten it up some more," she said quickly.

A few seconds later, they could both make out the image of a small, high-end pocket camera—and, more importantly, that of the photographer using it. The angle of the glass mirroring his reflection had captured part of his face.

"Do you realize who that is?" Chuck asked, surprised.

"Al Russo," she answered quietly, stunned by the revelation.

"He's supposed to be a quality guy. What's he doing following Gloria Green and taking cheesy photos like these?"

"I'll be sure to ask when I see him," Sister Agatha said.

"Come to think of it, maybe it's just part of the politics involved in a campaign. Campaigns can get rough, and in that game winning is the only thing."

The fact that Russo had supplied the photos Robert had shown Tom revealed that Al had been part of the blackmail scheme all along. He'd also been the first to arrive at the crime scene and had used that opportunity to remove his own handiwork. Now she'd have to figure out what else he'd been involved in besides blackmail and tampering with evidence.

"There's a lot more to Al than I'd realized," she said.

"Sister, no politician's hands are ever really clean."

As Sister Agatha sat still, trying to figure out what to do next, the *Chronicle*'s cleaning woman came into the office from a back room where she'd been working.

"Hi, Claire," Chuck greeted her absently. Then, hearing someone at the front door, he stood. "Be right back, Sister."

Sister Agatha remained where she was, lost in thought. Hearing a bump, she focused on Claire and saw her struggling to move a corner table so she could clean behind it. Remembering Mother's advice to see Christ in everyone, she immediately went to help.

"Thanks, Sister," Claire said, once they'd finished. "I couldn't help but hear you mention Al Russo. He's more than the cold businessman most people see, did you know that?"

"No, I didn't," she answered, then waited. Claire didn't disappoint.

"I go on walks along the bosque trails with my boy, Kevin, every Thursday morning. One day we went past the horse jumps, deeper into the bosque, and saw Mr. Russo, Mrs. Garcia, and her son, RJ. They had a blanket spread out and were having a picnic—a real special treat, too, judging by the white bags with the red JP on the sides. The sandwiches came from Judy's Place, and those big babies are *expensive*," she said, then added with a chuckle, "Mr. Russo was playing around, roughhousing with Robert Jr., and you could just see how much he loves that boy. The cold businessman we all know from around town was nowhere in sight that day."

"I've seen Al with RJ, and those two *are* great friends," Sister Agatha agreed. The sandwiches from Judy's Place had also given her an important clue she was definitely going to follow up.

"It's rare these days to see family moments like those," Claire said. "My husband, Jerry, used to play like that with our son, but Jerry's in Iraq now. I really miss him," she said with a sigh. Glancing up at the clock on the wall, she added, "I've got to hurry now, Sister. I'm running behind this morning."

"Thanks for taking time to talk to me," Sister Agatha said, thinking back to the last time she'd seen Al with RJ. They'd both had that same lopsided grin . . .

As Claire moved to the next room, Sister Agatha remembered her conversation with Scout. He'd claimed to have seen two people wearing Garcia campaign caps near the scene of the crime. Al had been the one to approach the body. Perhaps the second person had been Victoria.

When Chuck came back into the room, he gave Sister Agatha a long, speculative look. "What's happened?"

"I may have found a motive for Al Russo, but I'll need to check a few things out before I'm sure."

"He's already number four on my suspect list, Sister, but I'm willing to bump him up a notch or two. How about a sneak peek into that brain of yours? Remember, you gave me your word that I'd get the story."

"You will, but I need to verify a few things first. As I've learned the hard way, half-truths can damage people far more than anyone realizes, and I don't want to be guilty of that."

"Come on, just a hint? It'll stay between you and me for now."

She considered it for a moment, then nodded. "All right. The truth is that I could really use your help. I need to know what Al did for a living *before* he became Robert's campaign manager. I also need you to find out how long he and Victoria have known each other."

His eyes grew wide. "I see where you're going with this. If your suspicions are right, this could turn out to be one heckuva story."

"Slow down. I have no proof, so this better not find its way into print until we know a lot more."

"Count on it, Sister. I don't want to be sued or lose my job by jumping the gun. I'll start looking into it right away and get in touch with you the minute I know anything."

"Good."

Sister Agatha and Pax drove directly to Judy's Place. Getting a whiff of the marvelous scents that belonged to the breakfast menu, Pax barked happily.

"Nothing doing, old boy. We took a meal when we were hungry because we hadn't eaten, but we both had breakfast. Accepting food now would be nothing short of gluttony—a sin."

Pax whined softly.

"You heard me. No begging!"

Moments later, Sister Agatha knocked at the back door, and Judy came to meet her. "Good morning, Sister. Come in."

Sister Agatha accepted some of the café's special coffee, and the first sip convinced her that Judy's Place would be a fixture in their town for many years to come. "Everything you prepare is so good!" she said, and Pax whined.

Sister Agatha shot him a cold look, but Judy laughed. "How about some breakfast, Pax?"

"No, don't. He doesn't need it," Sister Agatha said, but before she could finish, Pax went over to Judy and placed one of his huge paws on her lap.

Judy burst out laughing. "I'll tell you what. We have some day-old tortillas . . ."

Pax barked once, and Sister Agatha sighed. "Go ahead."

Moments later, Judy returned with a plate of leftovers. "I have a soft spot for former officers," she said, looking at Pax, then back at Sister Agatha.

Sister Agatha took a few more sips of her coffee, which had the faint taste of freshly baked cinnamon rolls. "I know you pack huge crowds in here for lunch, and you probably don't remember one from the other, but I need to ask you a question. I've been told that Victoria Garcia comes by around noon sometimes and picks up a couple of takeout lunches—"

Judy raised one hand. "*Her*, I remember. Victoria acts like

Queen Victoria herself. She's really difficult to deal with, Sister. She always orders three lunches and is incredibly picky about one of them. No mayo, nothing with pork, no added salt. One time the waitress made a mistake and put a small container of potato salad in the bag. Victoria had a fit. She said that to someone like her friend who has a severe allergy to eggs, anything with mayo was nothing short of a death sentence." She rolled her eyes. "For Pete's sake, all she would have had to do was eat it herself or toss it out, but she made the most incredible ruckus." Judy shook her head and smirked. "Now, I always have two people check her orders."

After thanking Judy for the information, Sister Agatha went back outside with Pax. The possibility that Victoria and Al had worked together to eliminate Robert was looking more plausible by the minute. It was still all circumstantial, but the picture was certainly coming together.

There was one problem, however. Al Russo's time had been accounted for the day of the murder. He'd been campaigning and had also hung out with the kids from the local youth program.

Sister Agatha considered her next step. If those kids were local and had records, the *Chronicle* would have their stories. Maybe Al had found a way to exploit them, using the kids to establish an alibi for at least part of the time. It was also possible that one of them had pointed Al to a source for the date-rape drug that Tom and Robert had ingested.

Sister Agatha called Chuck and asked him to check his files. As she waited, she prayed they'd find a connection. At long last Chuck came back to the phone.

"According to a story I did on the group last year, two of the kids in the program dealt drugs at one time," he said. "One of them, Brent Corda, was eighteen, so his name was released. He was supposedly selling that date-rape drug when he got busted.

He got into trouble again several months ago and got kicked out of the Second Chance Program Russo takes part in. Brent's got new charges pending, though he's currently out on bail."

"Was he at the park on the Fourth?"

"If he was, he wasn't with Al—at least officially. Russo's on record saying that he won't deal with repeat offenders."

She'd have to pay Brent Corda a visit. "What's Brent's address?"

He hesitated before answering. "Sister, I know Brent. If you're thinking of paying him a visit, you shouldn't go alone. He's bad news. Besides dealing, his track record now includes assault and battery."

"I'll stay outside in plain view, and Pax will be with me. We'll be okay."

"Maybe, but without leverage, you'll get nowhere," Chuck said. "The dude's a bit of a loose cannon, Sister. If you're lucky, all he'll do is slam the door in your face." He thought about it for a second. "If you let me ride along with you, I may be able to help."

"How?"

"Brent owes me one. I testified on his behalf, and that's how he avoided jail the first time."

"Okay. Get ready. I'll swing by and pick you up."

Twenty minutes later, they drove into an area on the south end of town. Single mobile homes stood on quarter-acre lots across the railroad tracks from pueblo-style residences that dated back to the forties. The struggles of the residents who lived in this part of town were told mostly through the crumbling stucco walls, litter, and old junked cars in the backyards. These were tough times, but tougher on some than on others.

Even before she parked the Harley in front of the old house with the sagging porch and trash-filled yard, she knew what she'd be facing. Anger and hostility all too often followed long-term poverty.

As she reached for Pax's leash, a young man wearing baggy jeans and a loose shirt came to the front door, a bottle of beer in his hand. He glanced at her, then at Chuck.

"Hey, Chuck. You guys lost?"

"Nah, we're not lost. We came hoping to talk to you, Brent," Chuck answered. "Got a minute?"

"Depends. What's on your mind?" The underage boy took a sip from the bottle.

Something in his tone made Sister Agatha tense up. People who lived on the edge, slipping from one side of the law to the other, knew how to play the game. Getting information from them was often as easy as getting answers from a rock.

As she approached Brent, Pax suddenly growled. Sister Agatha stopped in midstride. Something wasn't right.

Chuck glanced down at Pax, then back up at Brent. "You packing?"

Brent patted a bulge in his waistband beneath his unbuttoned shirt. "Yeah, I'm expecting some people. Just being careful."

"If the dog sees your handgun, he's likely to react according to his training," Sister Agatha warned.

"I've heard about him—former police dog, right?"

She nodded. "We're not here to hurt anyone. Could you put that away, at least for now?"

He looked up and down the graveled lane, then nodded. "Let's go inside. I don't like making a target of myself."

Sister Agatha wondered how someone so young could stand living the way he did, always looking over his shoulder. If nothing else, it had to be exhausting. Remembering that Christ was in everyone, she tried hard not to judge him.

Moments later, they were sitting at a metal kitchen table. From where he sat, Brent had a clear view out a window at the road leading into the neighborhood.

"I can give you about fifteen minutes. Make them count," he said, looking toward the drawer where he'd placed the small semiauto pistol.

"You owe me one," Chuck said.

"Yeah. That's why you're getting fifteen minutes."

Chuck glanced at Sister Agatha and nodded.

"Brent, at one time you were dealing date-rape drugs. Then, while on parole, you joined a community youth program for offenders under twenty-one. I understand Al Russo was your sponsor," she said.

"Yeah, and that man really walks his talk." He met her gaze and held it. "I owe him big-time."

"Why is that?" Sister Agatha prodded.

"He helped me when he didn't have to, and as Chuck already knows, I respect that."

"We're not looking to nail you," Chuck said. "We're looking for a killer."

"So I've heard, but I wasn't even in town the day Garcia got capped. Ask the cops. They've already been by."

"Was it because of your connection to benzodiazepine?" Sister Agatha confronted him.

"Yeah." He glanced away, avoiding her gaze.

"You didn't tell them everything, did you?" Sister Agatha said, playing a hunch.

He laughed. "Sister, in my business you *never* tell the cops everything. That helps keep you alive out on the streets."

"We're not cops, so why don't you tell us?" Sister Agatha insisted.

"What's in it for me?" he countered.

"For starters, you'd be squaring the debt you owe me," Chuck shot back. "If it hadn't been for me, you'd have served time—no parole—three years, maybe more. Remember?"

"Yeah. That judge wanted to make me an example," he said, then walked to the side of the window, looking out but not exposing himself to view. "If I talk to you, that'll square us once and for all."

Chuck nodded once. "Deal."

Brent looked at Chuck, then at Sister Agatha. "The Second Chance Program required that we stay clean, and I did—for the most part—but then my old man got sick. He needed painkillers, and I needed some fast cash, so I started dealing again. Al found out, but he kept his mouth shut. He even helped me stay below the radar. When my caseworker told him about a surprise visit he had planned, Al came by to give me a heads-up. I had, like, less than an hour to get rid of the merchandise. There was no way. I don't even have a car. So Al told me that if I stayed clean from that point on, he'd take the stuff with him," Brent said. "Al kept his end of the deal, and so have I. I make my living doing other things these days."

"What kind of drugs did you have on hand?" Sister Agatha asked.

"Painkillers, a little grass, and some Rohypnol."

"Did Al ever tell you what he did with the stuff he took with him?" Chuck asked.

"No, he carted it off in a milk carton, and my guess is it ended up at the dump." He looked at Chuck, then at Sister Agatha. "I know what you're thinking. Word's out that both the sheriff and

241

Garcia were drugged, but I can tell you right now that Al wasn't involved in that. He's a straight arrow. The only way he would have ever killed anyone is if his own life had been threatened, or maybe if he'd been trying to protect someone else."

Sister Agatha thought about Al's relationship with RJ and of the times Victoria had been physically beaten. Slowly a new picture—a sad one, to be sure—began to emerge.

Sister Agatha stood, getting ready to leave. "You were given a chance to get your life together, Brent, but you're still as lost as you've ever been. If you turn to God, and ask Him to help you, He'll show you a way out."

"God doesn't visit my neighborhood anymore, Sister."

"You're looking for Him in the wrong place, Brent. He's not out there someplace," she said with a sweep of her arm. "He's within you." She tapped over her heart. "Unless you can find a way to connect, you'll never feel safe, no matter how much money or firepower you have."

19

SISTER AGATHA DROPPED CHUCK OFF AT THE PAPER'S OF-
fice a short time later.

"You're going to talk to Detective Marquez, aren't you?"
he said. "Brent'll just deny what he told us, you know."

"Undoubtedly, but the link between Al and that drug is serious. Maybe Frank can think of another way to follow this up, or
maybe he can offer Brent a deal."

"Do you think Al killed Robert on his own, or do you think
Victoria was involved?"

"I don't know. I'm not getting a clear enough picture yet.
There are too many possibilities. It could even have been someone else, like Mike Herrera. Mike's criminal record speaks for
itself. He's attracted to Victoria, taught her how to shoot, and
supplied her with a gun of the right caliber. A gun, I might add,
that's still out there somewhere."

"Victoria and Mike were my number one and two suspects

until now, so I agree—but we need more evidence. Call me the second you have answers I can print," he said, climbing out of the sidecar and giving Pax one last pat on the head.

Sister Agatha drove directly to the station. As she went down the long hall toward Tom's office, now being used by Frank, Millie came out of the break room.

"Hi, Sister," Millie greeted her. "Are you on your way to talk to Detective Marquez?"

"I sure am."

"He's been in a lousy mood lately—just a heads-up," she said in a whisper.

"What's happened?"

"Although he's come down hard on anyone connected with the Garcias, he's still having trouble getting straight answers. Al Russo, in particular, is giving him the runaround."

Though their methods had been different, Sister Agatha suspected that Frank had come to the same conclusions she had.

As she neared his office, Frank came to the open door. "I thought I heard your voice out here. Let's talk," he said, inviting her inside with a wave of his hand. "My bad mood is lightening a little," he added, letting her know his hearing was still top-notch.

"That's good to know," she said, weaving more than one meaning into his words.

He waved her to a chair. "I've got some photos of a badly bruised Victoria taken after one particularly nasty knock-down, drag-out fight between her and Robert. Turns out that the meter reader got busy using his cell phone camera a few of the times he was there. It's amazing what people fork over when you press them."

"I have some new information, too," she said.

Marquez closed the door and listened while Sister Agatha filled him in on what she'd recently learned about Al.

244

"What I'd like to do next is something that'll work best if both of us are on the same page," Sister Agatha said. "Let me go talk to Victoria—I'll wear a wire, and you can hear everything. I think she'll cooperate once I point out that we know she was having an affair with Russo and we can put her at the scene of the crime. If she stonewalls, I'll try a bluff. I'll say that we have her son's DNA from a hair sample, and we intend to find out who Robert Jr.'s father really is."

"That's a good plan," he said, his voice thoughtful. "Considering we're hard-pressed for any actual physical evidence at the moment, we need to rattle the cage."

"If we can persuade her to help us, evidence will be a lot easier to find. The district attorney could also use her testimony."

"Yeah, but this sting will only work if we can prevent her from getting in touch with Russo." He paused, then added, "I can have him hauled in here for questioning. That should do it."

"There's one piece of evidence that'll prove who the killer was—*if* we could track it back," she said slowly, thinking as she spoke. "I'm almost sure that Al took the signed baseball roster Robert had in his pocket when he died, then gave it back to RJ the day of the funeral. That roster will undoubtedly have trace evidence that may not readily appear to the naked eye but could be enough to convict Al of the shooting. We have a witness that saw the killer take it from Robert's pocket. That should be enough to convict Russo."

"*If* we can pull all this off. Play it by ear, and stay sharp."

Frank arranged to have a listening device placed on her. "You're a good detective, Sister Agatha. If you ever decide to leave the monastery, give police work a try. You're a natural."

Sister Agatha smiled. "Thanks, but I'm exactly where I belong."

. . .

Sister Agatha set out with Pax in the Harley a short time later. A passing squad car had already confirmed that Victoria and her son were at home. All she needed to do now was keep her cool and get the job done.

Sister Agatha pulled up the driveway and parked beside Victoria's car. As she removed her helmet, she was surprised to see Victoria and her son coming out the turquoise courtyard gate. Victoria was carrying a suitcase and an overnight case, and RJ had an Isotopes gym bag.

"Are you leaving?" Sister Agatha asked.

"Yes, but I'm not going far. I'll be putting this house up for sale, so we're moving to a new place a little at a time, beginning with tonight. I've decided to start fresh, Sister Agatha."

"I hope you aren't planning to leave town."

"No, not at all. I'm moving into a rental property about a mile and a half from here. Robert Jr. and I need a place of our own—a new home where we can relax and feel free to be ourselves. A team of Realtors is scheduled to come in later today." She smiled at RJ, then glanced back at Sister Agatha. "Is there something I can help you with? As you see, I was on my way out . . ."

"You and I need to talk. It won't take long."

Victoria glanced at RJ. "You can leave your gym bag on the front porch if you want, son, but let's go back inside. It's cooler there." She then gave Sister Agatha a hard look. "Please keep in mind that I don't have all day, Sister."

"Mom, can I stay outside and play with the dog?" RJ asked.

Victoria looked over at Sister Agatha, who nodded, then handed him the leash. "Don't go out of the courtyard."

"How about if we go through the house to the back and play ball on the lawn. That okay?"

"Sure, go ahead," Sister Agatha answered.

Victoria and Sister Agatha stepped aside to let Pax and the boy go ahead of them, then walked on into the great room and sat down side by side on the sofa.

Once RJ and Pax had gone out the patio door, Victoria glanced over. "So what can I do for you, Sister?"

"I know about you and Al," she said without preamble.

Alarm flashed over Victoria's features. Then, before Sister Agatha could offer any reassuring words, the fear in her eyes faded and was replaced by an unnatural calm.

That told Sister Agatha clearly what she needed to do next. "Hair samples taken from your son will prove that Robert isn't RJ's biological father, am I right?"

"Do something like that and I'll sue," Victoria said, leaning forward and holding her gaze. "I'll win, too, and the sisters will lose *everything.*"

"Law enforcement agencies would be the ones with the authority to order any tests, not me or the monastery. So I have nothing to fear from you. Even if you choose to sue the county or the state police, the damage would still be done. How important is it for you to hide the truth?"

"It's not a matter of hiding anything. My son stands to inherit a fortune from the only dad he's ever known, and I won't allow *anyone* to cheat him out of that. The Garcias owe him a future. RJ's gone through more than any child ever should. Do you know how difficult it is for a kid to see his mother getting beat up by his father? It would break my heart every time he'd try to stick up for me."

"I'm sorry—"

"Save it. The test stuff? That's all *your* doing. Marquez isn't that devious," Victoria interrupted. "Here's the way it is," she added, venom in her gaze. "If you ruin RJ's chances to get what's rightfully his from the Garcias, I'll find a way to take it from your hide, the monastery, and the archdiocese. The stink I'll make about your snooping will impact on the Church and everything else you hold dear. Think about *that* for a while."

Sister Agatha had her answer—and a measure of Victoria's desperation. What she needed to get now was Victoria's cooperation.

"What happened the night of the Fourth in the park? Someone saw you at the scene of the crime wearing one of the red campaign caps," she said, adding credibility to what was just a bluff. Scout wouldn't testify, even if she could find him again.

"I didn't drug either man, if that's what you're really asking me," Victoria shot back. "I didn't shoot my husband, either. I ended up there because I was following someone else, and when I left to go check on RJ, my husband was still alive and on his feet."

"You were at the crime scene long enough to see someone else—Al," Sister Agatha pressed. "A witness has come forward."

Victoria took a long, deep breath but didn't answer right away. Sister Agatha knew that her mind was working overtime, wondering what to say next, or, more to the point, what not to say.

"I don't believe you killed Robert, Victoria, but you know who did. If you don't come forward, an innocent man could end up in jail for a very long time."

Victoria shook her head. "You're wrong. Sheriff Tom Green has a lot of friends in this town. I read the papers and have heard enough to know he was drugged, too. That's a matter of record. Coupled with his long history of public service and a good attorney, he'll get off," she said firmly. "By trying to pin this on either me or Al—and we're not guilty—all you'll be doing is ruining a child's life. My son's."

"Tell the police what you saw that day, Victoria. If you with-hold information in a murder case, sooner or later you'll find your-self facing charges. Your son needs you more than ever now. How much are you willing to risk?"

"I saw nothing that can help the police."

"I know you were there, and the police will soon reach that same conclusion. I came to offer you some hope and give you the opportunity to come forward on your own terms. Robert Jr. doesn't have to be brought into this." Seeing the stubborn set of Victoria's jaw, Sister Agatha continued. "Once the police estab-lish your presence at the scene, you'll move to the top of their suspect list—if you're not there already. Seven figures of life in-surance is a very good motive."

Her eyes widened. "I did *not* kill him, Sister Agatha, but stu-pid accusations like those can do a lot of damage to me and my son. I've paid my dues for years, and RJ and I deserve the chance to make a new start."

"Then make a new start. Settle the past. This is your chance," Sister Agatha said.

Victoria walked to the window. By the time she turned to answer Sister Agatha, her expression had changed from anger to cold calculation. Her eyes narrowed slightly as she spoke. "Rob-ert taught me that the best kind of deal is one where everyone comes out ahead. With that in mind, I've got a proposition for you, Sister Agatha. The insurance check I'll be getting soon will set me up for life—with plenty left over. If you'll stop making waves—just go home and mind your own business—I can turn things around for you. I know that the monastery is about to close down from lack of funds. You now have it in your power to save the home *you* love. What do you say?"

For a moment Sister Agatha couldn't find her voice. Had she not been wearing a wire, would she have accepted the offer? She would have liked to think that she would have taken the high road and declined, but deep down she wasn't so sure. "I can't . . ."

Victoria waited, then, when Sister Agatha said nothing more, shrugged. "You had your chance, Sister. I certainly hope you can live with the choice you made." She remained silent for several seconds before she added, in a voice that held the echoes of fear and desperation, "I stayed with Robert because I had to, but let me be clear about something. My husband would have killed me one day. Of that, I'm sure." She reached into her purse and brought out a small tape recorder. After checking that her son was still outside with Pax, she returned to the couch. "I want you to listen to something."

Victoria switched on the player, and the first thing Sister Agatha heard was a loud crash. It sounded like wooden furniture being slammed into something and then splintering. That was followed by another resounding crash, then soft whimpers. Robert's voice came through loud and clear as he brought name calling to a new low. Although the insults were in Spanish, they were easily recognizable to anyone who'd lived in New Mexico for as long as Sister Agatha had.

Sister Agatha heard a slap, then a moan followed by a gurgling sound. "If I squeezed your throat just a little tighter . . ." she heard a man say.

Gasps, shallow coughs, and a desperate wheeze that tore at her heart followed.

"Robert, stop!" a faint but recognizable voice cried out.

Suddenly there was a loud thud and a man's deep groan. That was immediately followed by running footsteps. "Leave me alone," Victoria screamed, then a door slammed shut.

Robert retched, then cleared his throat. His voice came through next as a whisper, and the coldness of it made a chill run up Sister Agatha's spine. "You're bought and paid for, *puta.*

Your life is mine, and you'll pay a thousand times over for what you've done."

As the tape ended, Sister Agatha looked at Victoria in shock. "Al is RJ's dad, and Robert *knew*."

"Yes and no. There's more to the story." Victoria took a shaky breath, then continued in a slow, weary voice. "Robert was injured in college, playing rugby or some dumb thing, and doctors told him that he'd never father a child. I always thought we'd adopt, but after we got married Robert decided he didn't want to do that. He said he didn't want someone else's cast-off kid."

Sister Agatha's heart went out to her. A woman who wanted to have a child yet couldn't . . . for whatever the reason. She could understand that particular form of anguish far better than most.

"That's why I . . . went to Al," Victoria said in a whisper-thin voice. "Once I got pregnant I figured I'd tell Robert that a miracle had happened and that he and I were going to have a baby. Knowing him and his ego, I was sure he'd want to believe that, and wouldn't question it so long as I remained by his side."

"But things didn't go as you'd planned," Sister Agatha prodded after Victoria had been silent for some moments.

Victoria nodded. "Once the baby was born, I figured I was safe. No matter what, I knew Robert would never admit that the child wasn't his. My baby would be raised as a Garcia—with all the advantages that come along with that. For a while, everything worked out, too, but when other health concerns came up, and Robert got tested, he *knew*—and he was furious. He thought I'd gone to a sperm bank, so I let him go right on believing that. I even took a page from his own playbook and bribed a few people to back up that story."

"What you did . . . having your own child . . . cost you more than you ever realized," Sister Agatha said.

"Yes, but I don't regret it, not for an instant. RJ means everything to me—and I'll do whatever it takes to protect him." She met Sister Agatha's gaze and held it. "Reconsider my offer, Sister. You'll come out ahead, and no one, especially RJ, will be harmed."

Shaken to the core by the tape and uncertain what to do next, Sister Agatha stood. "Let me speak to Reverend Mother. I'll come back later."

"If I'm not here, I'm at 105 Chamisa Lane, the house with the lion sculpture on the front lawn."

Sister Agatha gathered up Pax and walked back to the motorcycle. Taking a deep, unsteady breath, she placed a trembling hand on the dog and waited before switching on the ignition. The feel of Pax's muscled and toned body beneath her palm steadied her. "I wish we could go home, Pax, but we have other business to attend to first," she said quietly.

She was well away from the neighborhood when she finally pulled over to the side of the road and called Detective Marquez. "I assume you heard all that, including the recording Victoria played for me."

"Yeah, but we still don't have enough solid evidence to arrest Russo," Frank replied.

"She won't implicate Al, so let's see what we can work out from the other direction."

"You want to put some pressure on Al next?"

"Yeah, I do. How about sending out a deputy to pick up Victoria and have her brought in for questioning. Then make sure Al sees her being brought in."

"I'm following you. I'll tell him that Victoria's being arrested for the murder of her husband. Then we'll see how things play out," he said.

"Once he's released, I'll push his buttons. I'll mention the missing piece of evidence—that autographed Isotopes roster. If he gave it to RJ, he's sure to want to get it back pronto. I think he already knows where RJ keeps it," she added, remembering the conversation the day of the funeral.

"Works for me. Prod him some more by pretending to let it slip that we'll be doing a full house search tomorrow for anything that might connect Victoria to the murder."

"He might try to go around us directly to the source, so we'll also need to make sure he can't reach RJ," Sister Agatha said. "How about if I tell him that RJ's spending time with his aunt since the Realtors will be at the house this afternoon? I'll say that with his mother in jail, Alyssa took RJ on an outing, but they'll be back later this evening, and she'll be spending the night with him at the house. My guess is that, knowing Alyssa's penchant for sleeping pills, he'll feel it's safe for him to enter the house to-night under the cover of night. If you plant cameras in critical areas and have someone tail Al, you'll get your evidence."

"Sounds good. One more thing. I could cut you some slack and give you time to take advantage of the deal Victoria offered you. If she signs a promissory note, that money—"

"Is still not ours," Sister Agatha said firmly. "I don't even have to ask Reverend Mother. I already know what her response would be. God provides for us. If we look away from Him and start looking to ourselves for answers, we've already lost a far big-ger battle than the one before us right now."

"I understand. Okay, then, I'll get busy. Where will you go after speaking to Al, Sister?"

"Home to spend some time in prayer. I need to prepare for the battle ahead. After that, if it's okay with you, I'll head to Victoria's and make myself comfortable in the little boy's bed-room."

"No problem. I'll be there by the time you arrive. Use the back door. The boy's room will have been properly staged by then, too. All that Al's going to find under those covers is pillows."

"Al will look, too. I've seen how close he is to RJ. I'm sure he'll want to take his son with him when he makes a run for it."

At the station some time later, Sister Agatha waited in the parking lot until she saw Al coming out the entrance.

"Mr. Russo," she said, going over to meet him. "I know about Victoria's arrest. I was there when the deputies came. They were looking for an autographed baseball roster they think might be important. I don't think they found it, but they did take her into custody. Did you get a chance to see her? How's she doing?"

"They brought her in a while ago, but we never got a chance to talk," he said. "Tell me, Sister, do you know what happened to RJ? I'm really worried about him now that his support system is breaking down."

"Don't worry. For now he's fine. Alyssa took him to an Albuquerque park so he'll be out of the way of the Realtors who are coming by the house this afternoon. Later tonight, they'll be back. With all the changes around him, they felt it's important for RJ to sleep in his own bed, so Alyssa will be spending the night there with him. I also understand that she plans to apply for custody of RJ if Victoria goes to trial. JD and Alyssa are very fond of RJ."

"If you say so, Sister," he said, his voice hard.

"Of course, we still don't know if Victoria's going to trial, and even if she does, it's still way too early to know if she'll be convicted. Either way, I'm sure RJ will be fine. The Garcias take care of their own," she said. "This isn't your problem, though.

You have to find a new job now that your boss is with his maker."

"Yeah. My future's at hand, and it's time for me to start making some plans. Thanks for the information, Sister. Have a pleasant evening."

Wondering which car contained the deputies who were tailing him, Sister Agatha watched as Al drove off. Shortly thereafter she was on her way back to the monastery. If there was ever a time that begged for prayer and help from above, it was now.

By the time the sun had set, Sister Agatha was back in town. Marquez's deputies, working in teams, had kept Russo under surveillance, and everything was running on schedule.

Sister Agatha parked the Harley along the bosque on the ditch road a quarter mile from Victoria's house; then she and Pax walked over. As they reached the door, it opened. Marquez stood just out of view.

"Glad you remembered to keep the Harley out of sight. We're all set up here. We've got cameras hooked up in several places, including the boy's bedroom," he said. "Let's just hope Russo comes tonight. This is a very expensive operation, and we even had to borrow a few low-light cameras from the Feds in Albuquerque."

"Where's Russo now?"

"My deputies said he's still at his house."

"He'll come," Sister Agatha said. "And RJ, is he okay?"

"He's staying at a private residence under the care of a court-appointed psychologist and a caseworker. As soon as we release his mother, they'll be reunited."

"Have you already searched this house?" she asked.

"We looked but didn't find the baseball roster. We had to back off in case Russo decided to come here in a hurry. Don't worry—if there's anything in there, we'll find it later."

Sister Agatha, Pax at her side, soon made herself comfortable in RJ's bedroom. The bump underneath the covers was nothing more than pillows.

No matter what other plans Al had made, she knew in her heart that he would stop by here tonight. He wouldn't leave town without his son.

She was busy praying the rosary an hour later when the phone at her waist vibrated. She answered in a whisper-soft voice and heard Marquez at the other end.

"Somebody came in the back door. There was a key we didn't know about under a brick in the patio."

"Russo?"

"No, not unless he managed to elude my deputies," Marquez whispered. "Stay put."

She listened, trying to stand absolutely still and keep Pax calm. Her heart was beating so loudly she was sure its crazy thumping could be heard miles away.

Finally she saw a spot of light, from a penlight, probably, farther down the hall. The light came closer, then vanished as a door somewhere close by opened noisily. Its sound was different, not like one of the bedroom doors. She heard a faint scrape from within the wall somewhere, then a metallic thunk.

"Yes!" she heard the person whisper loudly.

It was then she realized that RJ must have hidden the roster outside his room in the hall closet, and whoever that was had it now.

She inched toward the doorway, keeping a firm hand on the dog's collar, hoping to sneak a peek. Suddenly a hall light came on.

"Don't move!" Marquez ordered. "Set the gun down—very slowly."

"We're coming out, Frank," Sister Agatha called, not wanting to get shot by mistake. Pausing for a second, she stepped into the hall, Pax at heel. Seeing the scene before him, the dog stiffened and growled low and deep.

In the doorway of the bedroom across the hall, Frank kept his weapon trained on Mike's chest.

Mike Herrera looked over at her as he gently set a pistol down onto the carpet.

"This is unexpected," Sister Agatha said, surprised.

"It isn't what you think, either," Mike replied, standing slowly, then turning to put his hands on the wall and "assuming the position."

"You've done this before," Frank observed wryly. "You have any other weapons, Herrera?"

"A pocketknife. In my right front pocket. I can reach for it, if you want," Mike replied. "What are you two doing here?"

"Sister, have the dog guard him, please?" Frank said, ignoring the question.

"Pax, guard!" she ordered, letting go of his collar.

Still growling, Pax walked over to within three feet of Herrera and sat, his mouth open to show his weaponry in full gleam.

Marquez quickly frisked Herrera, then handcuffed him. By then a deputy had appeared.

"I just wanted to retrieve the pistol I loaned Victoria a few months ago." Mike turned his head toward Sister Agatha. "Okay, so I lied about getting rid of it, but she needed the protection.

When I heard she got arrested, I came to get it back before the deputies searched the house. If they found it here, they'd think for sure that she killed Robert, but she didn't."

"Because you did?" Frank countered.

"No way, man—and you can't prove that, 'cause it never happened."

"Get him out of here—use the back door," Frank ordered the deputy. "We might have another visitor to deal with tonight."

As the officer led Herrera away, Frank picked up the pistol by inserting a pen through the trigger guard, behind the trigger itself. He looked at the weapon closely, emptied the cartridges, checked the safety, then slipped it into an evidence bag.

Feeling the phone at his belt vibrate, he picked it up, said a few curt words, then looked over at her. "Russo's on his way here. I better turn off the lights again. Hurry and get back in place."

"Do you think we've been wrong all along and Victoria was the one who killed Robert?" she asked from the bedroom doorway.

"Russo's still a wild card, but Victoria's our number one suspect right now. This isn't the murder weapon—but this gun proves she's been lying. She claims she never handled a pistol before, but her fingerprints on this will prove otherwise. What I can't figure out is why she'd keep this pistol around knowing it could help send her to prison."

"Amateur killers make mistakes," she suggested, unconvinced.

Sister Agatha brought Pax back into the bedroom, her mind in a whirl as she weighed the possibility that Mike and Victoria had conspired to kill Robert. A few seconds later, the lights went out and the house became silent once more.

Ten minutes went by; then the phone in her pocket started vibrating. She picked it up immediately.

"Frank here. Al Russo's almost at the gates. Stay awake and alert."

"No problem. I have enough adrenaline in my system right now to keep me awake for years."

She heard a chuckle from down the hall. Then it was quiet again, except for the sound of a breeze picking up outside.

Pax cocked his head and looked at her.

"Just the wind, boy," she whispered, scratching him behind the ears. "Hang in there."

Minutes later, she felt the phone vibrating again. There was a slight rush of air in the tightly sealed room as an outside door was opened, then closed. She put the phone up to her ear.

"Russo came in through the back door. He had his own key."

"I'm ready," Sister Agatha said.

"Stay on the line this time."

Sister Agatha and Pax slipped into the corner just behind the half-opened door leading into the hall. Beside her was the life-sized cardboard cutout of the baseball player.

Marquez would monitor Al's location, but Sister Agatha was sure that things would be decided here in this bedroom. She heard distant footsteps, like before.

"Up the stairs," Frank whispered.

"He's coming for his son—and that baseball roster," she whispered back.

"If it's still there," he answered.

"Don't worry, Al will find it for us," she assured him. The footsteps were getting closer, so she froze, silent, and grabbed Pax's collar tightly.

Al came into the room a few seconds later. Without hesitation he went to the far right-hand corner of the room, directly opposite where she and Pax were standing, and moved the baseball mitt from the corner of the shelf. Behind it was a box. He moved that as well, then reached upward. She heard him curse as he struggled to get at something by feel alone.

Her nose itched, but she dared not move, knowing that if he looked up, he'd see two standing figures—and a dog.

Finally, with a muted groan, he extracted a piece of paper from the hiding place. Then, almost as an afterthought, he took the baseball that was nestled in the glove and slipped it into his jacket pocket.

Moving silently, he stepped over to the bed. "Hey, kiddo, I've got your Mitch the Missile personally autographed program and your team-autographed ball. What do you say we hit the road?" He reached down to shake the boy awake, then realized something was wrong.

"Crap!" he said, after tossing back the covers.

Sister Agatha stepped around the door and switched on the lights, letting Pax move closer to Al. The dog growled, standing tall.

"You made that hiding place for him, Al, didn't you?" she asked softly.

Blinking from the sudden brightness, he stared at her for a second, then looked back at the empty bed.

Before he could answer, Marquez came in and took the paper from Russo's hand, then placed it on the dresser.

"Al Russo, you're under arrest for the murder of Robert Garcia. Turn around and place your hands on the wall."

After Frank frisked him and applied the handcuffs, Al turned his head and looked at Sister Agatha. "Where's my kid?" he asked. "He *is* mine, Sister Agatha—but you already knew that, didn't you?" he added, studying her expression.

"Yes. I was also close by when you gave him the autographed Isotopes roster and told him to put it in his special place."

"Robert was a real sicko. He loved playing head games with

RJ—a kid—is that pathetic, or what? He'd hide RJ's favorite toy, making him come begging for it. He never hit RJ, but there are other ways to damage a child. The kid's so mixed up, even his mom can't control him half the time. You've seen him acting out."

"Proving that the victim was disturbed may work to your advantage in court, but you're still going to face a jury," Marquez said.

"I can live with that. But what about my kid? What'll happen to RJ?"

"In my gut I know that Victoria saw you that night and knows you shot Robert," Marquez said, "but I can't prove conspiracy, so she'll be released. Robert Jr. will remain in her custody."

"He'll be all right," Sister Agatha assured Al.

"Yeah, now that I've done what needed to be done." There was no satisfaction in his voice, just a weary acceptance.

Al had acted to protect his child, and a heart that was still able to love wasn't unredeemable. As Sister Agatha watched him being led away, she whispered a prayer for him.

"I can't help him, Lord, but I know You can. He's in Your gentle hands now. Show him the way back."

The following morning at the sheriff's station, Sister Agatha finished giving and signing her statement. She was on her way to say a final good-bye to Tom Green when he came out of his office to meet her.

"Russo's given us all we need, including the boot that left that unexplained footprint. We also got his recipe for hot dog relish," he added.

Sister Agatha smiled. "What about you? Are you back on the job?"

"Yeah, I sure am," he said. "Thanks . . . it doesn't seem enough."

"It is. I'm glad I was able to help."

"You did more for me than you realize, Sister Agatha. Gloria and I had a very long talk, and we'll be going to counseling for as long as it takes. We really do love each other, you know."

She smiled and hugged him. "That's the best news I've heard in a long time. God bless you both."

"And you?"

"I'm going back to the monastery to say a final good-bye. Then Pax and I will be on our way."

"No more Our Lady of Hope Monastery?"

"God's called us to serve elsewhere," she answered. "It's our duty to follow."

"I'll miss you—and Pax."

"I'll miss everyone here, too," she said, trying not to cry.

"Stay in touch," he said, bending down to pet Pax and looking up at her.

"I will, and I'll send you photos of our new home as soon as I can."

Sister Agatha went outside and, as she looked back at the station, wiped a tear from her eye. It was time for a new beginning.

"Let's go, Pax. The Lord's waiting to welcome us to our new home."